Helen Hays

Aspirations

Helen Hays

Aspirations

ISBN/EAN: 9783337179922

Printed in Europe, USA, Canada, Australia, Japan

Cover: Foto ©Andreas Hilbeck / pixelio.de

More available books at **www.hansebooks.com**

ASPIRATIONS

BY

HELEN HAYS

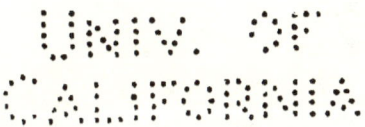
NEW YORK:
THOMAS WHITTAKER,
1886.

CONTENTS.

	PAGE
CHAPTER I. .	5
CHAPTER II. .	15
CHAPTER III.	26
CHAPTER IV. .	41
CHAPTER V.	47
CHAPTER VI. .	68
CHAPTER VII.	75
CHAPTER VIII.	90
CHAPTER IX.	103
CHAPTER X. .	114
CHAPTER XI.	124
CHAPTER XII.	136
CHAPTER XIII.	143
CHAPTER XIV.	156
CHAPTER XV. .	166
CHAPTER XVI.	178
CHAPTER XVII.	189
CHAPTER XVIII.	195
CHAPTER XIX. .	206
CHAPTER XX.. .	216
CHAPTER XXI. .	227
CHAPTER XXII.	234
CHAPTER XXIII.	244

CONTENTS.

4

		PAGE
CHAPTER XXIV.	. . . .	251
CHAPTER XXV.	. . . .	263
CHAPTER XXVL	. . . .	268
CHAPTER XXVIL	. . . .	279
CHAPTER XXVIIL.	. . . .	289
CHAPTER XXIX.	. . . .	302
CHAPTER XXX.	. . . .	312
CHAPTER XXXL.	. . . .	324

ASPIRATIONS.

CHAPTER I.

It was an old brown house, weather-stained and dreary looking, for there was not a tree to take it in a loving embrace and hide its old forlornness; hardly a shrub grew near it, and certainly there was no trace of a garden. All about it was sand, dazzling white sand; and beyond the sand was fog, miles of it, though once in a while a shaft of broad sunlight and a sharp west wind would gather up the fog and send it flying.

That is the way the house looked to most people. To old Abner Marsh and his wife it was no more dreary than the woodchuck's hole is to its inhabitants. They had lived there fifty years. Abner had fished, and mended his nets, patched his sails, and spliced his ropes, caulked his boats, and watched the varying signs of weather changes from year to year, without a thought of what his house looked like. Mrs. Marsh, in the same manner, had swept and scrubbed, and kneaded her dough, unmindful of domestic architecture, — unless the chimney smoked, or the roof leaked, in either of which cases she immediately, as a good housewife, attended to the matter without much aid from Abner.

But there was another pair of eyes under that old roof-tree, keenly awake to the rich coloring Time had given the old clapboards, still wider open to the long line of blue water meeting the horizon, the nearer green billows with their white caps, and the reflections of the fitful sky. Even the fog was not without charm for those eyes as they watched it come drifting down, blotting out all color except that of one great red tossing buoy in the near foreground; but better than all other aspects was that of the moon as she rose in queenly splendor from the waves. Then those eyes could not rest in slumber, but eagerly watched from the small window the grand pageant which had so few spectators; watched the gradual and dignified ascent of the Queen of Night to her throne, and wondered if the fishes were not glad to have their night lamp swung so high.

Turning from the window, a thin, flexible little hand would seize a piece of charcoal, made from a half-burned ember in the kitchen fire, and with rapid touches on the bare whitewashed wall reproduce long waving lines of water, the round moon above, and the outline of a far-away ship. Sometimes the ship would be nearer, and all sails set; again, it would be a shapeless wreck, cast against a jutting rock; and again, there would be only a fragment left, and hovering over this an uncanny looking gull. Murillo would have delighted in the tangled pate so intent upon these essays, and his own beggar children could not have looked forth from eyes of a duskier, dreamier darkness.

But whence came these eyes and this creative hand, so unlike the unimaginative Abner and his wife? Years ago a sailor lad had been born and bred under the old roof, a wild, roving fellow, and Abner's only son; glad to leave home and parents and humble labor for the varied fortunes of the sea, returning at long intervals, and bringing with him, as sailors do, the flotsam and jetsam of many voyages. Mrs. Marsh showed with satisfaction a camphor-wood trunk, a green silk umbrella with carved ivory handle, and curious Eastern looking stuffs by the yard, which Abner, jun., had from time to time brought home; but the greatest curiosity of all, the little curly-headed two year old boy, chattering Italian like a paroquet, was not brought forward as one of these treasures, though he had come in the same way, and though Abner, jun., had never returned from another voyage, which should have enhanced the value of his last gift. Who was he? Where had he come from? Mrs. Marsh was not quite sure that she could answer these questions; perhaps that was the reason why the camphor trunk and green umbrella had the precedence. Lillo certainly did not give half the trouble which Jack the monkey, Abner, jun.'s, first gift, had caused; and now that Jack was no more, owing the ending of his days to what the neighbors called a "spider dumpling," surely Lillo could take his place. He could and he did, and Mrs. Marsh was not unkind to him, and old Abner liked to have him about; and the child grew strong and lithe, a veritable sea-urchin, and but for

his "vagaries," as Mrs. Marsh bore witness, he would
have been quite a useful member of the household.
But what decent woman could tolerate a clean white
wall disfigured with a burnt stick? Not even the
mother of a Raphael.

And so Mrs. Marsh, having no knowledge of
Raphaels or Murillos, but having a keen instinct
that cleanliness and godliness were closely allied,
had recourse to her broomstick and scrubbing-brush :
with one she reproved Lillo, with the other she re-
moved the frescoes from the walls.

Lillo bore both with philosophic coolness : he did
not fear the broom-stick ; and when the glow of inspiration was over, the sketch once made, he did not
care what became of it, and so did not mind the
annihilating scrubbing-brush.

Conscious of the power to reproduce what he
wished, when it should please him, how did it matter
that the sketches were effaced? Already was he
prodigal after the manner of those who have much
to spare. And so he scrawled on, whenever it was
his mood so to do, — waves, flying-fish, sea-serpents,
and mermaids, and the invariable ship coming and
going under all sorts of conditions. From sailors'
yarns, from the figure-heads of vessels, from old
picture-books left by Abner, jun., he gathered his
material, and wove into it his own imaginings and
the varying surroundings made by wind and weather.

In vain Mrs. Marsh remonstrated and scolded, in
vain old Abner said, "Now, don't :" the fine frenzy
had to have its way; though after a while it left the
walls, and spent itself on shingles, bits of old board,

smooth cupboard-doors from dismantled schooners, clam-shells, and indeed any thing that offered a fair surface for the pencil. For the pencils were obtained from a peddler, who took in exchange any pretty shell the boy could procure.

There is this similitude of force in all living, growing things, — it will have its way; from that of the tiny seed pushing up through the black mould, and spreading out its small green fibres, to the power in a human being's brain, expanding, pushing out into the ideas that demand sun and air.

"Lillo, Lillo!" screamed Mrs. Marsh from the doorway one afternoon, shading her eyes from the glare which the sun made on the sand.

"Where *is* the boy?" she soliloquized, turning abruptly, and with a startled manner, towards a stranger, who suddenly appeared before her, and replied to her question.

"If you mean the little curly-head down on the sands, I can tell you where he is, madam."

"I mean our boy Lillo, sir," said Mrs. Marsh stiffly. "Every one knows him, in spite of his outlandish name, but no one can find him when he's wanted."

"I dare say not; he looks as independent as the wind, but he's to be found now on the other side of the big rock yonder. Shall I go after him for you?"

"No, I am obliged to you. He promised to bring the fish for supper; but if he's where you say, I'll get no fish this day. I'll warrant he's at his trumpery picture-makin'."

"He certainly is making a bold marine sketch, which I greatly admired," said the stranger very kindly.

Mrs. Marsh was not to be mollified. "I am not sure that I know what you mean, sir, but I wish it was a bold haul of a fish-net. My old husband is in his bed, and likely to stay there ; and what we are to do for food, I don't know."

"Is Lillo, then, your only dependence ? "

"Depend upon *that* boy?" she queried in blank amazement. "No, I depend upon myself, old as I am ; but he can, if he chooses, get a nice mess of fish or crabs or clams, when the picture-fit ain't on him. I beg pardon, sir, will you come in and be seated? I am not used to seein' many strangers."

The gentleman took off his hat, and entered, saying, —

"The boy interests me. You must know that it is very unusual to see so early a development of talent, and in so out of the way a place."

Again was Mrs. Marsh puzzled.

"Out of the way of what, sir ? "

"Of ideas, of the world's current of thought."

Poor Mrs. Marsh set her cap straight, untied and re-tied her apron-string.

"Mebbe you're a furriner, sir. My son Ab had travelled, that's the way he used to talk; but I'm not used to many people, and sence father took the palsy I've been less clear in my mind."

The stranger was evidently flattered to find his conversation resembled son Ab's, and looking good-humoredly about said, —

"What do you propose doing with the boy?"

"Oh, I don't do nothin' with him. I used to spank and to scold, but I'm past that now: he does as he pleases."

"But in the future? He's growing, you know. Do you intend that he shall be a fisherman?"

"I never intend any thing at all about that child. The neighbors want me to send him to Codtown to learn the house-painter's trade; but like as not, ef I did, he'd just be up and off afore the mast, as Ab was."

As she talked she drew out an oval mahogany table, which looked as if it might once have been in a ship's cabin, spread a clean, unbleached linen cloth upon it, and took from the dresser a few pieces of china and delf, and a pitcher on whose side danced a jolly tar.

"You'll stay to supper, sir, I presume; though I've not much to offer sence Lillo's forgotten the fish."

At this moment, kicking up the sand and trailing a conglomerate lot of rubbish behind him, with a whistle and a merry, happy-go-lucky air, appeared the youth they were talking about. As brown as a chestnut, and as slender as a young birch, his large eyes lifted their long lashes beneath the rim of a battered old felt hat, in some surprise at seeing a visitor; but though he grasped in one hand a variety of implements, — rod, net, boat-hook, and an extemporized sketch-book, — in the other he held aloft triumphantly a string of quivering fish, flashing in the sunlight and sending out sparkles from their silvery scales.

"There, granny, dear, I did remember after all, though you thought I wouldn't," was his salutation. Then turning to the stranger, he bowed as gracefully and as naturally as if in a drawing-room; though at the same moment he tossed his traps on the floor, sent his hat flying into a corner, and went into the kitchen pantry to make his ablutions.

"Now you see the sort he is," said Mrs. Marsh grimly, gathering up the various articles the boy had thrown down, putting them where they belonged, and preparing to fry the fish.

"Yes," said the gentleman, nodding. "I see there is more than Yankee blood in his veins. But where did he get his singular name, madam?"

Mrs. Marsh stooped over the frying-pan; her aged cheeks were a little flushed.

"Name? Oh, Ab gave him that name just as he gave the monkey his'n! I'd ruther it had been Jack for the boy, and Lillo for the monkey. But the fish are doin' nicely now, sir; so if you'll please draw up I will have your supper ready in a few moments."

"Can I not wait for you and Lillo?"

"We are not fit to sit down with you, I'm afeard; but, if you don't mind, Lillo will take his."

The boy came in laughing and *insouciant*, without any of the hesitation or self-consciousness of the rustic, drew his chair to the table, and began conversing with the stranger as though he had known him always.

"So you like our bay, sir, when it's smooth water? I think you said down at the rock that you weren't much of a sailor."

"No, I'm a landsman; but this salt air invigorates me, and the monotonȳ of the life is a rest," was the reply in an absent manner, as if the question had been asked by one who could better comprehend the answer: then rousing himself as he saw the boy's interrogating gaze, he added, —

"I should have introduced myself before. My name is Barclay; my health is somewhat broken, and my physicians won't let me work. Boston is a busy place, you know, and idlers have to leave it, so I have come here for a while. I am boarding at 'The Neck;' you must come over there and see my books and pictures."

Lillo's eyes widened.

"Pictures, sir, — do you paint?"

"Yes, after a fashion."

"And you use colors?" eagerly.

"Yes; you shall try them if you want to."

"Want to!" What was not expressed in that exclamation? Day-dreams, hopes, aspirations, which the boy could not have uttered had he wished to, so impalpable and unformed were they; and yet so entirely did they sway his thoughts, that the air suddenly seemed intoxicating, and this somewhat gray-haired man an angelic presence. The boy laid down his knife and fork and became perfectly silent.

"What is the matter, Lillo?" asked Mrs. Marsh.

"Nothing," said the boy; but his eyes were filling, his throat contracting. He jumped up from the table, and seizing his hat rushed from the room.

"Now, isn't he a crack-brained creature?" asked Mrs. Marsh, glad of this proof of her assertions.

Mr. Barclay smiled.   He fancied he could better understand the whims of talent than could this withered
old dame ; but, wiser as he was, he would have been
astonished had he seen Lillo, buried in the sand, crying as if heart-broken : for the boy could have given
him no reason for this outburst of emotion, and, when
it was over, dried his eyes, bathed his face, and went
into the house again, to find Mr. Barclay gone, Mrs.
Marsh attending to the sick man, and his half-eaten
supper waiting for him on a corner of the stove.

He ate his supper in solitary haste, gathered fire-
wood for his grandmother, and with an unusual alacrity finished up all his little duties and went to bed.
But his brain was too active for sleep.   The sough-
ing and sobbing of the waves, so familiar, so constantly heard as to be unthought of, disturbed him,
and he rose more than once to see if a storm were
brewing.   There were no indications of it : the moon
had not risen, but the stars were shining.   The black
mast of a schooner was dimly visible, and far, far
away gleamed the light which was the beacon of hope
to mariners.   At last he slept, but his dreams were
brilliant visions of kaleidescopic fitfulness ; and he
was awake again by the time the round red orb of
day was soaring out of the waves.

CHAPTER II.

MR. BARCLAY was a man of wealth, leisure, and taste, none of which he had gained by any effort of his own. The wealth was inherited, the leisure was its result, and the taste was due to education and refined influences, more than to any in-born quality. But despite this blooming hedge, the garden of his happiness had not been secure from sorrow. He had married a lovely woman, who had been the balance-wheel which kept his caprices from running away with him; and, after a few years of entire peace and delightful congeniality, she had died, leaving him bankrupt of that which he most valued. Despondency and ill-health had followed. Restlessness had sent him hither and yon; but the sights and scenes of foreign lands were not enjoyed, because of the absence of the eyes which could not share the pleasures, and of the mind which had always been so ready to grasp ideas. He had now conceived the notion that he must absorb himself in some pursuit. He had some little knowledge of art, he could make a fair sketch in water-colors; and, as the air of the seashore suited him, he had come down to "The Neck" before it should be given over to the swarm of pleasure-seekers, to see if time would hang less heavily than it had done, and if he could accomplish any thing to relieve his melancholy.

He had been here a week and had done nothing. The air was soft as spring sunshine could make it, uninterrupted by keen winds; and he had paced the sands dejectedly, living on his loneliness, morbidly allowing retrospection to have its way, deceiving himself with the belief that this was faithfulness, this was true devotion, to his lost love. It is needless to say that he had no children.

Before he had risen on the morrow, after his visit to Mrs. Marsh, there came a knock on Mr. Barclay's bedroom door. The house where he was staying had the usual barren nudity of a seaside lodging-house, and he had therefore encumbered himself with more than a small supply of luggage in order to make his transient home comfortable. He supposed the knock to be that of the man who lit the blaze which his delicate health necessitated, even on a spring morning: so he simply said, "Come," and turned over for another doze.

The door was pushed gently open, but no one entered; surprised at this, Mr. Barclay glanced that way, when he saw the curly pate and the brown eyes of the lad whose acquaintance he had made the day previous.

"Hallo!" was his exclamation, "you *are* an early bird, Master Lillo. Have you caught the worm?"

"Not yet, but I can if you want me to, sir," was the matter-of-fact reply, though his eager eyes were devouring the whole room.

"No, you needn't," laughed Mr. Barclay. "I

fancy *I* am the worm this time. Come in, come in.
Just lift up that shawl over there which hangs over
a door, go into the next room, and amuse yourself till
I am dressed. You will find enough to keep you
busy; but, should you get tired, there are pencils and
paper on the table: do what you please with them.
Have you breakfasted?"

"Yes, sir." His breakfast had been a cold potato
and a draught of milk.

The boy obeyed instructions and found himself in
a bewildering maze of delight. On the walls were
fishing-rods and guns, sketches and etchings; a beautiful crayon of a sweet-faced woman looked down be-
nignly upon him. A tiger-skin was stretched over the
hard wooden rocking-chair, a warm red cover was
upon the table, books and papers were heaped about
in all the corners, and altogether there was a warmth
and comfort which the lad could not have described
or analyzed; but his tireless eyes roved from one
thing to the other until he caught sight of an odd
volume the title of which he could not appreciate,
but by opening it he soon buried himself in the life
of Michael Angelo by Vasari.

Here Mr. Barclay found him, to his surprise, for
he had not supposed that his few books would be
any thing to the boy's liking, and, summoning him
to follow him, he took him down to share a second
breakfast.

This over, the mysteries of paints, both in water
and oil, were made known to Lillo, a good supply of
materials given to him, and his choice of the books
also allowed.

A miner just in possession of a huge bonanza could not have felt richer than did Lillo, but the miner could not have shared the exquisite felicity of this young creature as at the end of the morning he trudged home with his treasures. A new world was before him, with possibilities hitherto unthought of. He seemed to himself to have suddenly grown, like the fungus which in a single night comes up from the earth.

He trod not on earth but on air, and he entered the little kitchen with the exultation of a young prince. The very tins seemed to beam upon him, and the cooking-stove glowed a welcome; the cat purred at sight of him, and the sun showered its gold on the well-scoured boards. Mrs. Marsh came slowly out of her husband's room, looking more jaded than usual.

"Well, what's up now?" was her greeting.

"O granny, I am going to be an artist!"

"Humph!"

"See all the things Mr. Barclay has given me. I must work now in real earnest."

"At sign-paintin'?"

A look of supreme disgust was all the child allowed himself.

"Sign-paintin' or house paintin's both onhealthy, but you'll never do much more. Hev you seen your gran'ther lately?"

Like all sensitive children, Lillo hated illness: he hated the wan look of suffering, the nauseous drugs, the unnatural stillness of a sick-room. He had a rebellious sort of an idea that it was unnecessary, and that if one chose one could shake it off as he would a venomous insect. When called upon to do any little service for his grandfather, he made no resistance, but it was hastened through with as much speed as possible.

"No," he replied, "I have not seen him since day before yesterday. Does he talk any to you? He never says a word to me."

"No, he's past talkin'. I think he'll hardly live the day out!" And Mrs. Marsh threw her apron up over her face as she sat down in the rocking-chair.

Lillo was unutterably shocked; all the sunshine seemed gone.

"Granny, do you mean that gran'ther is dying?"

"Yes, child, what else?"

"Sha'n't I go for the doctor or the minister or somebody?"

"No use. They can't help a poor old body that's worn out. The cobbler can patch up old shoes, but no one can mend us when we've served our time."

Lillo crept nearer to the rocking-chair.

"Granny, don't cry: I am here."

"Poor boy!"

"And I'll try to take gran'ther's place. I can fish. I can manage a boat. I'll give up the paints if you want me to." What an effort it cost him to say this!

There was no answer, only the creak of the rocking-chair.

"You're tired, granny. Won't you go to bed, and let me cook the dinner?"

The old woman rose and suffered him to lead her

to the one little spare room, which had belonged to "son Ab." She was too tired to attempt to keep up. Then he freshened the fire and made the kettle boil, fried the fish and peeled the potatoes, set the table and warmed the plates. This done, he went on tip-toe to the sick-room.

It was dark, except for the light which came from a crack in the wooden shutters, through which also came the soft spring air. He went up to the bed, — spotlessly clean in its patchwork plainness. He was curious to see what change had been wrought, what death looked like. He had seen more than one poor sailor carried up from the shore, wrapped in tarpaulin; but their faces were as much hidden as their forms, and he could shape no idea of what this mysterious change consisted.

He walked up fearlessly and listened. It was so strangely still. The old weather-worn and storm-beaten face looked gray and rigid.

He spoke softly, as he was in the habit of doing now-a-days, —

"Gran'ther!"

No answer.

"Gran'ther!"

No reply.

He reached out to stroke the poor old hand, and drew back as if he had been struck, — it was already cold. But for the coldness, he was disappointed: he had supposed there was a grandeur about death, a great and lofty unlikeness to life. In this case there was a barely perceptible difference. The old face was no older, only more soundly, surely asleep.

Death had come too naturally, and released the old man too gently, to make the transition a very palpable one. He looked so comfortable and quiet that Lillo crept out again into the sunlight. It was he who seemed to be changed. His young eyes looked forth on a new world; the bright one of the morning still lingered in his mind, but its brightness was subdued, chastened. He must work now in sober earnest to be able to take care of his grandmother. The dinner waited all day. Towards night Mr. Barclay found Lillo digging for clams.

"How, now," he cried, "my young artist, how many sketches have you made?"

"None, sir, yet. Gran'ther is dead, and I must take care of granny now. The paints will keep, won't they, sir?"

"Yes, child, they'll keep; and when they're gone you shall have more. Take this to your grandmother." He had opened his pocket-book, and extended a little roll of bills.

"No, I thank you," was Lillo's proud refusal. "I don't think she would like me to take any money I have not earned."

"As you please," answered Mr. Barclay, putting the money back. "May I engage you, then, to take me boating every fine day? I want to study up the shore a little, and possibly I may be able to give you some hints as to your own sketches."

Lillo's eyes flashed their pleasure. The bargain was made on the spot, and Lillo went on with his clam-digging.

Thus began an intimacy which proved to be as

beneficial on the one side as on the other. To the
saddened man, whose sorrow absorbed his life and
colored all his reflections, this boy, with his youth
and eager talent, was a strengthening, revivifying
tonic. Mr. Barclay found him teachable ,to an extraordinary extent : he fairly devoured all the books
he could get, and then re-read them. The lessons,
which became a regular matter, included all the simple elementary studies which Lillo had begun in the
district school, and others which Mr. Barclay's pet
theories found advisable ; but, in addition to these,
the boy's keen eyes had picked up many a fact in
natural history, just as they had almost intuitively
learned the principles of perspective. Quick also in
the practice of his native instincts, his boating and
fishing were a constant impetus to Mr. Barclay, who
found him a lively, daring companion, ready to explore
any nook, follow any channel, or dive into any undis-
covered way. One thing which he could not be induced to subscribe to was a proposition made to him
by Mr. Barclay as the season wore on, the refusal of
which was their nearest approach to any real check
of friendly feeling.

They were sketching, as usual, together on the
rocks and in the shade of them. Mr. Barclay, tiring
of the work which would not yield its charm as
readily to him as to his young companion, had taken
up a book and was reading, partly to himself and
partly to Lillo, when a few strangers, who by this
time were numerous at the Neck, came peering at
them with the careless sort of rudeness which idleness is apt to beget. Mr. Barclay closed his book

impatiently, and with an air of disdain said to Lillo, —

"This is unbearable; why can't they let us alone?"

"Shall we go farther away?" asked Lillo, inwardly indifferent to the strangers, and caring very much to continue his sketching.

"No," said Mr. Barclay, "it would ruin your work; but *I* must go farther away. 'The Neck' is too much of a resort now to suit me. Will you go with me, Lillo?"

"Where? When? I don't understand you, Mr. Barclay."

"I wish to adopt you, Lillo, take you home with me to educate you and give you the advantages which you cannot receive here."

"That is very kind," said Lillo, flushing, but going on quietly with his sketch.

"Of course you will be willing to promise obedience and respect for my authority. That is hardly necessary for me to demand, you show so keen an appreciation for all that sort of thing. And after a while we will go abroad together, as soon as the schoolmasters will let us; for, pleasant as I find it now to teach you, I may not have quite time enough to be as thorough as I ought, or I may find myself too rusty; and " — Mr. Barclay was evidently planning pretty far on into the future.

"What would become of my grandmother, Mr. Barclay?" broke in Lillo.

"Really, I had not thought of her. I suppose she would have no objections. She has the good sense to see what is for your benefit."

"But she is alone."

"We can arrange matters so that she need not remain alone."

Lillo shook his head.

"I can't leave granny."

Mr. Barclay looked astonished.

"Not leave her? Why, child, she is already an aged woman with few years before her, while you have all your life to live."

"Then I ought to stay with her as long as she needs me."

"But she does not need you: any one can provide for her few wants. She would probably be much relieved to dispose of you, Lillo."

The boy again shook his head.

"I can't go, Mr. Barclay. You are very kind, but I can't leave granny."

"Why, child, you have no idea of the value of the offer I am making. It is not every day that a poor lad has the chance of education and a start in the world."

"I know it, sir; or I feel it, if I don't know it. It is kind of you; but as long as granny lives, I must stay here."

"Pshaw!" said Mr. Barclay. "You are not the one to decide this affair: you are too young and absurdly quixotic. Do you want to be sent to Codtown, as your grandmother proposes, to learn the house-painter's trade?"

"No," said Lillo frankly, "I don't."

"But that will be your fate, boy, unless you accept my plan."

Lillo worked on silently. His quick imagination had seized the possibilities of Mr. Barclay's project with an intensity and vividness which its author, sympathetic as he was, had no conception of ; but, widely as his fancy led him, the boy's thoughts came back to the poor old roof-tree and its one lonely occupant with undiminished faithfulness.

Mr. Barclay took up his book again. He was annoyed at being thwarted, as people are who are used to having their own way, and the more so as he knew his proposal was as generous as it was exceptional ; but he had no doubt that Lillo would finally yield, because it would be simply absurd for him not to do so. Nothing more was said at the moment. When the sketch was finished and criticised, and they were trudging home with the setting sun in their eyes, Mr. Barclay paused awhile before the little old house and said, —

"I shall come over and talk to Mrs. Marsh to-morrow, Lillo."

"Thank you, sir," was the reply, as the boy touched his cap, "she will be glad to see you ; but" — He hesitated, and then said frankly, "I hope you won't ask me to leave her, for I can't do it."

"Nonsense!" said Mr. Barclay. "She will be glad to be rid of you."

Lillo laughed.

"Perhaps, after all, he likes his wild life too well," soliloquized Mr. Barclay.

CHAPTER III.   .

Now that Mr. Barclay's whim had really taken shape and been put into words, it became an ardent desire. To develop the undoubted genius of this fisher-lad, to educate this quickly perceptive mind, and to make a gentleman of Lillo, had suddenly become the dearest wish of his heart, unsatisfied in its parental aspirations. He had in all his life encountered no serious obstacles to any of his reasonable desires, and he would not allow himself to suppose that there could be any impediment in this case. The boy must be brought around to a better sense of the offer, and for this purpose he sought the grandmother.

It was really very warm weather, and the Neck was getting crowded for this fastidious man who had no great interest in human beings *en masse.* He longed now to be on some mountain-top, listening to the wind surging through the pines, watching the purple shadows on the mighty peaks, far away from these thin, penetrating voices which saluted him even in the retirement of his own apartments. With his dog, his gun, and his book, he had always found peace; with Lillo added, there would be less for his devouring melancholy to prey upon. And who could tell what profound possibilities might be drawn from the education of this boy? Velasquez, Titian, Leonardo, Raphael, Rubens, were the pride of the Old World: why should not the New possess as powerful creative force?. He woke from his dreaming and started out for the little brown house. Mrs. Marsh was at home, silent and alone as usual.

She responded to Mr. Barclay's greeting by telling him that Lillo had gone into town on an errand very early, but would soon return, and that he knew his lessons. Then she supposed she had given all the necessary information, and she resumed her knitting.

The room was neat and cool, darkened by the heavy wooden outside shutters of the windows, which, being drawn, the sun penetrated only at their meeting.

The old woman sat up stiffly in a high-backed rocking-chair. Mr. Barclay occupied one equally straight and high backed, without rockers.

"I suppose Lillo has told you what I have come to talk about, Mrs. Marsh?"

"No: he hasn't been at any pranks, I hope?" said the old woman, with a startled glance over her spectacles.

"No: he's all right; and I find it so pleasant to teach him, that I want the pleasure prolonged."

Mrs. Marsh still had a questioning manner.

"I may as well put it in as few words as possible. I want you to give the boy to me, that I may make something of him; I want to send him to school and give him advantages impossible to gain outside of cities. He is so docile and affectionate that I have no hesitation in making this offer. Lillo will make a fine man. Will you give him to me, Mrs. Marsh?"

She looked incredulous: was this strange man in earnest, or was he beside himself?

"Hain't you a family of your own?" she asked.

"No, none very near to me."

"What makes you think he'll be a fine man?"

"There are many proofs of it. I have watched him closely and with interest."

"Seems to me, then, he can get along without help."

This was a new view. Mr. Barclay laughed.

"Yes, I dare say; but it will be harder for him, and he will have to do without the opportunities of cultivation and advancement which I can give him. The difference will be that of one who starts in trade with or without capital. I wish him to have the capital."

"There's no reason agin that, I'm sure; but seems to me you've made a mistake."

"How? Why?"

"Did you never take a crab up out of the water, and watch it wriggle back when you put it on the sand?"

"I don't know; I suppose I have."

"That's just the way it would be with Lillo if you took him away from here."

"I am willing to risk it."

"What does *he* say?"

"He would like the plan, I think, if he could be assured that you were willing; but he will not consent to leave you alone. I think I can arrange that, however."

"Does he show that much feelin'?"

"Yes, quite; it seems to be the one reason for his remaining here."

"Then I'll not drive him off," said the old woman firmly, taking off her spectacles to wipe away the moisture which had gathered upon them.

"But, Mrs. Marsh, you have not given this enough consideration; you forget that if I adopt Lillo I shall be in a measure obliged to see that his future is assured. I have some property. Should he prove worthy of my trust in him, worthy and grateful for the education I propose to give him, he will stand a good chance of being better off in a pecuniary sense."

"Pecuniary sense:" the old woman said the words over to herself, but made nothing of them. "Property:" yes, she understood that.

"It's well to have property. So you're a man of means, eh!"

"Yes."

"But I don't think so much of the eddication: it's apt to spoil poor boys."

Mr. Barclay smiled loftily, and glanced at the sanded floor.

"Yes, it's apt to spoil 'em and make 'em look down on their parents. There was Jim Macy: he went away to school, and it was the ruination of him; they never could do nothin' with him after that. He scorned bein' a Cape Cod fisherman, and I don't quite know whatever became of him. He had an uncle who did for him just what you want to do for Lillo; and the uncle was master of a fine coastin' schooner, which went ashore off Nantucket, and he was drowned. You're very kind, Mr. Barclay, but I guess Lillo'll stay with me."

Was there ever so persistent an absurdity?

Mr. Barclay rose impatiently and looked at the clock. There was no use in arguing.

"Take a little time to think of this, Mrs. Marsh. Tell Lillo he'll find me at my rooms. I'm going for a swim now."

But at this moment in came Lillo with a basket on his arm.

"How dark it seems, and how cool in here! there is such a glare on the sand, and those old beach-wagons creep like snails. How d'ye do, Mr. Barclay? You and granny seem to be waiting for something."

"We were talking about you."

Mr. Barclay, who had sat down again, felt the disadvantage of a chair without rockers. Mrs. Marsh was quietly moving back and forth in hers, knitting fast all the while. He waited till Lillo had put away his basket and was prepared to listen.

"I have been telling Mrs. Marsh what I told you yesterday, Lillo, how I should like to give you a start in the world."

"It's all very kind, Mr. Barclay; but my start's got to be taken here. I've engaged with Mr. Smears, granny, to learn house-painting."

"Lillo!"

"Yes, I knew your heart was set on it, and I might as well begin whether I liked it or not. Mr. Smears is to take me for three months on trial. It'll be a good trudge from here to Codtown every day."

Mr. Barclay said nothing; he was indignant and

hurt, and amazed that their ignorance could so thwart his well-intentioned plans, and do violence to their own prosperity. He drummed a tattoo on the pine table and was silent.

Lillo looked up appealingly.

"You see, Mr. Barclay, I had planned what I was to do before you spoke. I didn't want to learn a trade, and I don't want to now; but granny has been at me to do it for a long while, and now she's alone, I must try to please her; and this is what came into my head to-day when she sent me to town to buy flour, and I met Mr. Smears and he began to talk about it too. Granny was my first friend, Mr. Barclay; but you come next, and I hope you will believe I am grateful."

"There's nothing to be grateful for. You won't let me help you, so there's the end of it. Come, I have only a day or two, so I must be off, and make the most of my time. I want to row over to Seal Island after I've had a bath; the luncheon is already stowed, so you can get the boat ready. Good-morning, Mrs. Marsh, and good-bye. I shall not see you again, as I leave on Thursday. I must thank you for allowing Lillo to be so much with me. We have had very good times together."

"No obligation to me, sir, none at all. The boy has been happy in your company, and will miss you. I hope you're not offended; but, in truth, I couldn't spare him, and he's full enough of nonsense without eddication. You know the man in the Scripters whose learnin' had made him mad. I'm afraid it would have done that to Lillo."

She had risen, and was standing as stiffly erect as she had been sitting.

"Possibly," said Mr. Barclay, smiling grimly as he glanced at the bare, clean little room, with its shining tins, its sanded floor, and few comforts.

"Perhaps you are right, Mrs. Marsh : if he has any thing in him, he will make his way in the world yet, and no thanks to me either."

And so he departed. But he was very much vexed. So much vexed was he that he did not at all notice the change which had come over the day, the shifting of the wind, or the obscuration of the sun; neither did he notice how Lillo, as he dipped his oars, glanced over his shoulder at an ominous gathering of the clouds. Lillo saw that Mr. Barclay was angry, and knew that silence must be maintained; indeed, the boy had no wish to talk. Though he had forced himself into this antagonistic attitude towards his patron, he had not even the ordinary consolation with which those who have their own way solace themselves. He was not having his own way. He was doing that which displeased himself as much as it did Mr. Barclay, but he was acting from a higher motive than self-pleasing. The boy loved this wan, weather-beaten, rough old grandmother ; and in the refusal of Mr. Barclay, and the acceptance of Mr. Smears, he knew he should please her.

So they rowed in silence in the direction of Seal Island; for though Mr. Barclay had forgotten his bath, he had not forgotten his intention of taking his luncheon beyond the gaze of sight-seers.

Yet even in this was he thwarted. As the boat

bumped on the rocks, and Lillo sprang lightly out to moor her, he saw a flutter of white skirts, and two girls retreated behind the few cedar trees and huckleberry bushes which were about all the vegetation the island could boast.

Something very like "Confound it!" escaped from Mr. Barclay. "Not alone even here. Well, perhaps they will have the good sense to stay out of our way. Get out the traps, Lillo, and we will remain where we are, it's too late to go farther;" and Mr. Barclay drew a book from his pocket, spread his army blanket under a sheltering rock, and began to read. Lillo secured the boat, landed the provisions, and, with an eye to the weather, unrolled Mr. Barclay's rubber coat; then with customary habit in idle moments, and now as a resource from the discomfort of his friend's displeasure, he sharpened his pencil and sketched. His knees were his easel, and his canvas an old account-book; but a fallen pine, some grasses and cat-tails in proximity, and a scraggy mass of weeds were grouping themselves almost of themselves on his page when something of greater loveliness caught his quick eye. It was the face of a young girl, a child of his own age, peering at him from the thicket. Her figure was hidden, and her soft gray-blue eyes, shadowed by chestnut hair, seemed to belong to some creature of the woods. When she saw that she was discovered, she drew a branch across her place of retreat and hid herself; but a low grumble of thunder coming at this moment, she sprang from the trees towards Lillo, exclaiming, —

"What shall we do, what shall we do? It is going

to storm, and how can we get home?" Then pausing, and swinging her hat in her hand, with a blending
of fright, curiosity, and timidity she said, —

"Please let me look at your sketch. I wish I
could draw, but I can't. I can only drum on the
piano, and that has to be done indoors; and it is stupid
to stay in the house in summer-time, don't you think
so?"

"I suppose it is," replied Lillo bashfully, as the
child drew nearer, and her soft breath, like the odor
of violets, came over his shoulder.

"Oh, how pretty that is!" she went on. "You
draw beautifully, better than Grace. Grace is my sister. There she is trying to hide. But what shall
we do? We never rowed so far before, and we are
frightened half to death in thunder-storms, at least
Grace is. What a cross-looking man that is under
the rock! Is he any relation of yours?"

"No," said Lillo, smiling.

Mr. Barclay at this moment turned and certainly
scowled. He had been aroused by the thunder, and
was now considering whether it would be possible to
get to a place of shelter before the rain came; then
he heard the pretty, childish treble, and saw Lillo's
companion. At the same time another young girl
appeared, with a very alarmed countenance; but she
went boldly up to Mr. Barclay, saying, —

"I think this is Mr. Barclay. I am Grace Alden.
My aunt, Miss Alden, is a friend of yours, sir, I believe."

Mr. Barclay rose and took off his hat.

"I have the pleasure of knowing Miss Alden."

"I am so distressed! We have disobeyed aunt in coming so far alone, and now I dare not go back. What shall we do, sir? — Here, Pinky, come speak to this friend of aunt's."

"I am not 'Pinky' to strangers, Grace," said the other child, blushing, but coming forward. "Besides, it's raining; and if you're going to stand still I shall go back to the woods."

"Present me properly to your sister, I beg," said Mr. Barclay, amused, though he felt the rain on his nose.

"Miss May Alden, Mr. Barclay," said the other girl, putting up her sun-umbrella, but Miss May was already scampering away. Meantime, Lillo had closed his sketch-book and had begun cutting down branches to pile over the rocks, beneath which they could crouch for a while. On this he spread the rubber cloth which was always in the boat; and by the time Grace had brought back her sister, and Mr. Barclay had donned his rubber coat, the girls had quite a comfortable shelter ready for them. It was now pouring, and the sea dashing up on the rocks, the thunder pealing, and the air dark with the driving rain. Lillo, drenched to the skin, had hauled the boat far enough up to turn her, thus covering the lunch-basket.

Mr. Barclay stood grimly beside the rocks beneath which the girls sat, dry and untouched.

"Look at him," whispered May, "isn't he ugly? Just like a fountain in our square when it's covered with dried leaves in the autumn. Is it a Dryad or a Naiad, or a what do you call it, Grace?"

"Hush!" said Grace peremptorily, "he has been very kind to us."

"I am so hungry, Grace, it makes me cross, — and what will aunt say? She'll be worried and distracted. Perhaps her hair will turn white, and then always we shall hear her tell the story of it, — how we ran away and rowed out to sea, and she supposed us to be drowned, and the agony made her hair turn gray. Age will never be the cause, — as if it weren't gray already. Oh, dear, when will it stop raining? Where's that boy? Oh, you don't know how beautifully he sketches! He must be what aunt calls a genius."

"I wish you had the genius for keeping still," said her sister impatiently.

"Ah, two in a family can't have that. Come, Grace, let's just peek out a little. I do believe I see a little blue sky. There goes the fountain! Come, I don't care if I do get a little wet, now that he has gone," and she thrust her feet out into a pool. "Lovely for ducks!"

"Come directly back, May, or I shall certainly appeal to Mr. Barclay."

"There he comes again!"

"The rain is stopping, young ladies, but I am afraid there will be a succession of showers," said Mr. Barclay. "If you can tell me where to find your boat, I think we had better start for home."

Grace directed him where to look for the boat; but Lillo, coming up at this moment, reported, —

"It's breaking loose, and drifting out to sea."

This was a serious matter, and the children looked aghast.

"What if aunt should hear of that before we reach home! Oh, please, Mr. Barclay, get us home as quickly as you can!" exclaimed Grace. "I really am very sorry to give you so much trouble. We have been very foolish, but we can't help ourselves now;" and tears streamed from her eyes.

"What do you say to our starting, Lillo?" asked Mr. Barclay.

"It's an ugly sea, sir, but " —

"Oh, let us go!" exclaimed both the girls. "We are not afraid."

"Neither am I," said Lillo stoutly, "but " —

"Oh, please go!" chimed the girls.

"We will try it," said Mr. Barclay, and Lillo turned to obey orders. He knew Mr. Barclay was not strong, so the brunt of the labor would be his. He would do his best; and, if the wind went down, there was nothing to fear. But what if the wind rose, could he pull the increased load to shore?

The girls were now in feverish haste to be off. Mr. Barclay, however, insisted upon their taking some lunch, which, hungry as they had been, they could now scarcely swallow. This done, they quickly embarked. For a while all went well. The water was rough, but the swell was exhilarating. Suddenly the wind veered, and they were in an ugly, cross sea. Grace, in her fright, seized Mr. Barclay's arm; the boat lurched, he lost his oar, the sea poured in upon them. The rain came driving down again.

"We must go back," shouted Mr. Barclay. Lillo tried to turn the boat, but could not, and the rain blinded him.

The girls huddled in the stern together, like two frightened doves, white, and with much dripping plumage. Mr. Barclay became seasick, and grew absolutely unable to conquer his deathly faintness. Lillo looked up at the clouds: not a glint of brightness was there to encourage him. The wind was, however, getting around to the south, he thought: so, drawing in his oars, he began to bail out. They could wait a while. Mr. Barclay wrote himself down a fool for his attempt. They should have waited on the island. How could he have allowed himself to be led into such a scrape by two silly chits! What would that aunt of theirs think of him? But that was a small matter, so long as they were not drowned. Ugh! that horrible faintness.

"Lillo!"

"Ay, ay, sir."

"Get back to the island."

"Can't see it, sir."

"We are floating out to sea; I hear the breakers."

"I think not, sir."

"I am sure of it. Isn't there a line of rocks just about here?"

"No, sir. Hello! there's the lost boat."

Mr. Barclay saw it too, and eagerly reached out to grasp it, more to supply himself with an oar than because he cared to save the boat. As he did so, the deathly sickness seized him: he must have fainted, for he lost his balance, and went over.

There was an instant of horror, of indecision. The girls shrieked, and clung closer to each other. The waters seemed to have opened like a hungry mouth, and closed again. Lillo threw off all the clothing he could loosen, and pausing only to see in what direction he should go, plunged after his friend. Mr. Barclay rose a boat's-length away. He was no practised swimmer, but he knew enough not to struggle; and in a few moments Lillo had him by the hair, and was towing him.

By this time, the boats were drifting from them; but, as they rose on the swelling foam, they saw little May scramble into the bow of the "Water-witch," seize an oar, and manage to keep her with her head towards them. Grace sat with clasped hands, crying.

At last the distance lessened. Each wave carried them nearer, and with supreme satisfaction Lillo and Mr. Barclay tugged each other into the safe-keeping of the boats.

Just as they did so, a warm, broad flash of sunlight penetrated the driving spray, and they saw land: but, what was better, a stout craft coming to meet them. With what cordial appreciation of dry land Mr. Barclay stepped ashore that day, it is needless to mention.

Drenched and draggled and ill, he managed to restore his transient wards to their tearful relative; and then seeking Lillo, he said, —

" You've saved my life, boy. Do you know the obligation I am under ? "

" Indeed I don't, sir. It was an accident. I hope you'll be none the worse for it."

"And you ? "

" I mind it no more than a water-rat," said Lillo, shaking himself.

"I consider myself very much in your debt, remember."

"Not at all, Mr. Barclay. I'm only too glad to have been of use to you. We are friends again, I hope."

"Yes, we are friends," said Mr. Barclay. But he did not again urge his proposal.

The next day, instead of leaving the Neck, he found himself too ill to leave his bed.

Miss Alden was profuse in attentions, and Grace and May made daily inquiries concerning him; but a doctor and nurse from Boston forbade his departure until late in the summer.

CHAPTER IV.

THE fourth floor of a New York second-rate board-ing-house is not especially to be chosen as an abiding place when June is bursting her roses and scattering perfume on the air. Birds do not tilt on the window-sills and sing to the unhappy prisoners, neither do daisies beckon to the fields of clothes-lines below; but the rumble and roar of the city's chant of toil fill the air, already heavy with sewer-gas and petroleum.

No one could have been more conscious of these things, nor felt himself more a prisoner, than the person who at this moment is listening to a distant hand-organ, and seeking for a glimpse of sky above the barren ugliness of bricks which obscure his sight. He is a man yet young, as you can see by his beard and hair, which, though unkempt, are of fine color; but he is a man whose experiences have aged him. He has been unsuccessful, has invariably lost when others won, stumbled and fallen where others kept the path; has been baffled, pursued, defeated, in the battle all have to fight. He had begun fairly, as well as nine-tenths do, with high hopes, good cour-age, and no vices, but had neither satisfied himself nor other people. Undoubtedly there was a screw loose somewhere, perhaps in the original construc-

tion of the article; the nice mechanism had probably been too nice for its applied purpose, and when
overworked or rusty no one had been sufficiently interested to lubricate it.   It has now given token of
stopping altogether.   With the ceasing of the struggle has come a certain calmness which might easily
be mistaken for peace ; perhaps it is peace in an imperfect form, the perfection being attainable only in
another world.   At all events, this man has ceased
repining, ceased wishing for himself; but he has one
tender plant for whose blossoming he craves the sunshine and the dew of heaven.

"Ruth !"

"Yes, father."

"Where shall we go this summer ? "

The girl looks up with startled eyes from her sewing.   It is a piece of very plain sewing, — no filoselle
and canvas with sprays of lilies or meadow-sweet ; but
her fingers are lithe and active, and her needle flits
quickly in and out of the under-garment.   She is
very young, very small, and very like her father.

"I don't know, father," she responds ; "I am afraid
you are not strong enough for a journey."

"Very likely! we may have to go different ways ;
but where should *you* like to go ? "

"Nowhere without you, father."

"Not to some cool, shady, old farmhouse, where
the elm-trees make a bower overhead, and the robins
chatter among the cherries ? "

"No, father."

"Nor to the hard sandy beach, where wave upon
wave comes rolling up in foam, and you could gather
shells and seaweed ? "

"No, father."

"Nor to the hills overlooking the valleys, where the wind sighs in the tall pines, and its breath is the very elixir of life?"

"Nowhere without you, father."

"Come here, Ruth."

She goes to him, and he draws her down upon his lap.

"You are a very little girl to be left alone in the world."

She buries her face in his coat.

"If you cry, I can't talk to you."

"I will stop, father." And up comes the brave little head; and she bites her lips and swallows her sobs with an effort, which, after a while, becomes successful.

"I can't take you where I am going, Ruth, — I wish I could, — and I have no one with whom to leave you. All my relations are too poor, they have just as much as they can do to take care of themselves; and your mother's friends are all too rich and taken up with their own affairs to be bothered about a little waif like you. I used to visit at their houses, dance at their parties, and dine at their tables; and I know just how your poor little heart would ache to be a dependent among any of them. They are not wicked, but they are cold and selfish and narrow; and you would have to hear your father spoken of as an unlucky dog, who ought not to have married his pretty wife and let her die for want of comforts and luxuries which he could not supply, nor left his little Ruth to their charity. Ah, yes, child! I know how it

would be. No, I am not angry. I am not cross. I
am just telling you all this because when you grow
up you will have to know it all, and rather than let
you go to them I would put you in the orphan asy-
lum; but— There, there, Ruth! I know some one
who I think will be good to my little girl and take
care of her; some one who has always been good
to me, and would have bridged me over many a difficulty if I had let him know my trouble. Ah! we
were chums long years ago, — friends always, in
school and out of school. He always beat me at
every thing. I was always unlucky, but he never
crowed over me. He has had his griefs as well as I
mine, but they haven't put an end to him as mine
have to me. He has a kind heart, and can be trusted
with my one poor lamb. I will write to him and tell
him all about little Ruth, and he will come and get
her; and then I can go as soon as I please, —yes, just
as soon as I please."

Here the poor man had a wretched coughing turn,
which made talking quite impossible, and little Ruth
had to get his spoonful of sirup, and shake up his
pillows; and then she ran down-stairs for the toast,
which might be burned by the careless cook if she
did not attend to it.

She was quite breathless when she came back, and
found her father at his table with pen, ink, and paper
before him.

"I am only afraid, Ruth, that I can't go as soon
as I ought to on your account."

"Where, father?" said the child innocently.

"Oh! away, — altogether. I am stronger than I
thought."

" How glad I am, dear father ! "

" You shouldn't be, Ruth ; it is very wrong of me to keep you here in the hot city, pent up in this room. You look pale ; you need fresh air. Put on your bonnet and go to the square, and you may post my letter at the same time. I can't write a very long one. There, run off now."

" But the toast, father ; please eat it."

" Well, just to please you, dear ; but I oughtn't to," he murmured. " It's an injustice to her to keep the fire going, and just so much fuel wasted. But there's the trouble, I can't hurry matters ;" and laying his pen down he felt his pulse, with his watch before him.

" Pretty rapid, weak, too, goes by jerks ; it can't keep up much longer, I should think. I'd like to get the answer to this letter ; just my luck, however, if I don't. The parson says I mustn't call it luck ; but that's a bad habit of mine. I know better. I know it's God's will."

Here Ruth came back, with a brown straw hat shading her violet eyes.

" I am ready, father."

" All right, little wren."

The scratching pen and the hacking cough kept up a duet.

At last the letter was finished, signed, sealed, and stamped. The father drew his little girl to him with a kiss.

" You are just the best and bravest little daughter in the world."

" And you are the dearest and sweetest father."

With that she tripped off to mail his letter, glad to get out even into the dry and dusty streets.

He walked to his bookshelf, reached too far for a volume, the strain started his cough again. A bright red stream bubbled up and over his lips. He sank into the nearest chair. "Sooner than I thought," he said to himself; and then, though fainting and the darkness of the lonely valley shutting out the daylight, his thoughts were for his little one. "God keep her! God in his mercy temper the wind to the shorn lamb."

CHAPTER V.

THE letter sped on its way, its life and force continuing long after the hand which winged it was lying lifeless on the still heart. It reached the Neck soon after Mr. Barclay had been pronounced convalescent, and was allowed to have visitors. On the day of its arrival, Mr. Barclay was sitting at a window looking seaward. In front of him was a table with a bowl of ice, a bottle of claret, a heap of new publications fresh from the press, a bunch of flowers from a Boston hot-house, a sketch of a trim little yacht, on a rustic easel, and a tonic or two bearing broad labels of their virtues with magnanimous publicity on their fronts.

Beside him sat Miss Alden, crocheting.

Miss Alden is a person with a talent for other people's affairs, having few of her own. The talent takes a kindly form with her, for she is generous, warm-hearted, and fond of making all around her comfortable. She is a slender lady, of an unknown age, with a prepossessing countenance; her hair is tinged with gray; and she assumes a style of dress, which, though rich in material, is severely simple in form. She disdains marriage as a state of life suitable only for the very young and frivolous. Her charge of her two young nieces gives her ample occu-

cupation of a sort she enjoys, and the chance of ministering to her invalid friend, Mr. Barclay, is also a
piece of good fortune which she is making the most
of. She sent for the hot-house flowers, and one of
the tonics is a draught which she has never known
to fail. She has great faith in herself and in all her
prescriptions, and it imparts a happy placidity of demeanor and a certain force to all she says and does.
People confide in her and believe in her — unless, as
is sometimes the case, she makes a mistake and prof-
fers her services in the wrong direction. For all people are not equally ready to be taken under her wing.

Mr. Barclay is not wholly reduced to proper sub-
jection. She knew his wife, — for Miss Alden was a
woman grown when Mrs. Barclay was a schoolgirl, —
and she speaks of her once in a while in a way that
is not unpleasant to him, in a refined, gentle way, as
if Belle were still living, which makes him more
ready to accept her kind services than he otherwise
would be. Though outwardly placid, Miss Alden is
restless; she likes to scheme and plan, likes to travel.
When she is at home she often changes her hotel,
or at the hotel changes her apartments. In this
way she also occasionally errs, for her movements
sometimes disturb other people. But her manners
are unexceptionable, and often carry her over rough
spots where awkwardness might bring her to grief.
Few persons can resist kindness; even the grim
old uncles with lots of stocks and money-bags (in
novels) always have a tender spot which can be
touched beneath the hard crust of their ungracious
exterior.

The day is very warm; and as the man with the mail comes in Miss Alden puts aside her crochet, and gently stirs a large feather fan, sending the odor of roses about the room.

"Pardon me for opening my letters," Mr. Barclay says, with a little inclination of the head, somewhat hoping that his guest may go.

"Certainly, Frank" (she always calls him by his Christian name), "certainly. I will read my own at the same time." She has quite a budget of crested and monogrammed envelopes in her lap, and is soon absorbed in their contents. It takes her a long while; and when she ceases she looks up with a little start, to see Mr. Barclay surveying an open newspaper and comparing its date with that of a blue ruled letter-sheet before him. He looks pale and distressed. She rises, pours out in a little glass the strengthening liquid on the table, and says gently, —

"You had better lie down now, Frank; you seem tired. Your nurse is out too long; I must speak to him."

"Pray don't, Miss Alden: it bores me to death to have him here all the time." Then he takes the draught from her hand, and says, "Read that, if you please. I'm sure I don't know what I can do in the matter, situated as I am now."

She reads the letter, which runs thus: —

DEAR FRANK, — The memory of school-days and college-days, and many a happy time, suggests to me the idea of making you my legatee. I am very rich — in one little girl. This large fortune I bequeath to you. Be good to her, be kind to her. I am too near the end of my rope to explain matters. She is to be found at my present address.   I should be glad to hear that you will accept the trust, but, "*post factum, nullum consilium.*" I have no time to spare.   Yours in the grasp of death.

RICHARD MORRIS.

"What a strange letter!"

"He was always a strange fellow, poor Dick! And here's his death already announced."

Miss Aldén took the newspaper, and read the announcement.

"And you know nothing more than this letter tells you?"

"Nothing.   I haven't seen him for years."

"He has taken a great liberty."

"None too great for the occasion, if the child has no protector."

"But so unconventional."

"He was always that."

"It is very strange."

"It is indeed.   If I were not so helpless just now, I would go on to New York."

"Has he no relatives?"

"I am sure I don't know."

"But they are in duty bound to see to the child?"

"Not unless I declare myself disinclined to serve as guardian; besides, people are not always ready to do their duty."

"Has he property?"

"I fancy not.   I have lost track of him lately. We studied law together.   He married early; since then, I fear it has gone hard with him."

"But you are not obliged to accept such a trust?"

"No, not obliged legally, perhaps morally I am."

"It is very strange that he did not give you the choice of refusal."

"He rather honors me in supposing refusal impossible, and certainly a man in the grasp of death must look at life with clearer vision. He *has* honored me. I was somewhat dazed at first, not knowing just what to think; but of course I shall do what I can for the child, if she is of the right stuff."

"Ah, that is just the point! She may not be interesting."

"Nor tractable, which would be worse."

"An uninteresting child is so tiresome."

"I shall not promise to keep her with me; there are plenty of schools."

"Yes, a good boarding-school will have to be found; I know of several. Of course you cannot be cumbered with a child: that would necessitate a maid and a governess."

Miss Alden was becoming interested.

"You do not keep a governess for your nieces, Miss Alden?"

"No, I have only my maid. She serves them too, as much as I think well for them, — I prefer them to depend a little upon themselves, — and Grace and May go to school at home. My brother, however, is thinking of letting them go abroad with me this coming winter."

"I wonder what this ward of mine will look like — if she is as pretty as her mother was; that is quite an important element in this transaction."

"But the poor child — who is with her at this trying moment?"

"True! I will have to inquire. Poor Dick! so he is dead. Another friend gone!"

"Suppose I go to the city, and bring the child here for your inspection?"

"That certainly is a very kind proposal; I can, however, send a clerk on from Boston."

"Ah! but a young man might find it an awkward errand. She may need an outfit, and she may be delicate or ill or"—

"Heavens! what am I undertaking? Miss Alden, you open my eyes to the difficulties. I begin to recall my own childhood, — the doctors, the dentists, the schools, and the thousand and one demands made by the 'hostages to fortune.' It is somewhat odd, too, that I should be refused the child of my choice, and have the child of friendship forced upon me."

Miss Alden did not understand the latter end of his speech: so she only repeated her offer, explaining that it was nothing of a journey for her, she often went on to the city for shopping. May and Grace must take their sailing and bathing orders from Mr. Barclay until she returned; that would be the only compensation she would exact from him, if he were equal even to that.

And so it was arranged.

Miss Alden left the next day, combining her errand of mercy with one of convenience. Her summer gowns needed altering, and her dressmaker was in New York.

Three days afterward came this letter to Mr. Barclay.

My dear Frank, — I was just in time to attend the funeral, and see to the poor child. It was most fortunate that you allowed me to represent you. She needs *every thing*, and will be a very suitable companion for May and Gracie. She is *perfectly unexceptionable;* is small and slender, but much too quiet and pale for her age. It will take me a few days to get her mourning made. Her board was paid in advance by her poor father, who, I hear, was extremely honest, and though very, very poor, leaves no debts behind him. Should you change your mind in regard to her, I will adopt her myself. One or two relatives offered to take her, but she shrank from them all. Tell the girls her name is Ruth. I hope sea-air will bring a little color to her poor, pale cheeks. The city is terribly dry and dusty, and the noise is intolerable.

I hope my nieces are models of propriety and give you no concern, and that your health has improved.

Faithfully yours,

ALTHEA ALDEN.

P.S. — Ruth sends her love to her father's friend, Mr. Barclay. I hope you will permit her to call you uncle: it will sound more friendly. A. A.

Mr. Barclay smiled and groaned. The letter was extremely characteristic, but he began to realize what he was undertaking. No more should he be left to himself. Already had he become of double interest to Miss Alden, and hers would not long be the only finger in the pie. It was certainly easy enough for Dick Morris to walk out of the world leaving his child behind him; indeed, he had no alternative: the difficulty was left for the living man to adjust, and he too, having a kind heart, had no alternative. And then his sorrow, as usual, tinged his thoughts. If Belle had only been spared to him, how trifling would this obligation have seemed! With her tact and sweet temper, how happily every thing would have been arranged! But for her sake, as well as Dick's, he had no intention of refusing the trust imposed upon him. He would take a good look at the child, make some sort of an estimate of her points, consult Miss Alden as to her present needs, find a good school, and place her in it. Then, if the doctors had settled about his lungs, he would depart for the South of France when cool weather should set in, if only to escape the advice and suggestions which his guardianship would bring about his head.

Meanwhile, little Ruth, drowsy and dazed with grief, was being used as a milliner's block, and swathed and folded in crape. To get out of the boarding-house, with its perpetual smell of food, was a pleasant change, especially as the kind lady who took her about always came in a trim little coupé, and had a nosegay somewhere about her; but it was fearfully tiresome to stand, and be measured and fitted and discussed, to have gloves tried on, and bonnets tried on, and find herself black, dismal black, from top to toe. It is a singular way we Christians have of expressing our belief in a blessed immortality, this swathing ourselves in the most hopeless looking garments we can find.

But the preparations, though they seemed long to Ruth, were really finished in a short time; and she found herself with a tearful smile on her face, as she looked in the cracked looking-glass at her new attire, put on for the journey, and heard the men carrying away her luggage, and knew that she would never come back to this house of sorrow. For it is a great

relief to a child to get away from the scene of anguish
and mysterious pain which darkens all the sunshine
and compels silence and gloom.

She sorrowed none the less for her father, but
there was a little springing of hope, a few tender
blades of joy in her young heart, at the prospect
Miss Alden portrayed to her. And how honestly a
child allows itself to be pleased, to smile even through
tears ! it has no compunctions, no hypocritical desire
to look afflicted, and no immoderate demand for sympathy.

"Heavens ! what a rare, sweet face," said Mr.
Barclay to himself, as on the day of her return Miss
Alden led Ruth into his apartment, followed by
Grace and May Alden, who had at once, and with child-
ish effusion, taken their new acquaintance into their
youthful keeping. Aloud, he said, taking her hand, —

"I am glad to see you, my dear. You and I ought
to have known each other before, but you find me
laid up for a while, and so Miss Alden has kindly
done for me what I should have done for myself."

Ruth advanced timidly, and took the chair beside
the invalid. There was just enough resemblance
between the condition of this invalid, and that of the
one to whom she had so recently said farewell, to
make her feel at her ease, as well as to arouse her
sorrow and her sympathy. She made no reply to
his kind greeting other than to fix her gentle gaze
upon him with a sad tenderness that made Mr. Barclay look vainly around for the handkerchief he had
misplaced.

"Was your journey fatiguing? Have you ever

before been to the seashore ? " he questioned rapidly,
to hide his agitation.

" No, sir."

" A soft, low voice — an excellent thing in woman,"
again was Mr. Barclay's mental speech.

" Then you will find much to amuse you ; and
these lively girls will have to show you all the wonders of the deep, until I can get about again."

" But I think I would rather wait upon you."

" Oh, no, not at all ; I shall soon be all right.
Children need air and sunshine and merriment.
You must grow strong and gay with bathing and
boating."

" But I am used to taking care of things.   Father
called me his little nurse."

There was a gentle insistence and a pleading tone
to the soft voice, which made Mr. Barclay look at
Miss Alden despairingly.   Instead of his caring for
her, here was this bit of a creature desiring to be his
protector, for she went on to say, —

" I can drop medicine very steadily, and I can keep
the glasses and spoons so that they shine ; and I can
make a bed up very nicely, — so father said."

" Can you read aloud ? " put in Miss Alden with
gentle tact.

" Oh, yes," said Ruth eagerly, a tinge of rose coming to her cheeks.

" Well, I daresay Mr. Barclay will let you read to
him once in a while.   He has a nurse, you know,
else he would be very glad to let you show him all
your nice little accomplishments.   What have you
read ? "

"Oh, every thing that father liked, — 'The Princess,' and 'Aurora Leigh,' and 'In Memoriam,' and 'The Tempest;' but father liked 'The Essays of Elia' best of all."

"'The Essays of Elia' to a dying man;" this was another aside from Mr. Barclay. "Poor fellow, I don't blame him. He wanted to laugh as well as the rest of us, and he had precious little to laugh at."

"Father didn't like 'Artemus Ward' or 'Mark Twain.' He said they had no wit, it was all coarse humor; and that Tom Hood and Charles Lamb were like wax-candles, they gave such clear fine light."

"And what did your father say about the others, Tennyson and Mrs. Browning and Shakspeare?" said Miss Alden, glad of the diversion of thought for Mr. Barclay as well as for the child.

"I don't remember all he told me. I think he said Mr. Tennyson was very much like somebody else — a long Latin name" —

"Theocritus?" said Mr. Barclay.

"Yes, that was the name. And he said Mrs. Browning had wonderful power; and that, put them all together, every one of them, they wouldn't live as long as Robert Burns, because he" —

"He what?" urged Mr. Barclay, noticing the child hesitate.

"Because he wrote for poor people and was a poor man himself."

The child had hesitated because she knew she was not among poor people. The pictures, the comfort, the beauty of much that she saw gave her this impression; and she supposed she was committing a

breach of good manners to speak as slightingly as
her father had evidently spoken of those who were
well off in the world.

"And why would that make him live longer?"

"I don't know, sir, except that there are so many
more poor people in the world."

"How do you know that, Ruth?"

"Father said so, sir."

"Will you be as willing to quote my words, and
be guided by my wishes, as by those of the father in
whose place I am to stand, dear little Ruth?"

She looked into his very soul, it seemed to him,
before she answered; then the violets filled to the
brim with dew, and throwing herself down upon him,
she cried, —

"If you will love me as he did, I will do any thing,
any thing!"

Mr. Barclay kissed her in silence, and Miss Alden
drew her gently away, giving her in charge to the
two round-eyed girls, whose laughter generally had
to be checked, but who now were mute and still.
They wound their arms about Ruth as young fawns
caress a hurt doe, and led her off to their favorite
haunts on the beach where the dashing waves tossed
their silvery crests.

"So that is what you entitle 'perfectly unexceptionable,' my dear Miss Alden," said Mr. Barclay,
with a shade of sarcasm in his tone, when the children had gone.

Miss Alden was not expecting thanks for her
trouble. She knew that her services were fully appreciated, and she was not disposed to over-rate

them. But she did not quite understand Mr. Barclay's remark. So she smoothed her soft hair with just a touch of her taper fingers as she replied, —

"Yes, I *do* think so. You mustn't be troubled by this little outburst of feeling: it is extremely natural, you know, under the circumstances."

"I'm not troubled. It would have been odd had she shown less feeling. She is the loveliest little creature; as choice as a bit of Sèvres, as fine, as pure, as transparent, — too fine for a man's rough fingers."

"Ah! you exaggerate."

"Not at all. My eyes are fresh; but I cannot hope to convey my impression to one who only finds her 'unexceptionable.'"

"But, Mr. Barclay, my words are very high praise, I assure you. I am very *exigeante*. I suppose you allude to my letter. It was written in haste; but, after all, what more would you have had me say? I am not an enthusiast, and I have not the habit of over-praising."

"I beg your pardon, Miss Alden; I am rude. Illness has made me overbearing. The child to me is as exquisite as a lily. Did you notice the play of expression in her face, — the sorrow and tenderness mingling with happiness at the thought of her being of some possible use to me?"

"I saw less than you did, probably; but she has a delicate prettiness, I acknowledge."

"It is more than that, and will be as she grows. I am afraid I have undertaken too much."

"Shall I take her off your hands?"

"Not till I have made the experiment — and failed. But what shall I do with her at present?"

"Leave her to Grace and May. Children seem to understand each other."

"Yes; there seems to be a free-masonry among them. But she must have a maid."

"That is as you please."

"Lessons, I suppose, need not be thought of immediately?"

"No, not for warm weather."

"And she has every thing else she needs, thanks to your kindness."

"No thanks are necessary. She has a neat wardrobe, simple and becoming. You have no idea how destitute she was."

"Poor Dick! How hard it must have been for him to see such a sweet little thing deprived of all that she ought to have had. I wish I had known his situation; but pride and poverty go hand in hand, always."

"Yes, I suppose that is very true. There were relatives at the funeral who were abundantly able to help him. I told you about them, I think?"

"You mentioned that there was some sort of an offer made to the child."

"Yes, from her mother's uncle, a pompous sort of a man. He was quite surprised and annoyed that Ruth had been given to you, and tried to make her think it was her duty to go home with him."

"What could have been his motive?"

"Perhaps he was ashamed that he had not sooner befriended them."

"It is charitable to suppose so. What was his name?"

"Biggs or Boggs; Boggs, I think. I have not a very good ear for names."

"Did the child seem to know him well?"

"Not at all, and she shrank from even speaking to him. He had a certain superficial polish of manner, but he murdered the king's English. His coachman was in livery. There was an aunt, too, who, judging by externals, had wealth. She wore diamonds large as the tip of my finger. She was quite overcome at the funeral, and was profuse in attentions to Ruth, in a peculiar way. Her name was something like Venner or Vedder. I really am ashamed of my inability to remember names."

"What does it matter? We shall never hear of them again."

"No, I suppose not; that is, if you assume the guardianship alone."

"And why should I not?"

"Really, I don't know, Frank; it is not for me to dictate. Belle would have been glad to have you interest yourself in so kind and unselfish a project as the education of this young thing; but your relatives may find fault."

"I am not accustomed to consult them."

"No, I suppose not, but"—

"Well, Miss Alden, I wait for your 'but.'"

"I'll not give it; second thoughts are wise."

"Not always. Did you not say you were willing to assume the task if I concluded to relinquish it?"

" No, not just that.   I only asked if I should take
her out of your hands."

"You surely wrote, that, if I changed my mind, you
would adopt her yourself; at least, this is the impression your letter made upon me, and I cannot be so
utterly mistaken."

" I may have done so under an impulse of pity;
but, as I said just now, second thoughts are wise
ones.   I had not looked at the matter in all its
bearings.   Grace and May have the first claim upon
me, as your relatives have upon you, Frank."

"Ah! now I know what your 'but' means."

Miss Alden smiled and asked, " Is it not well to
look before you leap ?"

" Quite as well for Miss Alden, but I reserve the
masculine right to leap without looking."

And so their conversation ended.

Mr. Barclay did not regain strength rapidly, and
preferred to remain in his rooms "away from the
crowd," as he expressed it ; but Ruth came daily to
him, with cheeks that began to rival the seashells in
delicate color.   She was entirely under Miss Alden's
kind supervision, though the necessary maid, a decorous Irish girl (for Ruth knew no French, though
the Aldens chattered glibly to their Alsacienne), had
been provided.

While Mr. Barclay was still undecided as to plans,
and was living in invalid fashion, a card was one day
brought to him bearing "Boggs" upon it.   Mr. Barclay read it over more than once, " C. Boggs," but
failing to remember any acquaintance of the name
excused himself.   The card was then followed by a

message, saying that Mr. Boggs was the uncle of Miss Ruth Morris. Recalling Miss Alden's description of the man, Mr. Barclay at once sent for him, wondering what would be his errand.

"Ah, how d'ye do, Mr. Barclay," was the somewhat patronizing salutation of this unknown but none-the-less-at-his-ease individual. "Sorry to see you sick this warm weather, — very warm, very warm. I am quite out of sorts, too; shouldn't have thought of making such an exertion but for being on my way to the Vineyard. Suppose you want to know what brought me here; you'd admire to know, I suppose?"

Mr. Barclay expressed himself as reasonably inquisitive in so indifferent a manner as to contradict his words.

"Well, you see," said Mr. Boggs, using his handkerchief to mop his perspiring countenance, and displaying costly sleeve-buttons, "I wa'n't altogether satisfied with them arrangements that our friend and relative Dick Morris made before he departed this life. I'm a man of some pride of family, and Dick ought to have consulted me about his daughter. Now, I don't suppose you were very much flattered to be chosen as the guardian of Ruth; no more was I to be left out. I can provide for her, if I choose, handsomely; but I ought to have been asked. It is the least a man should do who wants a favor done him is to ask for it, as I used to tell Dick when I'd hear of his being in a tight place; but he'd only quote some darned Greek or Latin at me, and never give me no chance to help him."

Mr. Boggs paused, and Mr. Barclay felt obliged to respond.

"It was not very encouraging to one who was disposed to be philanthropic or benevolent, certainly, to be met in that sort of way."

"No, of course not. Glad you agree with me. Well, now, about Ruth. I've got children enough of my own, and responsibility enough; but I am sorry for the girl, and want to do well by her. But she can't expect to eat the bread of idleness.

Mr. Boggs seemed to expect assent to this on Mr. Barclay's part; but, meeting no response, he went on, —

"She ought to be brought up to earn her own livin'; and I've been ready to give a helpin' hand to more than one orphan in my time, and am not goin' to back out now if Dick Morris didn't do as he'd ought to. The truth is, Dick was a trifle above the rest of us in his own opinion: a college education didn't do him no good; it only set him up in his own conceit; took all the vim out of him for business. Now, I left school at twelve, and went right straight into trade. My father had money, but he wan't the man to let boys hang on to him; consequence is, I have a pile of my own, live in comfort, have the best of every thing, and don't feel like seeing a relation left to strangers as Ruth has·been."

"Very creditable sentiments, Mr. Boggs," was Mr. Barclay's rejoinder; but Mr. Boggs was not quite sure that he had gained Mr. Barclay's approval. There was a little mocking smile on Mr. Barclay's countenance, and a languor of manner as he tilted a paper-cutter on his fingers, that Mr. Boggs did not admire.

"Did you know Dick Morris intimately?" he suddenly asked, as if a new thought had occurred to him.

"Very," answered Mr. Barclay laconically.

"And his wife?"

"Not so well."

"He made an idol of her; spent his money on her as if he had been a rich man."

"Indeed."

"Yes, it was a foolish match."

"I dare say."

"Well, what are you going to do about the child, Mr. Barclay?"

"Nothing, at present."

"Would you like me to relieve you of the burden?"

"Thank you, no."

"But you can't be bothered this way without some compensation."

Mr. Barclay simply looked at the man with so astonished a gaze that Mr. Boggs was alarmed. Perhaps this invalid was subject to spasms preceded by a stare.

"I'm ready to come down with the cash and do my share, Mr. Barclay."

"You are really very generous, Mr. Boggs, but I shall need no assistance."

"I suppose you know your own business best; but, remember, I am a man of experience. This girl is very likely of the same stuff as Dick, and you oughtn't

to encourage fine-lady notions.   She mustn't expect
any thing from us if she doesn't work.   You will
send her to the common-school, of course, and then
she can become a teacher."

Mr. Barclay here rose, and, with an unmistakable
air of dismissal, said, —

"I thank you for your visit, Mr. Boggs, and for
your interest in my ward.   In assuming the relation
of guardian to my old friend's daughter, I beg to have
the honor of her entire control, and must ask you
henceforth to give yourself no trouble concerning
her.   I am deeply indebted to my friend for the trust
he has reposed in me, and shall endeavor to fulfil the
obligation to the best of my ability, without assistance
and without advice.   Good-morning, Mr. Boggs."

"Good-morning, Mr. Barclay, good-morning; happy
to see you, sir, when you come my way.   I am going
to camp-meeting when I leave here.   Ruth would
have to be a Methodist if she came among us.   But
I'll offer no more advice : you know your own business best.   But I've done my duty to the child, so
good-morning."

He mopped his blazing face again, and again displayed the showy sleeve-buttons.

Mr. Barclay gave a sigh of relief, lighted a cigar,
and murmuring, "Poor Dick! poor Dick!" picked
up a volume of Molière ; but he was in no humor for
reading.

"So I must make a schoolmistress of my little
wild-rose, no matter what her adaptiveness, no matter
what her general qualities.   Pour the jelly into the
mould while it is liquid and warm, and turn it out

according to recipe. Ah, well, the man might have been worse! He is only a type of an essentially practical and unmistakably vulgar class with whom success is every thing. But I do not wonder Dick wanted none of his help."

Ruth came in just then with May. They had been bathing, and looked like Naiads with their wet locks hanging over their shoulders.

"It is just too glorious to-day, uncle Frank," said May, who had lost all awe of her aunt's friend.

"It is, indeed, Mr. Barclay," repeated Ruth. "The air is like wine."

"Where did you get your simile, Ruth?"

"From some of my father's books, I suppose, Mr. Barclay. But please do come out; it will make you well, and we want you with us."

"Did you meet any one on the sands, Ruth?"

"Oh, yes!"

"But some one you knew, a relation of yours?"

"No, Mr. Barclay. Who was it?"

"Mr. Poggs was here."

The child's face grew pale and downcast.

"Did he come for me?"

"He cannot have you, Ruth. I shall keep you all for my very own."

CHAPTER VI.

But where was Lillo all these long summer days? long, and bright, and buoyant with promise. Was he skimming the waves like the sea-gulls, or dreaming out his pictures under the full-orbed moon?

Early in the dew of the morning, while the sojourners at the "Neck" were still slumbering, he was trudging off to the small hamlet with the very fragrant appellation of "Codtown," getting an occasional lift from a wagon on his way, and striving to do his best at the trade which was practised, only in the most primitive manner, at Mr. Smears's small shop. There had come a change in the boy's aspect and demeanor. Hitherto, he had been careless and light-hearted to a degree which made him more like the wild creatures of the forest than a being bound down by civilization. He had lived like the wild creatures too, in a measure, and his joyous abandon had known nothing of care or perplexity. Now the growth of the human was asserting itself, accompanied by a repression, a gravity easily mistaken for sullenness, and an alteration which even grandmother Marsh noticed. That the boy was striving to accomplish something which in its nature was foreign to his own, did not, of course, suggest itself to her. She was very proud of the determination he was showing, and unfeignedly glad at the prospect of what she considered to be usefulness. But even she missed that at which she had scolded and growled. There was no merry laughter, no whistling, no flinging about: all was staid and decorous. His spare moments were not now spent in decorating whitewashed walls and embellishing profusely in charcoal-sketches. His last sketch had been made the day after the stormy episode at Seal Island: it was an attempt to reproduce a laughing face set in a frame of interlacing boughs. It was crude and rude, but forceful. Though he did not sketch, he did read, and with avidity. In the intervals of paint-mixing and powder-grinding and oil-measuring, from the pocket of blouse or overalls was produced the book which happened at the moment to entrance him; for he had a goodly lot to choose from in the box which had been ordered up from Boston by Mr. Barclay immediately after his unexpected and disastrous bath. Certainly it was a mixed diet, but none the less digestible, all this feast of fat things in literature. History, biography, poetry, natural history, science, and classical fiction were all represented in Mr. Barclay's order, and in the handiest form were all the books bound. It would have grieved a lover of bindings to have seen these books stacked one upon another in Lillo's small garret-room, with a piece of tarpaulin over and about them, as protection from possible leaks in the roof; but no bibliopole could have surveyed them with greater affection than did the fisher-lad. They so far compensated him for his disliked occupation as to make him oblivious for the time of every thing but their contents. Two or three times, Miss Alden, Ruth, Grace, and May had tried to find Lillo at home, and, failing in this, had essayed to entertain Mrs. Marsh; but the old woman had shown so much reserve, and had so plainly given them to understand that she preferred her loneliness to their presence, that they had ceased their visits. Once in a while Lillo had seen their merry party on the beach, and had even followed their laughter of an evening on the water; but he managed to keep his own boat unnoticed, and would leave the allurements of the musical voices to fish for his granny's breakfast. If he had longings and regrets, they were buried in the first page that he next turned over.

Meanwhile, Mrs. Marsh was getting more and more feeble. With the absence of her life-long companion, many of her duties had ended; and, when the incentive to exertion ceases with aged people whose lives are spent in toil, there is often a very sudden decline in strength. Their interest in life wanes. This was the case with Lillo's grandmother. She still sat upright and knitted her stockings, when the domestic affairs were settled; but more frequently her head drooped, and her knitting fell to the floor. Sometimes Lillo would come home late, tired and eager for his supper, to find her still sleeping, with a pallor and expression of fatigue on her countenance which did not escape the boy. Very tenderly would he regard her at such times, and step lightly for fear of disturbing her; but it only irritated her to waken, and find the cloth laid, the fire rekindled, and the boy

preparing supper for himself. She did not comprehend her own weakness, and Lillo invariably received
a sound scolding for doing the most simple and necessary trifles. But his nature was too sweet to be
spoiled by any crabbed peevishness. He could assume a slightly saucy air of indifference, which, to a
younger woman, would have been exasperating, but
which was wasted on Mrs. Marsh's dulled percep-
tions, while it was a sort of armor to Lillo himself;
with it he could receive without injury any amount
of buffeting. And so he took all the scoldings and
fault-findings. To be sure, he had always been used
to them; but perhaps with his growth had come an
enlarged sense of justice, which made more apparent
the fact of their being undeserved.

At Mr. Smears's paint-shop, trade was dull; there
were no villas in the neighborhood to need frequent
new coats, and the boarding-houses waited for their
guests to go before they refurbished. A barrow or
wagon had occasionally to be touched up. But after
a few experiments it was found that Lillo, having a
natural faculty for tools, could be usefully employed
in more ways than one. Slight repairs, demanding
a good eye for straight lines and a skilful use or ad-
justment of old material, were assigned him; and
the boy, hating idleness, responded with alacrity.
Day by day the tasks grew larger and more numerous. Quickly and readily he accepted them, to the
surprise of all who watched him.

Mr. Smears's " bound boy," which as an apprentice
he was called, was often in demand.

And so the summer passed, and the summer

idlers sped home, and the lodging-houses were closed.

Lillo looked out over the vast expanse of water, with an incoming tide of hopes and wishes. His reading had widened his horizon. How could he reach the other side of that vast flood? When would this serfdom end, and he be master of himself?

Keen and sharp blew the east winds over the ocean, piling the sand-bars higher than ever. The little brown house stood as bare and lonely as always, taking the wind in its face; but long into the dreary nights a clear, bright beam shot from its garret window, like the thought which had wakened within and was sending rays out far and wide, scintillating and flashing on the wide waste of darkness.

Wildly the autumn winds beat about the little house, making it groan and creak and wheeze. They carried tales of wreck and ravage. They screamed their cries of bitter joy down the chimney; they hooted and howled their contempt of peace and ease and fireside joys, and they sighed that they could do no more. For the little house was undaunted, and sent up its curl of smoke from the chimney as if the winds had never breathed their fables. It had not stood before the ocean's mighty throe so long to be easily made the sport of the winds even in their wintry blasts.

Then the snow hissed on the billows and tossed its flakes, wreathing and writhing and twisting its drifts about till the house was nearly buried. But still shone that beam, as an eye from which no accident or misfortune or tempest could take the brave gleam.

When the long winter was over, and the sky was full of little downy clouds drifting like doves across its deep blue, Mr. Barclay returning from Florida, and *en route* to Geneva whither he had sent Ruth to school, desirous of making amends for an indifference and forgetfulness which hatred of letter-writing gave him the appearance of possessing, but to which he would not plead guilty, knocked at the door of the little brown house, without getting a response. He had noticed how tight and trim and snug it looked as he drew near, and now he saw that every window-shutter was barred, every loop-hole of ingress carefully covered. What did it mean? Had its inhabitants not wakened from their nightly slumber, or had they been hibernating all the winter through?

The nearest neighbor was a half mile away.

Again Mr. Barclay rattled the latches and hammered on the doors, only to hear the echo of his noise die into silence. Perhaps they had taken a holiday and had gone off visiting. So he cast about for a nook in which to wait. There was a rude bench near at hand where old Abner sat and wove his smaller seines. On it Mr. Barclay rested, looking as he did so at the curious scrawls and scrolls which had been evidently executed by Lillo. Even these gave indications of a luxuriant fancy and freedom of touch, though they must have been done when he could but just handle a knife.

Ah! if he could have had that boy.

He waited till patience was exhausted, then he drove to the nearest house. An anxious, angular woman gave him information.

"No, there was no one livin' there now sence Mrs. Marsh died. She died just as the old man did, only she was rather quicker. givin' out. 'When did she die?' Oh, jest after New Year's, and sence then nobody had seen the boy. He was bound to Mr. Smears, and give promise o' bein' amazin' smart at his callin'; but he had run off, and no one knew where he was. Likely as not had gone to sea. Most o' the boys about did that. It wa'n't at all to be wondered at, —nobody to care for him. S'pose he had smuggled himself into some passin' bark or gone down to Bosting. There wa'n't no use in tryin' to find out any thin' more, for no one knew nothin' about him."

CHAPTER VII.

TEN years have come and gone.

Science has spanned the ocean, and sent thought flashing along its wires, till time and space are as things of naught. Little need the novelist, therefore, excuse the annihilation of ten years, — a decade of transition and preparation for the record of which the future of the lives in which we are interested must be responsible.

It is an Italian night, and there is a ball given at the American Legation, in Florence.

The rush and crush and glitter of balls are about the same everywhere, but this one was in some ways exceptional. There was no little national pride in the giving of it, and rather more than usual national expenditure. Much space had been secured, many suites of rooms thrown open, and an unusually lavish display of flowers offered. Many Americans were at that time visiting Florence. There were also many distinguished foreigners; and a very successful portrait of an American poet by an American painter had just been received, and its exhibition was to be one of the attractive features of the evening.

Besides, a ball in a Florentine palace, with its

ample space, where silks and laces can have a chance to be seen to advantage, gives the wearer of them a finer background than a crowded drawing-room in our cities.

Of course, the invitations had been numerous, and a throng had gathered early. Among the guests were Mr. Barclay and Miss Morris, who, with an English governess, Miss Marchbank, were at this time staying in Florence.

In the ten years, come and gone, little Ruth has become a young woman. She has seen little of her native land, for, from the winter spent at Geneva with Miss Alden and her nieces, to the present spring, she has been constantly wandering with her restless guardian, — a winter here, a summer there; school for a time, then studying alone or with the temporary companions of a foreign watering-place, until Miss Marchbank assumed the direction of affairs.

Mr. Barclay has never been in vigorous health, and has never settled himself down to active pursuits. Having acquired the habit of seeking balmy airs, he has also acquired the habit of liking to wander.

Miss Marchbank is a counterpoise to this tendency. She prefers tranquillity, and likes to consider herself a fixture. From the day she began with Ruth, there was a marked difference in the child's education. All the loose or tangled threads were carefully pulled this way and that, and made into a nice, round, even ball, with nothing of the slovenly, unwound skein about it. There may have been a tendency towards hard-

ness in this method, but the girl herself retained
sufficient softness to diminish it.

And now here she is at a ball,—her first one.
She has seen plenty of people, and has many pleasant friends; but she has viewed society from its rim,
watching the sheen, the iridescent hues, the bubbles,
with a girl's merry glance, but wisely restrained from
quaffing the enticing cup. The time has, however,
come for her to take a sip.

As she enters the beautiful *salon* of an old palace,
surrounded by lights and pictures and flowers, we
will glance at her.

How can any one, who has even small charms, be
any thing but lovely at eighteen? And in a ball-
dress even an ordinary girl is a thing of beauty.

"Ruth is not of the *salvia splendens* order; the
arbutus is her type."

Some one said this of her; and some one else
said,—

"You mean our May-flower, do you not?"

Yes, she is like the New England May-flower,
delicate, tender, slight. Soft brown hair, violet eyes,
a well rounded face, with a color which comes and
goes, a wistful expression on the curving lips, and an
air of unconsciousness. She is all in white muslin,
prettily fluted and flounced (for Mr. Barclay likes
simplicity, and allows no dictation from costumers),
and her ornaments are the silver filagree from
Genoa,—just a pendant from a black velvet ribbon
round her throat has a few clustering pearls. Without any marked style or air of fashion, she yet has a
grace which is very effective. But who is this who

sweeps up to her after the presentations are over, and Miss Marchbank's gray satin spreads itself on a divan ?

Who is this *brune* in gauze and amber and Isabel roses, who wreathes two exquisite arms about her, and kisses her in true American freedom, and, dragging her away from guardian and gazers into a window's near embrasure, exclaims ? —

"Ruth Morris! to think that we should meet at last, and here!"

"When did you come? I wrote last. You knew we were here. Where is Grace?"

"I did not know you were here. Your last letter never reached me till we were in London. Papa sent it over, and you said then that you expected to go to Germany."

"So we did; but Miss Marchbank persuaded Mr. Barclay to stay here. She is afraid he is beginning to be homesick, and she won't cross the Atlantic. So she inveigles him into the idea that I must study art."

"I am so glad.—Grace, come here. Aren't you delighted? Hasn't Ruth blossomed out wonderfully? —Now you can be our cicerone. You must know all the churches by heart. Oh! isn't Isola Bella lovely, ravishing? I am just out of my head with Italy.— Grace, come here."

And Grace came. Even Grace looked pretty in a fluffy, graceful toilette, glittering here and there with jewels. But her face wore a wearied expression which contrasted ill with her attire, and she was almost pettish in her salutation.

"Dear me, Ruth, you have grown! No wonder you look so fresh: you have an easy time. Mr. Barclay indulges you immensely, does he not?"

"I suppose he does, Grace. He is very kind. Where is Miss Alden?"

"Oh, she never goes to balls! She sent us with Mrs. Jones. Aunt is getting to be a dragon, Ruth. I think she dragged us abroad for fear we should become entangled in some noose or other. For my part, I should think it was time to be rid of us. I hate travel, and aunt knows I hate it."

Ruth was a little shocked at the way Grace spoke.

"Miss Alden used to be quite as kind and considerate as my guardian."

"So she is still," put in May impetuously. "Don't mind what Grace says. She is out of sorts — a little blue."

"Not any more than usual, I am sure, May. I am tired to death of every thing, and of balls more than any thing. You would make me come to this, and now what am I to do with myself?"

"Enjoy it, to be sure," said Ruth lightly. "There are hosts of charming people here, and there is to be a contadina dance in costume, the *saltarello* or *tarantella*, I don't know which, — something very pretty. And hark! is not that music delicious?"

"Do you dance?" asked May, her agile foot tapping the floor impatiently.

"No, Mr. Barclay does not allow me to."

"How horrid! I shall have to remonstrate."

"No, don't. I care nothing about it."

"Oh, what a fib! Breathes there a girl with soul

so dead, who never to herself hath said, this is my favorite waltz?"

"Then I may claim you for it, Miss May," put in a voice; and away whisked May, like Aurora, trailing her mists behind her.

The crowd was thickening, and Ruth had a bright smile or a word for many. She had introduced two or three youths to Grace, but Grace had snubbed them all, and still stood discontentedly pulling a rose to pieces. Ruth, sorry for her friend, whose mood was so out of tune with all the brilliancy about her, refused several agreeable offers to survey the dancers, and remained beside her.

"Why, Grace!" she remonstrated, as a cavalier of imposing appearance, making his profoundest bow, and tendering his attentions, was refused, "do you know that is the British *chargé-d'affaires?* You don't know what you have lost."

"Nor do I care, Ruth. Aunt is shocked at my indifference to society. She is the veriest toady to people of distinction."

"Oh, Grace, don't talk so! We nobodies all like to see how great people bear their honors. But, in truth, that man is delightful; has seen much, been everywhere, and yet when he dines with Mr. Barclay, as he often does, is just as simple and nice as anybody else."

"Well, it doesn't matter to me. I suppose you like all this hubbub."

"To be sure I do. Aren't the dresses exquisite? Look at that *ciel*-blue satin and point-lace, and the rose garniture. Ah, Americans know how to dress!"

"And how to paint. Have you seen the portrait?" said some one.

"No," replied Ruth.

"Allow me, then, to show it to you."

"Come, Grace," and she presented the one friend to the other.

"So you think Americans know how to paint. How do you dare assert so remarkable a truth surrounded by the works of Raphael?" asked Ruth.

Her friend was the son of an American sculptor living in Florence, but, though born and bred in *Firenza la bella*, was violently patriotic.

"I claim that every thing which an American attempts to do is done well. Have you been much among the studios here?"

"Very little."

"We must make up a party to visit them; I mean the studios of our own people."

"Florentines, then?"

"No; Americans. Ah, you want to tease me! Will you care to see some of our aspiring youths?"

"To be sure. The Aldens will go with us; will you not, Grace?"

"May will, with pleasure."

"And you too, — ah, here is the picture."

There was a reverent host of admirers about the venerable head which always commands admiration, and plenty of outspoken enthusiasm for the artist. The picture was hung excellently, with drapery specially arranged, and candles carefully placed. But in a moment, at the ceasing of the wind instruments and the twanging of a guitar, the throng surged away towards the central apartment, where a group of gayly dressed *contadini* were preparing to dance for the benefit of the foreign visitors.

It was a very pretty scene ; the brilliant lights, the sheen and shimmer of silks and jewels, the peasants in their gay colors and gold necklaces, forming a picturesque foreground against the surrounding mass of more conventionally attired people, upon whom had fallen the hush of expectation.

Then began the dance, which, "like all popular dances, represents a courtship or love-making, in which the lover is passionate and impetuous in his advances, and the maid is coy, shy, or coquettish by turns."

The two dancers (for only two perform it, the others waiting to relieve them when fatigue obliges them to pause) whirled in circles about each other, snapping their fingers, ringing the bells of the tambourine, and thrumming the guitar. Their movements were almost too violent for grace, though they acted their parts with sufficient spirit; the man advancing, the woman receding, now balancing, now whirling, keeping up a constantly amorous warfare, until utterly exhausted. Then two more advanced, and went through the same actions even more wildly, with more abandon ; and these two sang as they danced. Then another couple replaced these, ending with the complete subjugation of the lover, who dropped on his knee before his panting sweetheart, who triumphantly beat her tambourine to announce her victory.

There was great applause and much praise bestowed upon the dancers, who, their labors over, withdrew.

May came rushing up to Ruth, with, —

"Was it not pretty, charming, delightful? How I wish I could dance it! — Mr. Barclay, you are an ogre for not letting Ruth dance."

She had Mr. Barclay's arm, and looked up at him defiantly. He only answered in his quiet manner, —

"I dare say, but Ruth submits very placidly."

"That's because your tyranny has reduced her to a state of absolute subjugation."

"So you like the *tarantella*," was his unmoved remark. "You should witness the *saltarello* danced in the open air in or about Rome, to see it perfectly done. It loses by being indoors. I think, too, there is some restraint when they have an audience of this sort."

"Very likely. — How did you like it, Grace?"

Ruth had been absorbed in the dance and enjoyed it, but, happening to glance at Grace Alden, had noticed her watching the dancers with a painful interest, which, as they ceased, left her pale and *distraite:* so quickly turning towards May, she whispered, —

"Let her alone, she is troubled about something;" then aloud she said, "Mr. Barclay, it is proposed that we visit some of the studios; Mr. Potter will introduce us. Can we go to-morrow?"

"If you are up in any sort of time, I can go; but my afternoon is engaged."

"Then we have only to secure Miss Marchbank, for of course May will induce Miss Alden to go."

"With two chaperones you can dispense with me, I think."

"But we want you," said Ruth and May simultaneously.

"Well, I'll go get you some ices now."

"Take me with you, please?" asked Grace, going off to join the matron under whose care they had come to the ball.

"What *is* the matter with Grace?" demanded Ruth, as cosily ensconced on the same ottoman, she and May ate their confections and sent Mr. Potter off for more delights of the same kind. The refreshments were not of the light, Italian order only: there was a grand spread in true American style; and Mr. Potter, finding the viands to his taste, made his stay long enough to enable the girls to chatter confidentially.

"*I* think it's a love affair. Aunt says it is all nonsense."

"Really, do you think so, May?" said Ruth with a shade of awe.

"I am afraid it is."

"But why should you be afraid?"

"Oh, because!"

"Really, you make things clear."

"Well, there's time enough for Grace. Why does a girl want to bother about such things, when there's so much else to enjoy?"

To Ruth this view was inexplicable. To love and be loved seemed to her the acme of bliss, which every poem she read, every song she sang, every thing lovely in nature or in art, confirmed.

"So much else to enjoy?" she repeated; "what else?"

"Why, a thousand things, — dancing, flirting, riding, driving, travelling, dressing, — eating even, when you get as good things as these sweet biscuit. What are they made of? — cream, jelly, and sponge cake!"

Ruth laughed, a clear, silvery laugh. A slender fellow looking out at the stars heard the sound, and turned. Surely he had seen that face before. Yes; as she watched the dance, he had observed the sweet purity of her look, and her delicacy of color; but he turned from Ruth to her companion with still more interest. What a dashing beauty the clear *brune* had, and how well her costume accorded! The amber beads, the yellow roses, set her off bewitchingly; and how her eyes sparkled! The girls did not heed him, and went on talking.

"And does the possession of a lover banish all these delights?" asked Ruth.

"Certainly: one then has to be solemnly earnest, severely sincere, — no more fun after that. Don't you see how it affects Grace? She is as sour as lemonade."

"She seems unhappy."

"So she is, critical and censorious and disagreeable. I wish aunt would let her marry, and be done with it."

"You cruel girl! You never used to allow any one to abuse Grace."

"Nor do I now. It is just because I love her that I see her fatal mistake, and the flaws in her are all occasioned by it."

"Fatal mistake?"

"Yes, she is irretrievably in love, though aunt ignores it."

"With whom? May, quick, here comes Mr. Potter, tell me, with whom?"

"An insignificant clerk, a tradesman, a "—

The end of her sentence was lost in a profusion of thanks to Mr. Potter for the delicacies he was piloting towards them.

Then the music began again, — an entreating melody which May could not resist, and she was off again like thistle-down; while Ruth wandered to the conservatory with Mr. Potter.

It was a very jungle of perfumes, roses, lilies, and violets pouring out their lives for this one night's pleasure.

Before a bank of cut flowers, Ruth paused.

"Ah, what a slaughter of the innocents!" she said regretfully.

The same slim fellow who had been looking at the stars heard her exclamation, and responded with a quick glance of sympathy. Ruth only saw that his dark eyes flashed as he passed her.

"How many strangers are here to-night!" lazily drawled Mr. Potter.

"Are there? I know so few that I cannot judge."

"Yes, there are lots of them. Here comes one of the kind I most dread, — a specimen of the sort who represent us all over the Continent, and give us our unenviable social reputation."

"Oh, Mr. Potter, Americans are well thought of everywhere!"

"For their money-spending, yes, and that is what I object to."

" Yes, and for their good-nature."

" It would be better if they had less and demanded more, — their money's worth, for instance."

Ruth laughed. "I don't care a fig whether they get it or not," and she drew her muslin away from the rose-thorns.

"Ah! girls can be indifferent; more especially when they are" —

"What ?"

"Heiresses."

"I am not an heiress."

"Oh, no! I suppose not," said Mr. Potter dubiously

"I assure you I am not," repeated Ruth; "and, if this is the general impression, I beg that you will correct it."

Here the short, stout person whom Mr. Potter had said was one he dreaded approached more nearly. She was entirely clothed in black velvet, richly covered with lace. Her diamonds were prominent, and her hair was a structure worthy of an architect. She looked to be forty-five. She came up to Mr. Potter without embarrassment, and asked for an introduction to Miss Morris, in a voice which had no sweetness of modulation, but was not unpleasantly loud or strident.

Ruth courtesied distantly and wonderingly, as Mr. Potter presented Mrs. Vedder. She did not care to know the woman, and made no effort to conceal her indifference. Mr. Barclay, himself reserved, had by his example taught Ruth to be so; but she was not haughty, and at once had some pleasant little trifling word for the stranger.

"My dear," was the very unexpected rejoinder, "you have forgotten me. I am an aunt of yours, — a great-aunt, I suppose I must call myself. Your mother, Ruth, was my niece. And how you have grown, to be sure! The last time I saw you, you were only so high," — measuring with her hand about three feet from the floor, "a little, thin, pale girl; and now you are — Well, 'praise to the face is open disgrace.' I never flatter people; it's not my way."

Ruth gazed at the woman, and spoke not a word.

Could this be a relation of hers, this coarse, common woman, whose manner and voice were so distasteful? Yet, as she gazed, the face grew less unfamiliar. Where had she seen it? From the depths of her memory came a vision of this face, associated with dull, dark days of childish sorrow. The very smell of crape seemed to emanate from the heavy folds of the woman's velvet gown.

"Don't you remember me at all, Ruth?" she queried, "your aunt Abby Vedder?"

"No," said Ruth, faltering, — "and yet" —

"Now, just try and think. It was summertime, at the funeral" —

"Oh, don't!" said Ruth quickly. "Yes, I remember. How do you do, aunt, Mrs. Vedder?"

Mr. Potter seeing that something was impending, and that Ruth deprecated more explanations, here interposed kindly, —

"You will have to postpone reminiscences, Mrs.

Vedder, for I must just now take Miss Morris to Miss Marchbank. She will be delighted to renew your acquaintance, I have no doubt, on some future occasion;" and he offered Ruth his arm, which she took eagerly, only halting a moment, as she saw Mrs. Vedder's crestfallen look, to say kindly, —

"You must send me your card, please. — She *is* an aunt of mine, I really believe," was her honest avowal to Mr. Potter, whose comforting reply was, " Relations have an inexpressibly stupid way of turning up when they're not wanted;" and then they joined Miss Marchbank, who was yawning behind her fan.

In another half hour the ball was over for Ruth, — her first ball, — and she had come away with a confused sound of trailing silks on marble floors, whirling waltzes, buzzing voices, sweet reed-instruments, and a general depression of spirits; for over all other sights and sounds came the apparition of the woman in black velvet, and the commonplace voice saying, "I am your aunt Abby Vedder."

I wonder if balls do not oftener depress than elevate. Is there not always some sting of disappointment, some ache of unsatisfied vanity? And yet, Ruth had nothing of these to annoy her. She was artless, and disposed to enjoy every thing that was put before her. But in spite of the charms of the evening, the real pleasure of which she had partaken, there was a faint regret.

CHAPTER VIII.

"Slowly, Ruth, slowly," said Mr. Barclay.

They were sitting in a frescoed room, near a balcony filled with growing plants, and the soft, Italian sunshine bathed them in its light. Far away the hills were to be seen in waving outline against a clear blue sky; nearer a fountain rippled and gushed in its marble basin. Ruth was reading aloud (as she did for an hour every day) Ruskin's "Remarks on the Nineteenth Psalm," in which are these words: —

"The Bible is, indeed, a deep book, when depth is required; that is to say, for deep people. But it is not intended particularly for profound persons; on the contrary, much more for simple and shallow persons. And therefore the first, and generally the main and leading, idea of the Bible is on its surface, written in plainest possible Greek, Hebrew, or English, needing no penetration nor amplification, needing nothing but what we all might give, — attention.

"But this, which is in every one's power, and is the only thing which God wants, is just the last thing any one will give him."

Ruth stopped.

"How is it possible for any one less gifted than Mr. Ruskin to give the attention which he here goes on to describe ? For instance, I suppose he understands Greek and Hebrew enough to get at the exact meaning of each word."

" Yes, very probably ; but go on, and see what else he adds."

" We are delighted to ramble away into day-dreams ; to repeat pet verses from other places, suggested by chance words ; to snap at an expression which suits our own particular views ; or to dig up a meaning from under a verse, which we should be amiably grieved to think any human being had been so happy as to find before. But the plain, intended, immediate, fruitful meaning, which every one ought to find always, and especially that which depends on our seeing the relation of the verse to those near it, and getting the force of the whole passage, in due relation, — this sort of significance we do not look for ; it being, truly, not to be discovered, unless we really attend to what is said, instead of to our own feelings."

" That demands study," said Ruth.

" Of course," responded Mr. Barclay.

Ruth resumed her reading ; but again Mr. Barclay had to check her rapidity, at which she closed the book and said, —

" My mind wanders so that I have lost the thread of meaning. I was thinking how difficult it is to apply Bible teachings to every-day life, not how difficult it is to read them properly."

" Has the ball had this influence ? "

" Not exactly, and yet something happened there which may have started my thoughts in this direction."

"What was it?"

"A Mrs. Vedder was introduced to me, who calls herself my aunt."

"Humph!" said Mr. Barclay. "You did not tell me of this last night."

"No, I had no opportunity; but I did not like her. I was annoyed that she spoke to me, and I think I was rude to her."

"And all that was contrary to Bible teaching?"

"Yes, I think so."

Ruth had long ago learned the ease of confession, and always opened her heart to her guardian, whose worldly wisdom was sometimes sorely puzzled just what to advise. Sometimes she was the teacher, as the young, the pure, and the unworldly can be.

Mr. Barclay enjoyed these confidences, and never chilled them by any unresponsiveness.

"Perhaps you are not a good judge of your own actions, my dear. I doubt if you were rude."

"Yes, I think I was."

"Sometimes we are so placed that we have to defend ourselves by a little hardness of conduct."

"That is not the law of love."

"It is expediency, I admit."

Ruth looked perplexed. "I don't think I like it."

"You are a little Puritan, my dear. Don't lay too much stress on small matters: there is danger of forgetting the large ones."

Ruth made no reply. She submitted meekly to her guardian's wisdom. She was very docile.

A plate of polished umber chestnuts was on the table. Mr. Barclay began opening them, saying,

"So an aunt has turned up way over here in Italy. I thought you were safe from any approaches of that sort on this side of the ocean."

"Who is she, Mr. Barclay? Do you know her?"

"I do not know her. I suppose she must be a sister of Mr. Boggs."

"Oh!" ejaculated Ruth in a tone of horror.

"You have no devoted attachment for him, I believe?"

"No, indeed!"

"How about the law of love now, Ruth?"

"But, Mr. Barclay, he was rude and unkind to my father."

"Perhaps he did not mean to be; it was only his coarser nature clashing against the finer qualities of your father's."

"I suppose so."

A card was here brought in.

"Is the lady waiting?" asked Mr. Barclay.

"No; it was delivered at the door."

Mr. Barclay handed it to Ruth.

On it was inscribed:—

"*Mrs. Vedder. Casa Doria. Wednesdays.*

"To-day is Tuesday; to-morrow I will go see this aunt of yours."

"And I too, Mr. Barclay."

"You are not obliged to."

"But I would rather."

"As a penance?"

"The '*amende honorable*' instead."

Here Miss Marchbank entered, all ready for the morning excursion.

Miss Marchbank was a thoroughly practical person; always punctual, always suitably dressed, always attentive to proprieties. She was scrupulous in appearance this morning, in black silk, lavender gloves, and a bonnet that matched her gray hair.

"Not ready, Ruth? Ah, my dear child, how shall I ever teach you to be on time?" and out popped her watch.

"We have been a little discursive in our reading to-day, Miss Marchbank," apologized Mr. Barclay.

"I am afraid so; you are a quarter of an hour late," and the watch was pocketed again with a little click of the case.

"I can slip on my things in a moment," said Ruth.

"Oh, no! don't do that; you will not be tidy. Change your whole apparel."

In another quarter of an hour Ruth stood equipped, —no daisy could have been daintier,—in two or three shades of brown, with some fresh field flowers at her waist. They drove to Miss Alden's hotel, and found her party ready.

In spite of being ten years older, Miss Alden wore a round hat, which so displeased Miss Marchbank that she could hardly be polite.

"How shocking is such an affectation of youth, my dear Ruth!" she whispered, when the chance availed.

Ruth smiled, and said, —

"Ah! if you knew her, you would not be so vexed."

There was a little flutter of caresses, and kind inquiries, and salutations, and comparison of experi-

ences; and, this interchange over, they started on
their studio inspection with Mr. Potter.

I do not propose to follow them. Miss Alden was
bland, Miss Marchbank critical, Mr. Barclay amused,
Grace Alden indifferent, May as bright and bubbling
as champagne, and Ruth contemplative. The artists
received them cordially, and made a good display of
their works. Labor of months was quickly discussed
in as many moments. In the home of art one becomes either very reverent or very indifferent.

In one large room of cloister-like stillness, where
several youths were at their easels, and where several
fine frescoes impressed the visitor, a young man, who
had seen the gay party entering, turned hastily towards his canvas, and remained absorbed until they
had completed their survey. He was not more than
twenty-three, and, though among Americans, bore
unmistakable marks of foreign parentage. The olive
tint of his oval face, the dark, flashing eye, and the
close curling hair were not Yankee in their origin;
but when he spoke, as he did soon after, his English
was undefiled.

"Why did you work so zealously? The girls were
pretty, and deserving of attention," asked a student.

"Yes; I saw them last night."

"All the more reason for being civil to-day. Besides,
Mr. Barclay has the reputation of being a good buyer;
he is said to be choosing works of art to carry home."

"Indeed; when does he go?"

"Ah! that I know nothing of. But I see that you
now regret your inattention: filthy lucre has greater
weight with you than I supposed."

"As if you had not purposely made mention of that which was most pleasing to yourself."

"No, no! I deny it. But see, here is a fan that one of them dropped; will you just run out and return it? I can't leave this wet bit of color."

"Give it to me, if you choose; but I'll not go after them now."

"How will they get it?"

"I know Mr. Barclay. I will return it at my convenience."

"You know Mr. Barclay? Why the deuce, then, didn't you speak to him?"

"I was not ready to."

Meantime, our party proceeded to luncheon. Miss Alden had secured their presence for a very pretty festa, and they were all weary enough to enjoy it in an unceremonious manner.

"What a bore all this sight-seeing is!" exclaimed Grace Alden to Ruth, as she stripped a fig of its purplish-green coat.

Ruth answered quietly, "I am sorry you think so; perhaps the churches will suit you better."

"No; they're all mummery and moonshine."

"Pardon, Grace. They are to those who have no religious sentiment; but to others they are the revelation of the Divine."

"Ruth! Oh, but I suppose you mean Roman Catholics!"

"I mean nothing of the kind. I mean those who see in these beautiful structures the aspirations of humanity after all that is pure and beautiful and spiritual."

Grace laughed thinly, a sharp, satirical little laugh.

"What a little saint you are becoming, Ruth! Mr. Barclay will have to be careful, or his destined bride may enter a nunnery."

Ruth too had a fig in her fingers, which she now dropped; and turning with an astonished and alarmed expression towards her companion, her color rising, she said, —

"I cannot hear such words, Grace. I cannot imagine why you wish to offend me."

"Oh, I'll take it all back!" said Grace carelessly, seeing the vivid color, and the look of mingled anger and pain in Ruth's gentle eyes. "But you know it's not an unnatural supposition."

"It seems to me *very* unnatural and — I beg your pardon, Grace — very unrefined."

"It's the way of the world: so don't be a little prig, Ruth."

Ruth had been so sorry for Grace, so eager to sympathize and do a friend's deed for what she supposed to be real suffering, that to be thus wounded in return seemed doubly hard to endure. She turned from her now, for they were scattered about the room at small tables, and quickly sought the corner where Miss Marchbank and Miss Alden were eating salad, and discussing mosaics. May was having a tilt with Mr. Barclay, who liked her vivacity. Mr. Potter was skimming the cream on all sides, but seeing Grace alone went up to her. Her tongue had certainly been tasting bitter herbs, for she put him out of temper too; and so he sauntered back to Ruth.

"If your friend were a little older, I should think her a disappointed old maid; but " —

"What's that you say about old maids, Mr. Potter?" said Miss Alden. "Have a care, or Miss Marchbank and I will arm for battle."

"I have no weapons that can match yours, so I'll retreat behind Miss Morris's intrenchments. We are not going to say another word about old maids or young ones either; we are going to talk about art. — What were your general impressions, Miss Ruth, after all we saw this morning?"

"They were vague and varied, Mr. Potter."

"You saw too much?"

"No; but after the galleries, the Angelicos and Raphaels, the Titians and the Del Sartos, modern art seems so timid, so crude, so young."

"I should say there was nothing vague in that impression; it is remarkably distinct, and if I were an artist I should feel squelched."

"Then I should have erred in speaking, for it was. but half my thought: while their efforts seem timid, they yet excite my admiration by their industry and hopefulness."

"Young Marsh is making a name for himself. I don't know whether you saw him; he was in the last *atelier* we visited."

"Yes," said Ruth indifferently. "What does he paint?"

"A little of every thing. I don't think he has quite settled down to any one branch. He comes out occasionally with a strong head or portrait, then again landscape seems to attract him. He is not as well known as his pictures; he seems to shun society."

"I should think one would have to, or his work would suffer."

"He calls himself an American, but he looks two-thirds Italian."

"What did you say was his name?" said Ruth, striving to rouse herself to be interested, for art in its essence and abstract influence was more to her than the artist; and yet she wanted to forget the stinging pain of Grace Alden's speech. "What was his name?"

"Marsh — A. L. Marsh. His name is wholly out of keeping with his appearance."

"Who is that you are talking of?" queried Mr. Barclay.

"A compatriot, an artist, and a genius by the very plain patronymic of Marsh," responded Mr. Potter.

"How long has he been here?"

"Really, I don't know, — two or three winters. He keeps himself very much to himself."

"Can it be Lillo, I wonder!" said Mr. Barclay to Ruth.

"Lillo! Why, I never thought of him as any thing but a boy! Marsh was his name, to be sure; but would he not have recognized us?"

"I do not know, so many years have elapsed; but I must follow this scent, and see for myself if we have unearthed him. Come, we must make our adieux. — We owe you many thanks, Mr. Potter. — And, Miss Alden, we must compare programmes, that our young people may be together as much as possible. It quite revives old times."

"So it does, Frank, so it does; and you are not a day older than when my mischievous May ran away, and gave me such a fright and you such a wetting, do you remember? and that talented fisher-boy swam after you."

"Yes," said Mr. Barclay, shrugging his shoulders. "We are just speaking of him. I think perhaps he has turned up again."

"Really, how romantic!"

"Yes."

Here Miss Marchbank, who was not in the least interested in these reminiscences, made so strenuous an effort that they positively did go; but not before Grace made another languid attempt to pacify Ruth, which Ruth ignored.

It may have seemed unforgiving in Ruth when she coolly put aside Grace Alden's apologetic caress, but she justified herself by thinking that it would have been hypocrisy had she consented to it. Her self-extenuation had the basis of honesty. She was hurt and displeased; but though Grace had made her angry, she really tried to excuse the girl, as she always did when any one offended her. Never before had Mr. Barclay been spoken of as Grace spoke of him, and certainly never before had the possibility of a different relationship presented itself to Ruth. Not only was she hurt, but she was indignant; and the longer she dwelt upon the matter, the more involved became her thoughts.

Could it be possible that other people regarded

them in this light? Was every one so stupid, so commonplace, as to think that there could be no affection between two people except one that ended in matrimony? Was there never a parental or fraternal relation without kinship? Did she not prove daily that she bore a daughter's love to the man who had taken her, a friendless little orphan, from her dying father? Her very unconsciousness that there could be any other state of affairs was witness to its absurdity. But now she could no longer be unconscious. And she had no one to whom she could unburden herself. Always she had gone to Mr. Barclay with her griefs. This was something not to be spoken of, not to be thought of; and so she cried a few vexatious tears, and went down to Miss Marchbank for an hour's study, striving hard to forget that distasteful insinuation.

Mr. Barclay came home late from his engagement and his drive on the Casino, to find Miss Marchbank on a sofa asleep, and Ruth on the balcony watching the sunlight fading over the hills in all the soft gradations of color peculiar to an Italian sky. She did not greet him with her usual kiss and merry welcome, but stood mutely waiting for the first word from him.

"Tired, little Ruth?" said he, coming to her and putting his arm around her.

She almost shrank away from him, and said coldly, —

"No, I am not tired. Will you have tea?"

"Yes, dear child. But you *are* tired, and your hands are too cool; we mustn't run any risk of malaria. Come in and sit down beside me. I think I have found our old friend Lillo."

She overcame her coldness and embarrassment with an effort, calling herself a simpleton and an ingrate, and, drawing a cushion beside him, laid her head on his knee, vowing that those hateful words should not control her.

Then he told her where he had been, and the inquiries he had made, and whom he had met, and what he had seen, and how he had left a note for Mr. Marsh ; and when she had heard it all she rang for the tea, which she never allowed any one else to brew for him, and wakened Miss Marchbank, who always protested that she had not been asleep, but had only "just lost herself" a moment, and had heard every word that had been spoken.

CHAPTER IX.

MR. BARCLAY, somewhat *ennuyé* with travel and idleness, had lately become much interested in the founding of Protestant schools in Italy. Without taking any active part in the immediate conduct or control of these institutions, he had used his influence for them by interesting others, by writing home concerning them, and by raising money. He had thus been very useful, aud had drawn to him those who were similarly interested, as well as those who were simply curious to watch the experiment. But he would not allow Ruth to even have a class in a Sunday school, eagerly as she desired it. To all her arguments he opposed the conclusive one, that, were he to allow her the privilege she asked, his labors would then become of negative value ; for the police would soon contrive to make his residence uncomfortable, and, not being combative by nature, they would worry him into a withdrawal of all effort. But Ruth's missionary spirit had been aroused, and, though acquiescing to the necessities of the case, her mind was not at rest. She was longing for an opportunity to do good in some plain, practical way to which her powers might be equal. She did not give utterance to this longing ; on the contrary, so fearful was she of mis-

interpretation that she did not even venture to make
it known to Miss Marchbank, who, however, had
been instrumental in fostering it, by her own accounts of life in English towns, where she, as well
as her friends, had done so much for the poor, the
sick, and the needy.   So Ruth smothered her wishes,
and watched with envy the Sisters of Charity on
their rounds, the Brethren of the Misericordia, and
the pale, patient nuns, whose lives were spent in
deeds of mercy.   She had not become infatuated
with Roman Catholicism ; neither did she ignore
much that impressed her as useful and beautiful in
the system.   She had not been educated to the Puritan horror of its principles ; though she had been
taught to remember, with a salutary propriety, the
massacre of St. Bartholomew.   But living, as she
had done, so much abroad, the sharp edge of her
Protestantism had become dulled enough to allow her
to pray even more devoutly in a cathedral than she
would have done in a conventicle.   She thus was
ripe for a movement of some sort.

"Well, Ruth," said Mr. Barclay, the day after
their inspection of the studios, "shall we pay that
visit to the Casa Doria?"

"I suppose we must, Mr. Barclay."

"Or do you prefer the dentist's?"

"If the choice were given me, I think the one
would be preferable to the other."

"Your aunt would be flattered, would she not?"

"I don't think it would matter to her.   That is the
worst of our petty sacrifices : nobody cares really that
we make them."

"Then the sooner it's over, the better."

They were in their neat little English phaeton in a moment, and went bowling along to their destination. They passed a somewhat gorgeous equipage, from which a gloomy, red-faced woman bowed haughtily.

"That is one of my most energetic co-laborers," said Mr. Barclay.

"Who may she be?" asked Ruth.

"The Duchess of Stickingham, a very sensible, good woman."

"She looks cross, and as if her roast beef were too rare."

"Her looks belie her. I do not believe a person of simpler habits is to be found."

Again they passed a showy turn-out, but this time a pale face of great beauty saluted them.

"That is another ardent worker," said Mr. Barclay.

"She is American, I am sure," exclaimed Ruth.

"You are right. Her zeal only equals her love of splendor and show. She gives as generously as she spends, whether for schools or for laces."

"Why do I not meet these people, Mr. Barclay?" suddenly asked Ruth.

"I prefer to have you all to myself," said Mr. Barclay lightly, little thinking of his words, and in truth regarding Ruth as too young yet to be generally introduced, having even allowed her to go to the ball with reluctance. His words would have been taken with the same lightness, but for Grace Alden's unhappy suggestion. Now they made Ruth grave and uncomfortable and embarrassed; but also so angry

with herself, that she could have cried. The Casa
Doria — the hotel where Mrs. Vedder was staying —
was before them. It was a gloomy-looking structure,
old, sombre, and not very clean. They were ushered
into a small *entresol*, and then a maid came to conduct them up a broad flight of stone steps. She was
Irish and untidy, and very much overdressed for her
station. Opening a door, she said, —

"Will yees plaze to walk in ? Mrs. Vedder's not
well."

They walked into a high-ceiled apartment, where
Cupids were dancing and wreathing flowers, to find
Mrs. Vedder upon a lounge. She was still clothed
in her pall-like velvet, — only it was cut to conceal
rather than to uncover her charms, — and over it was
wound a coarse-looking shawl. Her tresses were
dishevelled, and the braids, awry from lying down
upon them, gave a comical aspect to a face which was
not devoid of good looks.

She rose at once, in opposition to Mr. Barclay's
request that she should not do so, and was profuse
in her welcome.

"I can't tell you how glad I am to see you," she
said. "I am so tired of being alone. My sons leave
me to myself, and I don't speak French or Italian,
and I hate the horrid cookery of the Continent ; and
I am not well, and it makes me *so* homesick."

Her very eagerness was repulsive to the quiet
Ruth, but at the same time she began to pity this
relative.

"How long have you been here, and why did you
leave home ?" asked Ruth.

"Oh, I have been away ever so long! My sons wanted to travel, and I thought I should like it ; but I don't. Do you?"

"Yes, very much."

"Ah, you care for the things that I don't know any thing about! I try to get up an interest in the pictures and statues ; but, the truth is, I don't care for them. When they are all undressed, they make me ashamed ; and when they ain't, I can't make them out, unless I read the guide-books."

She was certainly honest, and her hearers smiled, as she hurried on in her talk, as if afraid they would go before she could finish all she had to say.

"Now, my sons have had education, and know all about the classical antiquities, as they call them ; but I might as well be in Egypt, for all I can understand."

"And your sons leave you to yourself, I understood you to say," said Mr. Barclay.

"Yes. I s'pose its natural. Young people are eager to see and hear every thing that's going, and I don't want to be a drawback to them. That's the way I came to go to the ball at the Legation. I never go to balls, never ; but, just to please the boys, I dressed up and went, and took cold, — got overheated, stood in a draught, — and all the queer, foreign doctor gives me is lemonade. Bridget, the girl you saw, is the only creature I've got to talk to. She came over with me. — And so you are really Ruth Morris. You look like your mother. — She was a pretty woman, Mr. Barclay, wasn't she?"

"I agree with you, Mrs. Vedder."

"And Dick was a queer chap. Though I was your mother's aunt, Ruth, I was not more than a year or two older, being the youngest of a large family; and your mother's mother, my oldest sister, — her name was Margaretta, — she died soon after your mother was born. Your mother was Ruth, the same name as your own; and until she went off to her grandfather's, and then to school, we were playmates. She was a quiet child and very different from me; but we were fond of each other, for all that, and when she was sent for I cried all night long. We used to meet as schoolgirls; but I never cared to study, and Ruth was always talking about something I didn't understand. Then she married your father, and none of our family approved of that: so they didn't care to be intimate, and I don't blame them."

"Are you related to Mr. Boggs?" asked Ruth, thinking it just as well to know the whole of her family history at once.

"I should think I was. Cauldwell Boggs is my brother; but I may just as well say that we're not over-fond of each other. He is always scolding me about my boys, thinks I don't know how to manage them. People can give advice so cheap, you see. By the by, Mr. Barclay, he wants to know what you are going to do with Ruth."

Poor Ruth had borne all she could, but her patience was not equal to this: she rose and began to examine a distant picture, leaving the field to Mr. Barclay, who responded laughingly, —

"Do with her? Eat her up, I suppose, when she is plump enough."

Mrs. Vedder looked puzzled; then, regarding Ruth curiously, said, —

"She is very genteel, very."

"Now I can't agree with you," replied Mr. Barclay.

"Why not?"

"Because she is much too nice for that."

"Why, isn't it nice to be genteel?"

"No, not at all."

Mrs. Vedder laughed good-naturedly. "I don't understand you, but seems to me she is too fine to make her own way in the world."

"There I *can* agree with you."

"Then I suppose you intend to " —

Ruth lost the rest of the question, only hearing a very emphatic —

"Nothing of the sort," from Mr. Barclay, who now rose to go.

Mrs. Vedder began coughing violently, but squeezing Ruth's hand begged her to come again.

"What a relief," said Mr. Barclay, "to have that over!"

Ruth was silent. Unpleasant as had been the interview, she wanted to hear more of her mother; and, though Mrs. Vedder was not at all to her taste, she felt sorry for her. She seemed to be a person of good heart and honest nature, whom circumstances had forced out of the homely, simple sphere she might have enjoyed. To Mr. Barclay's surprise, Ruth announced her intention of going again to inquire about Mrs. Vedder on the following day.

"My dear, be careful. She will bore you dreadfully if you give her the chance," was his injunction.

"She is ill and a stranger, and I ought to show her some attention."

"Don't promise to go about with her."

"No danger: Miss Marchbank is on guard. She is to leave me and call for me to-day."

So again she went, carrying a bunch of violets.

Mrs. Vedder was much worse and really in need of sympathy. She was dull and feverish, and tears came to her eyes when Ruth entered.

"This is very kind of you, very kind, for I am sure Mr. Barclay does not approve of me. Oh, you may speak plainly to me! I am used to it. I see the difference in people. Mr. Barclay is a proud man, and you are the apple of his eye. I don't wonder. You are like your mother, Ruth, very like her. She was so sweet. I don't mean to flatter you. I am not complimentary. I thought perhaps you would like to hear about your mother."

"Of course," said Ruth, putting down her flowers, and touching the rumpled pillows gently, on which her aunt was leaning; "but let me make you comfortable; there, is not that pleasanter?"

"Yes, much. Ah, how I wish I had a daughter! But I suppose it would have been the same with her as with the boys, — she would have been seeking her own pleasure."

"Where are your sons?"

"In Rome, I believe; but I am not sure. They don't write punctually, and I'm no hand at letters."

"But they will come to you soon, will they not?"

"I don't know, I never know. They are making collections to take home. I wish I was at home; it

is all I want. Cauldwell told me I was foolish to come
to Europe. He said I wouldn't enjoy it. But I never
like to do as he says : he is so opinionated, and scolds
so about the boys; says they are spoiled, and will run
through their money and mine too. I'm sure they
are welcome to mine. What use have I for it after
my clothes are bought ? Are you fond of dress,
jewelry ? 'A little.' Well, just open that wardrobe.
The key turns hard. Keys and locks and door-han-
dles are always out of order in Europe. There, what
do you think of those things ? "

Ruth was amazed. Silks, satins, and filmy fabrics
were laid over one another in glistening profusion.
Jackets and capes of costly lace had been flung on
top of them indifferently. Instinctively, Ruth, with
girlish deftness, folded each article as she surveyed it,
until they occupied a third of the compass they had
been in before.

"Ah, how nice that is ! Bridget is so unhandy ;
but she is kind, and so I put up with her, and give
her all my old things."

Ruth, not accustomed to seeing servants arrayed
in cast-off finery, mildly suggested that plainer clothes
would be more becoming.

"Do you think so ? Well, then, I suppose it must
be correct. Mr. Barclay knows, of course ; but it
pleases the girl, and makes her think she is somebody. Now open that box. Here's the key on my
watch-chain."

Ruth opened a large leathern-covered case, and
her eyes were dazzled again. Rubies, emeralds,
amethysts, turquoises, in necklaces, bracelets, and

pendants, shone upon her. A diamond cross and a pearl locket were side by side.

"Open the locket, Ruth; it may interest you."

Ruth obeyed. In it was an old-fashioned daguerreotype of a child. Suddenly it seemed to her that she was looking in the glass, that the face was her own.

"There, that is for you. It is your own mother's likeness," she heard Mrs. Vedder saying.

"Is this my mother?" she asked, closing what might have been a small shop, and locking in the brilliants from their source of life and power.

"Yes, it is. We had our pictures taken together; and I cut out the face of this one day, and slipped it in here."

"Cannot you take it out for me?"

"Why should I? Keep it as it is."

"Oh, not in this valuable case!"

"Pshaw! that is nothing — a few pearls more or less. Put it in your pocket and think no more of it."

And so Ruth carried home her mother's picture, which Mr. Barclay acknowledged to be a very pretty gift.

Again and again Ruth went to inquire for her aunt's health, and after each report Mr. Barclay made less opposition to her going, until it came to be a daily affair. Sometimes it was only a question and answer, sometimes she sat for an hour. Miss Marchbank went too; and, though she saw reasons why Mr. Barclay could not admire Mrs. Vedder, she upheld Ruth in the duty of kindness to her lonely and evidently unhappy relative. But to Mrs. Vedder, Ruth seemed a ministering angel, much more of a heavenly visitant than the marble-winged creatures in the church.

CHAPTER X.

It was with a curious mixture of regret and pleasure that Mr. A. L. Marsh responded to Mr. Barclay's invitation to visit him, and sauntered forth from his lodgings one evening in May for this purpose. The regret arose from his entire indifference to society, and a preference for his quiet, almost monotonous seclusion. Having no family ties, his whole time was given to his profession ; and his Bohemian manner of life, though quite innocent, unfitted him for the etiquette and conventionalities imposed by society. The ball at the Legation had, however, been an opportunity which he could not afford to let pass, for his eyes had to be fed ; and while there he had discovered that the two American girls who had most interested him were the friends of his childhood. Towards Mr. Barclay he was also most kindly attracted, remembering the spur his good friend had given him, and how sincere an interest he had manifested in him. But how far away those early days seemed ! — days of toil, of vague and restless aspirations, — and yet how clearly came back the recollection of the little brown house, the broad, shining sands, the rocks at the Neck, and the old grandfather and grandmother whose life of hardship he

had shared, and for whom he had the warmest affection! Yes, he recalled now Mr. Barclay's generous
offer and his own refusal, — for the sake of the poor
old grandmother whose last hours he had been able
to cheer. How glad he was to think that he did not
leave her! and with what natural pride he contem-
plated those early struggles, the hard toil on ship-
board, when, leaving home behind him and the graves
of the two old people, he had started for the goal of
his artistic hopes, the land of his birth!

For Lillo knew that he was Italian; and besides
the charm which Italy had for him, there was beneath
all other thoughts the hope of discovering something
about his mother.

As yet, he had been unsuccessful. After his
grandmother's death, he had found a few papers and
letters which looked as if they might afford some
clew. The letters, however, were in Italian, and he
had been unable to read them. Among them was a
silhouette cut in black paper, a profile of a girl whose
clustering locks fell over her brow as his own did;
and it so pleased him that he made from it a sketch
in color, using his own eyes and other portions of
his face to supply the deficiencies which the silhouette could not give. But then, in the pressure of
work, these things had been forgotten, and remained
packed away in his trunk.

It was not unnatural, that, in the prospect of renew-
ing his acquaintance with Mr. Barclay, these thoughts
should arise.

The evening was enchanting; and his long walk
led him over the Arno with its boats, the amber

water tinted with the last rays of the setting sun, past the *cafés* where people were smoking and playing dominoes, and where there was much clashing of dishes and glasses.

The flower women and the dealers of early fruits were going home ; but he was able to secure a bunch of sweet double violets, and then he found himself at Mr. Barclay's door.

The room was full, — Miss Alden and her nieces, Ruth and Miss Marchbank, Mr. Potter, the Duchess of Stickingham and the pale-faced American beauty, Mrs. Coit, with several gentlemen whom Lillo recognized having seen at the Legation. It was hardly a time for reminiscences ; and Mr. Barclay made no allusion to them, but presented him to Ruth and Grace and May as an old friend.

"Of course we remember you perfectly, Mr. Marsh, as the courageous boy who jumped overboard after Mr. Barclay, that day we all had such a hard time together at the Neck," said May, with one of her bewitching smiles. "Ruth was not with us. — It was before we knew you, Ruth."

"Yes," said Ruth, smiling, "but I have heard the story related so often, that it seems as if I must have been one of the party."

"Perhaps you did not hear what courage one of the little girls of that time showed, and what a good oar she pulled," said Mr. Marsh, glancing at May, and noticing the merry flash of her gray-blue eyes. "Only half of the story was told, I fear."

"Ah, my lesser achievement was forgotten in the greater one of yours!" answered May. "Besides, I doubt if the misdemeanor of our escapade did not balance any merit of mine. I know I received a famous scolding, and aunt has never fully trusted me since."

"That is not to be wondered at," said Ruth demurely. "You have the faculty for getting into scrapes of all sorts. — But we must have a little dance now. You dance, I suppose, Mr. Marsh ? "

" No, not at all."

"Neither do I. Then you shall come and turn my music for me, as I must play."

The dancing, however, did not last long : the evening was sultry, and the elders were discussing the school question. The duchess left early, and Mrs. Coit was planning a garden-party with Mr. Potter, who had promised to aid her. The gardens belonged to an old and wealthy Italian family whose estates were in litigation, but who allowed the keeper of their domain to rent the gardens for his own benefit. Mrs. Coit wished to aid the Protestant schools, and chose this way to do it. The party was to be in the morning ; and, besides music and dancing, there must be a little bazar, — just one table of pretty trifles for the girls to sell, and where they could also dispense claret punch and flowers.

"But," interposed Miss Alden, "how are we to have time for all this ? None of us, I presume, intend to stay much longer in Florence. I am to leave on the 30th. How long do you remain, Mr. Barclay ? "

Mr. Barclay glanced at Ruth, but she was listening to May's lively chatter over some engravings Mr. Marsh was inspecting.

Here Miss Marchbank interposed.

"I am trying to induce Mr. Barclay to visit Spain, since he has abandoned Switzerland."

"Spain in summer?" said Miss Alden.

"Why not? It will be no warmer than would be a return to the States; and Spain is so comparatively fresh to the traveller, it would be a great advantage to Miss Morris."

"Very fatiguing, very. Are you then really thinking of home again, Frank?"

"Only thinking, Miss Alden; I assure you I have no definite plans."

"But it is time you did have, Frank; you will lose all your nationality if you stay abroad so constantly. Besides, Ruth is to be considered. Do you think it altogether beneficial for a girl to have no settled home?"

"How do you find it affects your own nieces, Miss Alden?" asked Miss Marchbank.

Now Miss Alden was quite willing to accept Miss Marchbank as a part of Mr. Barclay's establishment, but not quite so ready to accept her as a personal friend; for she had noticed what had appeared to be a certain aggressiveness in Miss Marchbank, which was distasteful to her.

"My nieces have the advantage of my personal care and affection, Miss Marchbank," she said with hauteur; not caring to explain, what was the truth, that she had come abroad with Grace in hopes of breaking up an undesirable attachment. "Ruth, of course, is fortunate in having a man of leisure for her guardian, but that hardly suffices for a home, in my opinion; and Mr. Barclay has always been wise enough to value that."

Miss Marchbank had not lived in the world fifty years for nothing. She was used to snubs, and bore them philosophically; besides, Miss Alden snubbed only in a lady-like fashion.

"But, Miss Alden, you forget that Miss Morris is still continuing her studies " —

"And if we go home we shall lose Miss March-bank's inestimable services," said Mr. Barclay, feeling it time to interpose.

"Well, of course you know best, Frank, as to the necessity of further study. I should think Ruth must be by this time quite an accomplished woman."

"So she is, in her quiet way."

As Miss Marchbank now glided off to see that Mrs. Coit's black lace and glittering diamonds were properly cloaked for departure, Miss Alden leaned confidentially towards Mr. Barclay, and said, —

"It is rumored that you intend to marry Ruth, Frank. May I ask if it is true?"

"What intolerable nonsense! It is indeed time for me to go home if I am thus to be the subject of gossip. No, Miss Alden, I have no thought of such a thing, and pray don't let it get to Ruth's ears."

"I am afraid it has done so already."

"Then she shows her good sense in not being affected by it."

"Ah, these girls are a great responsibility. There's Grace, whom I thought always a most sensible child, has taken it into her head to become attached to a poor young man in no way her equal. To be sure, she admits the folly of it, and yields to my wish that for a year at least there shall be no intercourse; but her temper is quite spoiled by it, and she will not be even civil to any other man."

Mr. Barclay smiled. He knew Miss Alden's preference for birth and fortune.

"Who is her friend?"

"Oh, a Mr. Bainbridge!—a nobody, a clerk in some office."

"What are his attractions?"

"You must ask Grace. I see none."

"And May—are her affections disengaged?" said Mr. Barclay lightly, glancing over at the three girls, who, with Lillo in the centre, were listening to something he was relating with vivacity.

"As far as I know, they are; May is too fond of variety and excitement to bear the restrictions of an '*affaire du cœur.*' She laughs at sentiment."

"Take care: she may be the more in danger," said Mr. Barclay prophetically.

"No, I have no fears for May; but Grace is a serious trouble."

But now they were drawn into general conversation. It was decided there would not be much time for elaborate preparations. Mr. Potter promised to levy on the colony of American artists for contributions, and Mrs. Coit was to defray every expense of hiring attendants. The *fête* would have to be on the 25th, just two weeks off; for after that all the Americans would be on the wing.

After all the other guests had gone, Mr. Barclay drew from Lillo an account of all the intervening years since the beginning of their acquaintance. It was a modestly told tale of earnest labor, to which Ruth listened with deep interest. She knew that her guardian had wanted to adopt Lillo as a lad, and she could not help comparing their two lives, her own and his. While she had been given every advantage, every means of culture, all that wealth and influence could command, he had striven alone single-handed against the world. From the time he had turned the key in the door of the little brown house on the sands of Codtown, and had gone with his bundle on his back to the fishing-smack which was to meet an outward-bound vessel, he had worked unaided. Landing at Havre, he had obtained employment on the wharves until money enough was earned for the railway journey to Paris. In the same way at Paris he had lived on scant earnings by day, that he might study in the schools at night. From Paris he had gone to Vienna, to Dresden, to Munich, and at last to his beloved Italy.

"And what have you to show us for all this labor?" asked Mr. Barclay.

"Nothing much," responded Lillo. "You must remember I am yet a student. My work has been desultory in its choice of subjects until now. I have now something on my easel which I think will determine me in future."

"What is it?" asked Mr. Barclay eagerly. "You will let us see it?"

"No, pardon me, not yet. It is not far enough completed to be exhibited; and, when it is finished, America must have my first offering."

"But our interest is so great, we should be privileged observers," urged Ruth.

"And to Mr. Barclay's kindness I owe so much, as my first patron."

"Yes, if you choose to put it that way; though I much dislike the word 'patron' so applied."

"Thank you. It is a mere phrase: no man is more independent of patronage than the true artist."

"I agree with you. You will let us, then, see your work?"

"Yes, when it is a little more advanced."

"And you will give us some trifle for our *fête*, — the merest sketch?"

"Certainly, with pleasure."

"That is one of the abominations artists have to submit to, even if it takes the very bread out of their mouths," said Mr. Barclay.

"But it may put some in Mr. Marsh's this time," said Ruth archly, "for you know he will have us to sound his praises. There will be lots of rich people come to the *fête*, all the English and American nobility, — I mean American 'distinction,'" she said, correcting herself, — "and we will point to his sketch, and say how kind it was in our distinguished young compatriot to give it to us when he is so very, very hard at work; and then they'll begin to think they ought to know something more about this clever Mr. Marsh, who paints so charmingly, and they will hunt him up and buy him out. Ah! you must have plenty of things ready to sell, for you will become the fashion at once."

Lillo smiled at Ruth's ardor. It was very sweet

to hear her, though his whole soul scorned such diplomacy.

But Mr. Barclay opened his eyes in amazement.

"Ruth," he said, "do I hear aright? have you become such an intriguer?"

"Oh, all girls have more or less artfulness!" she replied, "and this is certainly nothing very deep or dreadful."

Mr. Barclay still shook his head. "You are advancing in worldly wisdom rapidly. We will have to seek the retirement of a New-England village."

"And be twice as treacherous and gossipy."

"Nous verrons que nous verrons."

But Mr. Barclay had not the slightest idea of going home. Europe suited him, and in Europe he intended to stay, at least for the present.

CHAPTER XI.

If Miss Alden had been of a less courageous nature, she certainly would never have attempted to thwart destiny, in the shape of Cupid and his darts, by going abroad; for, so far from its proving curative, it had been distinctly an impetus in the wrong direction. But that she could hardly have known beforehand, so perhaps her courage on the whole was experimental. Letters came and went with regularity: the promise of no personal intercourse only had been acceded to; and, as this would have been rather difficult under the circumstances, it was not much of a compromise. She reasoned, she sighed, she scolded; but the reasoning was scorned, the sighing slighted, and the scolding taken as a dose, with a wry face.

Grace acknowledged that Mr. Bainbridge's prospects were not brilliant, nor her choice a wise one in a worldly way; but she never wavered in her allegiance to her lover. She argued that her father had not been a rich man when he married her mother, that everybody could not begin life with equal promise of success, and that she would live and die an old maid unless allowed to do as she pleased.

"And this you might much better do than accept the cramped, sordid, miserable life which poverty

entails," replied her aunt, smoothing down the folds
of her heavy silk, and adjusting the rich and delicate
lace at her throat.

Very naturally she considered her own condition
an enviable one. No sentimental nonsense had ever
disturbed her serenity. But Grace thought it the
very refinement of cruelty when her aunt would close
these unsatisfactory discussions by saying, —

"It is absolute selfishness in a woman to consent
to a marriage with a man of small means. He has no
chance to rise, he is tied, fettered; family cares soon
rob him of all ambition, and he becomes a household
drudge."

Then, as Grace looked her despair, May would
scream with laughter: "Aunt Althea, how ridiculous you make things appear! Why, Grace has no
attachment for a waiter-man or a bootblack!"

But May herself was also a source of great uneasiness to her worldly aunt, whose choice of friends
was very exacting. Never had Miss Alden allowed
herself to be drawn into any connection with people
whose ancestry, habits, personal appearance, or manners were in the least questionable. She had a high
standard, and she adhered to it. She was not of an
unkind disposition: she could tolerate chance ac-
quaintances, who were perhaps not up to the mark,
in a graceful way; but she stood guard over the
portals of her friendships.

Now May, well brought up, tenderly nurtured in
an atmosphere of refinement, had a most remarkable
taste for people whom her aunt considered deplorably
vulgar, — "loud" would have been the word which

would have expressed her meaning, had she ever used slang, — people who wore diamonds on all occasions, and who were very prominent at hotel-tables; who gave champagne suppers, and drove fast horses; who were anxious for the acquaintance of titled foreigners; and who by their acts and attitudes demanded the attention which nothing in themselves deserved.

Miss Althea Alden's appreciation of money never led her into the mistakes of these people, and she could not at all comprehend May's tolerance of them for an hour.

But May, full of life, spirit, vivacity, charmingly pretty, dazzled by glare and glitter, fond of fun as a child, had been drawn into dangerous intimacy with some of this sort.

A Mrs. Godfrey Gray had made ardent love to May, petted, admired her, invited her to visit her, and asked her to go about with her. But Miss Alden had steadily refused.

In Mrs. Gray's train were two or three young men, idle, rich, and with no apparent object in life but amusement.

May's innate good taste would soon have tired of them, — as it was, she ridiculed them constantly, — but her aunt's horror of them aroused a spirit of opposition, a childish love of teasing and mischief, which induced her to encourage rather than discourage their attentions. And Miss Alden received no sympathy from Grace when May disobeyed orders and went to drive with Mrs. Gray.

"I wonder that you are so shocked, aunt. Mrs.

Godfrey Gray is a very *rich* woman. I have heard her say just how many servants she kept, what high wages she paid, and how entirely her household is ruled by them. She never goes in her kitchen, rarely in her nursery ; and her expenses are enormous. She is so well versed in the price of diamonds and India shawls, that she can make a close guess as to just what was paid for them by the person who may be visiting her ; and she always travels *en prince.*"

Miss Alden listened patiently, and returned quietly, —

"You are young, Grace, to attempt satire. I am no devotee of wealth. I am simply prudent. When you have lived as long as I, your judgment will, I trust, be riper. I do not approve of Mrs. Gray ; she is one of those who misrepresent us abroad, and one whom people of refinement at home shun."

"Not exclusively. I have noticed that she mentions many people whom you visit."

"New York is cosmopolitan, I allow."

Grace shrugged her shoulders and went on with her letter. Little did she care for her aunt's burden of responsibility. She was selfishly absorbed in her own affairs, and she was honestly in love. Mr. Bainbridge would have been astonished to know upon how high a pinnacle she had placed him ; for he was a modest, unassuming, and apparently unaspiring man, and bore his share of their difficulties in a much gentler spirit. Perhaps the necessary but unromantic calculations suggested by the thought of marriage tempered his views.

It was a charming day, and May danced into the

room where her aunt and Grace were sitting, with a gay and naughty carelessness which nearly disarmed Miss Alden; but she rose at once and left in silence.

May made a little grimace, saying, —

"Aunt can be very dignified: I would much rather she scolded."

"You deserve her displeasure. It was outrageous in you, May, to go so directly in opposition to her wishes."

"I could not get out of it, Grace. I positively *was* cornered. I could not say, 'Mrs. Gray, my aunt won't let me drive with you,' as if I were a child six years old. Besides, she is awfully jolly, and the drive was delicious. We went to the Pitti Palace first, and afterwards in the direction of those gardens where Mrs. Coit is to have her *fête.* They surround an old gloomy prison of a palace, which is only partly occupied."

"And who went with you?"

"Arthur Smith and Mr. Morton."

"How can you tolerate them?"

"Oh, they are innocent sort of nobodies!"

"Innocent?"

"Yes; they have not force enough to be bad."

"Does it demand force? I hardly think so."

"You're in a preachy mood, Grace. You always are when you are writing to brother Bainbridge. I don't know any bad men, and so am not competent to judge just what badness does demand. But I always have supposed a villain had to have some native genius. Now, these fellows are just without one spark of that sort of thing. Why, they laugh at what I say as if I were a professional wit!"

"You are far from stupid."

"Ah, that is a nice little concession! Come, I'll reward your sisterly kindness now with a confidential disclosure. Mrs. Coit's *fête*, you know, is to be on the 25th. Well, it will all be over by evening, and that night there is to be a *bal masqué* at the 'Carlo Alberto.' Of course, aunt would never consent to our going. Nothing would move her, and I don't mean to trouble her by asking; but I'm going all the same, without asking. Oh, you may look as horrified as you please! All your thoughts and hopes and fancies revolve around brother Bainbridge. But I am free as air, as sunshine, — and I have always wanted above all things to see a *bal masqué.* It must be so droll, so delightful. Mrs. Gray is going to the *fête*, and will bring us home; but she will arrange to have a little accident, a detention at a wayside inn, where we can change our dresses and assume our masks; and then we will go on and have our fun, and nobody need be distressed about us."

Grace looked at May in silent astonishment.

"Why do you glare at me that way, Grace?" cried May.

"Because I cannot believe my own ears."

"Why not? What harm is there in having a little fun for one night?"

"You know exactly as well as I do."

"No; I protest I do not. All you do is to sigh and look sour, and care for nothing but the post; while I am glad to have some diversion. Aunt is so rigid and tiresome, that I might as well be in Kam-tchatka."

"But this *bal masqué*, — how do you know what sort of an affair it will be? what people you will meet?"

"What do I care? No one will know me. It requires, of course, a little daring, but it will be great fun."

"And aunt, — how do you reconcile your con-science to deceiving her?"

"Please don't put the thing in such a serious way. There's no conscience in the matter. I want to see something of the world. Aunt would have me wear smoked-glass spectacles all my life, and I prefer to use my unassisted eyes. I am not going to deceive her."

"You will if you do not tell her."

"No, I won't. I will manage somehow. I am a person of resources."

"And much self-deception, I fear," thought Grace, quite alarmed, but hoping the freak would not be carried out. She knew that remonstrance would arouse antagonism, and her letter was not yet fin-ished: so she bent herself to its completion, while May tossed over the contents of the trunks, and carolled a little song, putting off for a more conven-ient moment the duty of asking her aunt's forgive-ness, which she really coveted, now that the excite-ment of her day's pleasure had passed. As she did so, Ruth Morris was announced, and followed the servant into the room, with the freedom always ac-corded her.

May rose from the trunks, and Grace from her writing.

"I am so glad to see you," said May in her impulsive way, kissing Ruth, and leading her to a comfortable chair. "I am in disgrace, and doing all sorts of wicked things, and need sympathy."

"You look very distressed, to be sure," answered Ruth, surveying the graceful, pretty girl with admiration; "but I too come claiming sympathy."

"How is it possible, you who have every wish of your heart gratified?"

"Envy me not, Grace," answered Ruth, with assumed solemnity. "No one escapes trouble in this weary world. I have just come from my aunt, Mrs. Vedder."

May and Grace both knew who Mrs. Vedder was.

"Then no wonder you want pity," said May, with one of her mischievous grimaces.

"No, dear, it is she who needs it. I only asked for sympathy. I have determined to go home with her."

"You!" screamed the girls.

"Yes, I."

"But will Mr. Barclay allow it?"

"He has given his permission."

"Why, Ruth, how could you ask it?"

"I did so, because Mrs. Vedder is ill, and in need of kindness, and because — Well, no matter for any other reason."

Grace was stung to the quick.

"I thought you were above being influenced in that way," she said; adding, however, "I shall never forgive myself for my foolish speech to you."

"It did hurt, I acknowledge, Grace."

"But surely you will not leave Mr. Barclay on that account?"

"No. I have no idea of leaving him permanently. I love him too well to do that. But Mrs. Vedder really needs me, and I can be of great service to her, while Mr. Barclay can spare me for a while; and then, perhaps, the silly talk will have died away."

"And Miss Marchbank, what will become of her?"

"Oh, she is already in correspondence with a family who have been trying to get her for a year past!"

"But, Ruth, do you know what you are doing? what sort of people you are going among?"

"I have an imperfect idea," said Ruth, with a deprecating look.

"And you will leave this lovely, lovely Florence, a summer in Switzerland, another winter perhaps at Nice, to go — where — to what part of our beloved land?"

"To New York, first; afterwards to some quiet, little spot in the country, I hope."

"*Tiens! c'est malheureuse,*" said May; whereupon Grace turned scornfully about with, —

"Pray give us none of Mrs. Gray's execrable French phrases, May. She is not content with contaminating your manners only, but" — She stopped abruptly.

May made another grimace in reply, and answered with less severity, but equal maliciousness, —

"Positively, you envy Ruth's return to her native land."

"And if I do, what then?"

"Why, go with her! I would if I were you."

"I wish I could," said Grace regretfully.

"Really, you are the most absurdly love-lorn creature the world ever saw. — But, Ruth, what romantic idea possesses you to leave dear, kind Mr. Barclay for that stupid creature, Mrs. Vedder?"

"She is my aunt, May."

"I beg pardon, so she is; but that gives her no claim, I am sure."

"I am not so sure; she loved my mother."

"But nobody cares very much for relations now-a-days; besides, yours have virtually given you up."

"Yes, I know I am a"—

May sprang up, and stopped whatever detracting word was coming with a kiss.

"You are a darling, an angel, a treasure! I love you, Ruth, and so cannot allow you to say a disparaging word of yourself. This kindness to Mrs. Vedder indicates what you can do in the way of self-denial. You make me good in spite of myself, and so now I am going to find aunt and make my peace with her; I have offended her awfully. Adieu." May fluttered away like the butterfly she was, trailing her pretty silk after her.

Grace sighed.

"I wish I could influence her as you do, Ruth."

Ruth smiled, for she knew how self-absorbed Grace had become; but she made no reply.

"May is dazzled by that dreadful Mrs. Godfrey Gray, of whom I could believe any thing. I dare say she is a *divorcée*, or something of that sort."

"Why, Grace! don't be uncharitable," remonstrated Ruth.

"I cannot help it; she is an injury to May, and —
will you believe it? — intends taking her to a horrid
masked ball."

"Your aunt will never allow it."

"She is not to know it."

"Oh, Grace, she must!"

"No; May told me in confidence, and declares she
will go."

"But you must tell her that it is not at all a place
where girls are ever allowed."

"Pshaw! she laughs at every thing I tell her. She
says Americans are a law to themselves, and can go
where they please."

"She forgets that modesty and reserve are just as
essential in one place as in another. She would not
do such a thing in New York or Boston."

"No, of course not."

"We must prevent her going, Grace," said Ruth
earnestly.

"I sincerely hope we may."

"Shall I consult Mr. Barclay?"

"Perhaps it would be as well."

Then they talked of the garden-party, and the
various contributions for it that had been received.

"The artists have sent some charming sketches,
and the duchess has bought some mosaics," said
Ruth.

"The duchess! How grand you have become to
have her for a friend, Ruth!" exclaimed Grace.

"Really, I don't appreciate the elevation. She is a
very earnest supporter of the schools, and a thoroughly good woman; but she is much more Mr. Barclay's

friend than mine. To tell the truth, I find her hard to talk to."

"And Lillo, — Mr. Marsh, I mean, — has he given any thing for the bazar?"

"Yes. We were at his rooms yesterday; he works with many others in a large studio. I took my choice from a portfolio of studies, — a lovely little head, a child's, not unlike one of the Angelicos in the Uffizi Gallery. He was at first disinclined to offer it, as he said it had peculiar associations, — what, I could not of course guess, — but he relented at last and gave me the sketch. I knew it would please Mr. Barclay. He has already bought it."

"What is Mr. Barclay going to do with all the beautiful things he has gathered about him?"

Ruth's face saddened in expression as she answered, —

"I do not know: he seems too restless to ever settle in one place, and yet he may one day tire of travel."

"And you, Ruth?"

"I have no choice, except that for a few months I shall visit Mrs. Vedder."

CHAPTER XII.

"AH! signore, why will you let people come to these poor shabby rooms?" was the exclamation of Lillo's landlady the day after Mr. Barclay and Ruth's visit.

"And why not, Bianca?"

"Because, indeed, they are so bare, so unfit *an appartamento* for ladies to enter."

"Indeed! then why do you not lessen my rent?" exclaimed the practical artist. But, seeing Bianca's crestfallen look, he glanced out of the window, and with a stretch of his hand toward the .hills said, —

"This view atones for all shortcomings within. What care I for the broken-down *sedias,* or the cracked *tazzas?*"

"But the signorina, was she not shocked? The Americans are so grand, and to mount way up to this *piano* must have tired her."

"Not at all; she enjoyed it. American girls like variety, adventure," he said, more to himself than to his listener.

"The signorina is *bellissima!*" sighed Bianca, glancing at her withered old face in the small mirror, giving a touch of her duster to the table, and gathering up the various household utensils which she had been using, for a spasmodic fit of industry had seized her. Days and days went by with little or no attention to the quiet inhabitant of these upper rooms; but now that an American gentleman and a beautiful young lady had condescended to explore his fastness, she must be more alert. Who could tell what might happen should they be as foolish and romantic as the young signore, and prefer an outside "view" to interior elegance? There was no telling what those barbaric Americans ever would do; and Bianca began calculating how much more she would increase the rent.

But Lillo had already forgotten Bianca and her apologies. He was thinking of the delicate beauty of one American girl, of her gentle manners and sympathetic appreciation of his work. He was wishing he had such a friend, one that would take pride and pleasure in his achievements, one to whom he could confide his aspirations, one who could cheer and stimulate him, and for whom he would be so glad to strive and conquer fortune. Not often did he allow himself these thoughts. He was too strong, too determined, to yield easily to vague desires of this kind. But the strongest have need of affection, and Lillo often longed to know something of his mother.

Had she been young and pretty, or staid and saintly? Was she living or dead, and who was she? Ah, he dared not ask! He feared some mystery, some stain, would perhaps deface the image he had formed within his own breast; some dark cloud rest upon the memory of one of whom, so long as he knew no ill, he could believe every thing good and pure and lovely. Yes, he would not seek to draw the veil which circumstances had placed between him and the past.

But it was a strange past; for besides the little brown house on the sands, the gray fogs, the long, rolling waves and their thunder on the beach, the two old people whose weather-beaten visages were ever present to his memory, there was another picture, less distinct, much more shadowy, perhaps only a dream, but it was this, —

It was of a night, balmy sweet, full of soft airs and shining with stars; of a garden where roses grew, of a fountain falling from dolphin mouths into marble basins. And then the garden changed to a ship, creaking and pulling at the ropes which held it to a wharf piled with bales of goods; the scent of roses gave place to the smell of tar, the dripping fall of the fountain to the splash of waves and the hoarse cries of seamen. Some one bent and kissed him; he could not tell whom, but it seemed to him it was an old woman, and that her swinging bead necklace, as well as a tear, touched his cheek. Then a man held him in his strong arms, and he looked up into a kindly face, not unlike grandfather Marsh's, but it was redder and rougher than grandfather's. Then the ship sailed out into the night, and the stars twinkled in the water as well as in the sky. But ship and water and stars ended as they do in dreams, with a start; and he was again seeking clams at the Neck, or tugging at an unruly sail, or dragging home a string of fish for grandmother Marsh to fry.

"Tut, what foolishness to dream in this way!" he would say to himself, giving another glance at the heavenly blue sky, and watching the flight of some pigeons from a neighboring window; then he would draw his easel near, and arrange the colors on his palette, and with rapid touch block out a picture.

He was doing this now, when a knock was heard at his door, followed by a familiar, "*Buon giorno!*"

"Ah, I have bearded you in your den this time!" said the same voice, and Branly Potter stalked in. "The lovely Bianca informed me I should find you here. I'm drumming for that confounded garden-party, as you may suppose. What a bore it is to be in the train of a lot of women who have nothing to do but get up fairs and *fêtes* and fal-lals!"

"I should have supposed it entirely to your taste, almost a vocation," responded Lillo dryly.

"Yes, I dare say you would; but you are mistaken. I'm tired of even being decently civil to them all, and I think I'll go break stones on the roads before long."

"Really, this is serious. Had you not better become a courier?"

"Worse and worse, — more women to trot round after. No, thank you. I'm going to the States in the fall."

"What to do?"

"Any thing that turns up; run for Congress, perhaps."

"But what has happened to annoy you just now? Has the fair one refused to smile?"

"All the fair ones are frowning. Each has her

own particular fish to fry.   One needs to be a Machiavelli to understand them.   Mrs. Coit is at the head of this *fête*, and was amply able to carry it through without assistance.   But so soon as the duchess's name was mentioned in connection with it, the flutter among the females became fearful.   So many applications have been made to take part in it, that half the foreign population will be enraged to have their services declined, and there is danger of selling no tickets."

"Now is the chance for diplomacy.   Use your skill."

"No; I shall let them fight it out, and then wash my hands of all such affairs in future.   I am tired of being a 'vagabond,' as May Alden politely puts it."

"She is saucy."

"Yes; so is her sister.   They are both bright girls."

"Very."

"Miss Morris is so much quieter that she is thought to be dull."

"It's a mistake."

"So I think.   She wasn't dull when she faced that Vedder woman.   By the by, do you know her sons?"

"Whose sons?"

"Mrs. Vedder's."

"No; I never heard of them before."

"They have persecuted me.   They consider me an authority on art, and consequently consult me about all the rubbish they are going to cart home.   Do you know Mrs. Vedder is Miss Morris's aunt?   And it is rumored she is going back with her."

"Going to leave Mr. Barclay?"

"Yes. It's a queer move; I am quite sure she knew little of her before they met here. But this is all gossip. What trade would you advise me to take up, Marsh, since the courier suggestion is unavailable?"

"Bag an heiress."

"Thanks. Your suggestions have a spice of satire, as if my accomplishments were only in the line of social life."

"As they are, unquestionably."

"Then you painter chaps think I'm only a squire of dames?"

"Oh, I did not limit your powers!"

"But you calmly leave it to be supposed that is all I am good for. Now, in return, let me tell you that I am going to the States to work, not to dabble in art or literature, but to work for my daily bread — with my brains if I can, but with my hands if I can't."

"Good! Shake hands. I hope the bread will be sweet, in spite of your fling at my profession."

"You know well enough what I mean, for you are in earnest, and will make your profession subservient to your purpose, — viz., the elevation of humanity, — where others make it only the vehicle of selfish vanity. Do you know whose face is coming out now on your canvas?"

"No, I am only experimenting."

"Nevertheless, it is a good likeness of the little Mayflower, Ruth Morris."

"That is a good name for her. Where did you get it?"

"I don't know, — the Aldens may have suggested it."

Lillo went on painting. He was making studies for a group of Puritans going to church in the simple, primitive Colonial days of New England. Sternly devoted to duty, despite the danger from their treacherous foes, the men indicated the need of caution, not only in the expression of their faces, but in the weapons carried, ready for use, in their hands; and the women were no less courageous.

"Yes, I will get her to pose for me," thought Lillo. "She is just the sort of girl who would have faced these dangers with resolute calmness."

He quite forgot his companion, until Mr. Potter asked him for his contribution to the *fête.*

Then he explained that Mr. Barclay and Miss Morris had chosen a sketch, which had gone to be framed, and which would be duly on exhibition, although it was sold.

"Lucky fellow, to have such good friends," said Mr. Potter. "Well, I'll go then. But be sure you are on hand on the 25th, for I don't propose to be the only sacrificial offering to the fashionable mob."

Lillo smiled. No man less needed an ally than Branly Potter. Everybody liked him, and he liked everybody, though he pretended to great fastidiousness.

CHAPTER XIII.

IT may be as well to explain how it had come about that Mr. Barclay had given Ruth permission to follow the bent of her inclination in joining her aunt for a while — for a little while only, as he said to himself. He had no intention of surrendering her to her relatives. He was a whimsical man, as we know, and being so made him indulgent to the whims of others.

Ruth had come to him one day, fresh from Mrs. Vedder's lonely rooms in the Casa Doria, with a pitiful tale of her aunt's sorrows.

"I never saw any one quite so homesick as my poor aunt Abby, Mr. Barclay; she enjoys nothing, not even this lovely spring weather, and only longs for her sons to come. But they, selfish fellows, now write that they prefer spending the summer abroad, and seem quite indifferent to either her loneliness or her wish to return. If you could spare me, my dear guardian," — Ruth rarely used this word, but she was now in an excited mood, — "I would be so glad to take her home."

"You!" exclaimed Mr. Barclay.

"Yes. The poor woman would be immensely happy, and I — Well, I should feel as if I were doing just a little good."

"My dear little Samaritan, have you considered what you are talking about?"

"I have indeed," replied Ruth.

"But, Ruth, you do not like Mrs. Vedder."

Ruth blushed.

"I do not like her unrefinement, but I have really learned to look a little below the surface. She has a very kind heart."

"Does that atone for the thousand and one things that are lacking?"

"I am not sure, I cannot say; but I would like to help her."

"And leave me?"

"Only for a while, Mr. Barclay."

"I, too, have been thinking you should have some choice in the matter of your own actions, Ruth."

Ruth looked up quickly.

"Yes, you are no longer a child."

"You do not suppose I have any wish to do any thing you disapprove, Mr. Barclay?"

"No: you are very transparent, Ruth, and perhaps a little too docile for your own strength. I think I will not thwart you in this desire to be of use to Mrs. Vedder. You will learn more than you think, but you must be prepared for disagreeables and difficulties."

"And you will not think me ungrateful?" said Ruth pleadingly.

"No, dear, no."

Ruth rose and kissed her guardian with a bright smile, saying,—

"Mrs. Vedder will be so glad."

"She ought to be," was the emphatic reply.

Then, as Ruth left the room, Mr. Barclay soliloquized.

"I shall be very dull without her,—she is a dear child. My old friend, Dick Morris, never did a wiser or kinder thing than in leaving her to me. She has made my life worth living; but she is, in truth, no longer a child."

And then Mr. Barclay, who was walking up and down the room, stopped before a mirror and surveyed himself.

He saw there the slender figure of a man whose habits had not been productive of muscular development, but who was nevertheless of an erect and graceful carriage. The face did not indicate the exact years that had passed over it, though the hair was beginning to be more than silvery. The eyes were clear and bright; and if at their corners there were some lines which time had traced, they were no deeper than the furrows which care and toil also produce in younger visages. On the whole, Mr. Barclay, who had no overplus of vanity, and who was quite willing to acknowledge his forty-eight years, had to be honest with himself and admit that many younger men might envy his appearance. But at the same time he felt really older than he was. When he lost his wife, sorrow had made him its prey. He had loved her deeply, truly, entirely,—as a man only loves once, so he honestly believed,—merging his whole being into that of the object so loved; and his heart had never rebounded from the shock of her loss. This had aged him, and made him indifferent

to much that interests other people. He hated
novels, with their everlasting study of the affections;
he avoided music of the sentimental order; he would
not go to see a tragedy; he was as sensitive to the
sight of lovers' bliss as if he had been jilted, — and
yet his old friend, Miss Alden, had asked him if he
were going to marry Ruth.

That question had recurred to him again and
again; and, though to him its absurdity equalled its
vulgarity, it had helped him to decide this matter of
Ruth's departure. He would prove how false and
foolish the world had been in its surmises, and how
well he could do without her gentle presence; but he
was afraid the poor girl would suffer from the contact with her vulgar relatives.

And so, with not a suspicion that Mr. Barclay knew
the gossip she had heard, Ruth arrived at the same
conclusion that he had come to; viz., that it would all
be forgotten in her absence.

Of course, Mrs. Vedder was made happy.

"You have done more to make me well than all
the doctors in the world could do," she said to Ruth.
"I wouldn't have believed you could be so kind, that
first night I met you. I thought you were awfully
stuck up, — you were as stiff as a poker, — but you
ain't. You're a sweet little wild-rose, just such as
I've often picked in the woods at Berryville."

Ruth laughed.

"Tell me about Berryville, aunt Abby."

"I will, — only too glad to, — but first you tell me
how Mr. Barclay finds it in his heart to let you go
away from him. I thought — people say" —

The look in Ruth's face checked her.

"Well, I don't suppose I have any call to inquire, so long as he does me such a favor; but I really don't see how he can do it."

"He seldom refuses a reasonable request, and he has always been as kind to me as if he were really my father."

Ruth emphasized the last words of her sentence; and Mrs. Vedder gave a little shrug to her shoulders, around which were wrapped a costly shawl, that, from its dinginess, might have been worn by several pashas.

"Now about Berryville, Ruth. It's an ordinary country town. Your uncle Cauldwell Boggs has built lots of houses there, and it's not so nice as it used to be; but I like it, though the boys don't. They hate it. The old homestead was a real comfortable old place. Your grandmother — my oldest sister Margaretta — was born there; and there she died, leaving your mother. But her father took her away when she was little. Old Mr. Sanders was very queer. He didn't like us, and we didn't like him."

"I suppose he is dead," said Ruth casually.

"No, he isn't."

"What! have I a grandfather, then?"

"Yes, such as he is."

Ruth could not help smiling at the dubious reply.

"Well, he is queer, you know," went on her aunt apologetically. "He is very learned, people say. He has out-lived all his sons and daughters, and he doesn't seem to care about any thing but his books. When brother Cauldwell told him that you had been left to Mr. Barclay, he only said, 'Ah! indeed!' and that made Mr. Boggs mad; for, if he ain't very agreeable, he has some spirit, and he didn't like the notion of any of the family being sort o' begging of a stranger."

Ruth winced. What dreadful things this aunt could say, and do it, too, as if entirely for her auditor's entertainment. She hardly paused to take breath: it was so long since she had been favored with so good a listener.

"He had never cared for Dick Morris, who ran away with your mother, you know; and he had no sort o' feeling for Cauldwell's not likin' Mr. Barclay, —for Cauldwell didn't like his offer refused."

Seeing Ruth's mystification, she explained, "Mr. Boggs wanted to take you from Mr. Barclay, but he wouldn't listen to him. Perhaps it has turned out for the best, for Cauldwell is a hard man. People are apt to be who work for their livin' as he has done, and men *are* so cantankerous."

Ruth smiled at her aunt's philosophy, and strove to draw her out on a more interesting theme than chronology; but Mrs. Vedder was very fond of going into the deeps of family history, and of climbing the branches of her ancestral tree.

"The Boggses are all inclined to be proud; and Cauldwell thinks because he has made a fortune he is something very remarkable, and he is afraid my boys will go through all my money. It wouldn't matter much to me if they did. Money is a great bother. Mr. Vedder might have been living now, if he hadn't worked so hard to get it."

Here Mrs. Vedder whisked a tear away, and went on, —

"Mr. Sanders lives all alone in the city: we never see him, though."

Ruth suddenly interrupted her.

"Don't tell me any more about my relations, aunt Abby. What kind of a place is Berryville? Is it very rural, with arching elms and maples, such as I have heard are so beautiful in New-England towns?"

. "Well, you'll have to wait and see; I ain't a good hand at describin'. I like the city and all the shops. It's awful dull in the country, and — I say, Ruth, do you think you are going to like bein' with me, after all?"

There seemed to be some doubt in her aunt's mind; there certainly was in her own, but the girl strove to conquer it.

"I want to make you happier, if I can," she said modestly.

"Well," replied her aunt, "it is kind of you to give up so much for me; but, now tell the truth, ain't you tired of joggin' all over Europe a-sight-seein'?"

Ruth laughed merrily, and shook her head.

"Well, it's very queer: the boys like it too, — Jim and Charley. Oh, won't they be surprised to hear I'm going home! Let's see, we leave on the 28th. They'll get my letter in time to come and say 'good-by' if they want to; but I don't believe they want to. They're so fine now that they're sort of ashamed of me."

"Oh, Mrs. Vedder, aunt Abby!" exclaimed Ruth, pained to hear a mother speak thus of her sons.

"It's just the truth, anyhow; and Cauldwell would say it served me right."

Ruth inwardly revolted at this admission. Sorry as she was for her aunt, this was one of the things which made affection for her impossible, — this want of proper reserve, this absence of self-respect and dignity. Ruth could only pity, but she could not admire her aunt. The prospect of spending months in Mrs. Vedder's society was not an agreeable one; but in doing it she had not expected pleasure: a higher motive had impelled her, and, inspired by that, she had no intention of withdrawing. Nevertheless, it was a relief to get back to Miss Marchbank's calm and quiet presence, and to Mr. Barclay, waiting for his tea.

Although they were in a great, gloomy Italian palace, the room had an air not wholly foreign. Mr. Barclay always carried as many comforts about with him as an Englishman is charged with doing. His books, pictures, and papers, his wife's portrait, his tiger-skin rug, his American lamp and folding-chairs, all gave the apartment a cosiness not due to the lofty walls, the deep embrasures, and the flowery balconies. Miss Marchbank was never without her work-basket; and now, in addition to all these things, the table was set for tea with Mr. Barclay's own Japanese service. Ruth sat down with a little sigh, partly of fatigue, partly of satisfaction.

Mr. Barclay regarded her with a curious sort of glance, questioning without words. Miss Marchbank, too, seemed expectant.

"It is quite settled," said Ruth; "we are to go on the 28th. Have you heard any thing definite from your friends, Miss Marchbank?"

"Yes. A letter came this morning. I am to meet them on the 25th, at Genoa. From thence we start for the Pyrenees."

"But you will not then stay for the garden-party?"

"Impossible, my dear! — And you, Mr. Barclay, will you remain here?" asked Miss Marchbank.

Ruth looked eagerly at her guardian.

"Yes, for the present."

At that moment Mr. Marsh was announced. Lillo came in at the right moment. Ruth began to feel as if her courage had been overestimated, when these separations were so near. This talk of departure was painful. But now the current turned. Mr. Marsh had brought the picture for the *fête*. It was a lovely head, — a child's soft-featured face, with great, glowing eyes, and a tangled mass of curls; just such a child as one might see at any time down beneath the balcony, tossing pebbles with its companions. The picture was set in an old frame of niello-work, mounted on garnet velvet.

"How lovely!" "How picturesque!" came from the ladies.

Mr. Barclay looked at it critically.

"Where did you get your model?" he asked.

"I had none," replied Lillo, laughing

"But how can that be? The face is familiar. It looks like some one I've seen before."

"That is not improbable. The commonest Italian child has a typical face."

"Yes, that is true. But where have I seen this? Ha! I remember, now. It looks like the boy I saw

at Codtown, years and years ago, — your own self, I
verily believe."

Lillo did not deny it. On the contrary, he told
them that it had been worked up partly from his
own features, partly from a silhouette which he
possessed.

Ruth compared it now with the man's face before
her, and also saw the likeness; though it was, of
course, more in feature than in expression. There
was the same dreamy depth in the eyes; but the
child's face had a delicacy and richness of color, and
the subtle, imaginative qualities which were due to
the artist, and not to his model. Perhaps Ruth saw
more in the man's than in the child's face to admire;
it certainly was one of strength and penetration and
fine expressiveness. But looking at first, as she
would have done at any two things, to compare them,
she suddenly became conscious that one of them was
not a picture; for her gaze drooped under the return
glance of admiration and inquiry, which quite as
innocently had been bestowed upon her.

The evening was warm, and they all drew near the
balcony. Mr. Barclay and Lillo discussed art and
artists. The elder man was fluent, and a good con-
versationalist; the younger a better listener, but by
no means backward in responding. During the discussion, Lillo mentioned that the duchess had paid
him a visit, and commissioned him to paint her a
picture.

"Ah, did I not predict good fortune for you?"
queried Ruth.

"Yes. The visit was due to the fact that she had

seen the picture destined for the *fête.* She came across it at the frame-maker's, where she was ordering work. I am quite surprised to find her so simple and plain a person. I had the rustic idea that a duchess would be rather unapproachable."

"The Americans outrival the English in exalting rank," observed Miss Marchbank, tossing back her cap-ribbons.

"Is it not natural that all imaginative persons, Miss Marchbank, should environ those who occupy exalted positions with a little halo of superiority?"

"I don't know, Mr. Barclay, I am not sufficiently gifted to be able to say; but I do know that tuft hunting is as much practised by those who live under a republican as a monarchical government."

Lillo laughed, as he said, —

"It matters nothing to me whether Mrs. Smith or the Duchess of Stickingham buys my pictures. Appreciation is what an artist most covets. I should even spurn their money, only that it is a proof of the estimate put upon one's work."

Ruth gave him a sympathetic little nod of approval, but Mr. Barclay laughed at the youthful zeal.

"Ah, my dear fellow, you will outgrow that sentiment!"

"Never," said Lillo firmly. "I hate the commercial spirit. It is ruinous to art; it degrades and defiles."

"You look at it in the wrong light. Trade is one of the necessary evils of civilization."

"I decline to believe in necessary evils."

"Perhaps that word was not well chosen. 'Evil'

is a strong term to apply; 'barrier' would have been better."

"Truly trade is a barrier to aspiration, to cultivation even of the moral faculties."

"Ah, you run away with an idea! I did not mean you to take it in that sense. It is the barrier to greed, to man's trampling upon the right of another. It is one of the things to be used and not abused. In its simplest form, what was it but a mere exchange of necessities between barbarians?"

"It has outgrown all the limitations of necessity."

"I am not so sure. Certainly, values are factitious; but that is because we are no longer primitive men. Even our wants are of an abstract nature. We no longer have to depend upon our skill as marksmen for our meat, nor upon the hides of animals for our clothing; but we must have beauty, grace, order, repose, companionship, — things that delight the mind, — or we starve intellectually and socially."

Ruth listened eagerly for the reply.

"And are these a matter of barter, Mr. Barclay?" questioned Lillo.

"More or less, yes."

"I cannot agree with you," was the response. "These things are to be wrested from the world by the individual, as truly as the savage won his daily food by his own prowess."

The talk went on after this in a leisurely way. The soft south wind bore upon its wings the odor of violets; the tinkling bells of tambourines sounded in the distance; the splash of the fountain in its marble basin lulled its little melody. In a human heart had a sweeter melody begun. Who knows just when and where love is born?

As the conversation languished, merry voices broke upon the stillness, and Miss Alden with her nieces entered.

CHAPTER XIV.

THE 25th of May dawned, as a day set apart for a gracious purpose ought to dawn, benignantly. It was indeed the perfection of spring and early summer, — a warmth and breeziness, a fresh, dewy, sweet-scented atmosphere, and a sunny sky.

Early in the day a throng of pleasure-seekers set forth for the Romano Gardens, where Mrs. Coit's *festa* was to take place; and to the glad ring of merry voices came the answering song of hundreds of birds. The hedges were white with roses. The oranges were in blossom, and the locust-trees were hung with fragrant tassels.

In the carriages were bright toilets, vieing in freshness and color with the blossoming shrubs; and everywhere — from the silken bodice of the belle, the buttonhole of the dandy, to the ears of the horses, and the padded breasts of the liveried servants — were flowers, flowers *en masse*, or in a single creamy bud.

Ruth had gone out early with the Aldens to superintend the arrangement of the bazar, but Miss Marchbank had vetoed the wearing of any badge or costume; her only concession to the wishes of the others was in allowing Ruth to appear in white.

The road leading to the Romano Gardens commanded fine views, but became on nearer approach merely a private path, hardly wide enough for two vehicles abreast, and quite shut in by a dense growth of forest trees ; so that the impatient guests found it pleasanter to dismount and walk to the arching entrance, which, with its carved buttresses and heavy iron gates, looked, as May expressed it, "more like the approach to a cemetery than to a palace."

But palace there was, — at least such as remained untouched of Time ; and, though the solid stone showed modern additions of brick and stucco, there was still an imposing breadth and grace in the structure.

Architecturally it bore evidence of age, and diversity of taste on the part of its builders. With the revival of Greek learning in Italy, came also renewed admiration for the noble forms of Grecian art ; and the student could trace in this Romano Palace various types, — from the remains of its barbaric beginnings as a stronghold, to the lighter Corinthian capitals decorating the peaceful façade.

The habitable portion was closed and barricaded, the uninhabitable portion left to the embrace of moss and lichen and overhanging vines, — less useful, but more picturesque.

The gardens, however, were in very beautiful order, owing to the fact that the gardener reaped a harvest from them both in flowers and in fruit. Devotion to the family might have induced him to keep out intruders, but hardly to spend on them the time and trouble to which their careful appearance bore witness. But the gay procession quickly sped past beds of broccoli and asparagus, to the brilliant parterres which yielded less substantial delights; and even beyond the roses and violets, to the dense shrubbery of ilex and pine, and the more stately growth of forest trees. For here was shade and coolness; and here were splashing fountains and rustic arbors, and gnarled roots twisted into seats; and here was spread the table of pretty trifles, with also the refreshing ices and light viands which a bevy of gay girls dispensed.

The scene was pretty enough for a Watteau.

The dense foliage, lightened by the glittering sunbeams; the velvet sward; the beautiful glimpses here and there of distant fields where cattle grazed, —all forming a charming background for the people.

Mrs. Coit's delicate face and figure beside the Duchess of Stickingham's robust charms were like the lily and the pæony; though both were in costumes which were the contempt of many of the beholders from the absence of cost in their preparation. What was the use of being a millionnaire or a duchess if one could not dress better than that?

Mrs. Coit was in a lilac muslin, as delicate as the wistaria blossoms; the duchess, in leafy brown of two or three tints, —and neither wore diamonds. Their deficiency in that respect, however, was made up by Mrs. Godfrey Gray, who sparkled and flashed like a prism. She had a dainty little person, and her robes were a marvel of the dress-making art. No wonder, with her *chic* and dash and love of splendor, that she disdained lesser luminaries.

"Positively, I never saw such a fright as that Englishwoman," she said to May, whose white silk and rose-wreathed hat became her wonderfully; "and Mrs. Coit is dressed like a shop-girl."

"Or a shepherdess," put in Mr. Morton lazily.

"Nothing could be more appropriate," said May; "she is a picture just as she stands."

Mrs. Gray smiled scornfully. She liked May Alden in spite of the decided way in which they often differed. "But come," she said, "let us look at the fancy things. I haven't much interest in the Protestant schools. The Italians make better Catholics. But the money may as well go one way as another, and the fun is in spending. One never expects their money's worth in a place like this."

As she approached the tables, Grace Alden whispered to Ruth, "Behold the tempter! How she jingles and jangles! And May is as a spider in her web. That slender youth, who looks as if he hadn't two ideas beyond the cut of his coat, is Mr. Morton. He is one of our *jeunesse doré;*" and Grace sighed, thinking how far, far superior was her poor young lover, toiling away at his clerkly duties, and how unjustly the good things of life were divided.

Ruth had no time to reply, for already Mrs. Godfrey Gray, with one ear for the waltz which the band had struck up, and the other for the sallies of a young naval officer who was one of a gallant deputation from an American man-of-war lying in the Mediterranean, was stripping the table of its prettiest treasures.

"How much, Miss Morris?" she was saying, at

the same time pouring out gold pieces from the silken
meshes of a dainty purse, when her eye caught sight
of the picture of the Italian child, which in its velvet
and niello-work frame was a conspicuous ornament.
"How much? Oh, but I *must* have that! *Sold!* do
you say? Oh, no! I will pay ever so much more, and
you can get the artist to paint another."

"The artist must speak for himself," answered
Ruth, turning with a graceful movement towards
Lillo, who had just drawn near. "This picture has
passed out of his possession, and is not to be had,
Mrs. Gray."

The words were uttered by Ruth in a firm, though
gentle, manner; but Mrs. Gray pouted and fretted
with almost childish petulance, attracting the attention of everybody, and there was then quite a crush of
people. One person stopped and looked with near-
sighted inspection at the coveted picture. As he did
so, he drew out his glasses, exclaiming in Italian, —

"Remarkable! peculiar! interesting!"

Then turning to Ruth, he said in broken English, —

"I could show you something very like this in the
château over there," pointing towards the chimneys
of the palace, which were but just visible above the
trees.

"Indeed!" said Ruth, glad of a diversion from
Mrs. Gray's assumed anger. "Are strangers allowed
to enter?"

"Not usually," replied the gentleman, "but I can
get in if I wish. Would you like to go?"

"Very much. And here is Mr. Marsh; I am sure

he would enjoy such a privilege if there are any art-treasures to be seen."

"Permit me, then, to introduce myself as M. Petitspains, a solicitor attached to the Romano family," answered the stranger politely. "I have the honor to know Mr. Marsh by reputation."

Ruth glanced at the spare, dried-up, little old man, and wondered if her guardian would object to her going to the palace under his guidance. Miss March-bank was making her adieux to friends here, there, and everywhere; Miss Alden was nowhere to be seen. Grace could not be induced to go. She had a letter to read in her pocket when occasion offered, and this would be the occasion if only they would all go and leave her. Lillo was ready to act as escort. He had never seen Ruth looking lovelier. She was in white, gauzy, filmy, delicate white, with the jauntiest little cottage-bonnet trimmed with daises. Her cheeks were just pink enough to redeem them from the charge of pallor; for the heat was apt to whiten rather than redden them, and she was getting tired standing so long.

Mrs. Gray had gone off with May in her train, and all her courtiers laden with spoils. Dancing had begun, and the throng had left them.

"I shall be delighted to see the palace," said Ruth, "but I wish I could find Mr. Barclay. He might think it strange for me to go without him."

"Oh, no, he won't!" said Grace, nervously anxious to be rid of them. "I will tell him where you are, and perhaps he will follow. There he is now!" she exclaimed.

"We will have an opportunity of seeing the palace, Mr. Barclay," said Ruth, presenting the solicitor.

"Yes: well, I will go to, if permitted," was the response: so they strolled off, the little solicitor glad of so interested an auditor as Mr. Barclay proved himself.

The way was not the one open to visitors, but through by-paths; and these were so overgrown that more than once Ruth's delicate lace was caught by briars. She tried to free herself, but each time had to allow Lillo to disentangle her. The little solicitor was delighted to find that Mr. Barclay preferred French to Italian, and was now deep in an account of the Romano litigation, which to him involved all Italy.

In that charming saunter, with the echoes of the music following them, and the silence of the grim old *château* beckoning to its mysteries, a word or two was said never to be forgotten.

Is it well to attempt to delineate too closely the delicate bloom, the first fair freshness, of a blossom, unless we have the brush of a genius, the power of a master? Will not the effect of color answer the purpose?

Did Mr. Barclay notice the elation, the light joyousness of these two young people? or was he too absorbed in this curious mosaic work of legal difficulties which his enthusiastic companion was pointing out to him?

They reached the *porte cochère* of a side entrance, and paused while M. Petitspains went off to procure keys. He soon returned, followed by an old man, who scrutinized them closely, but made no observations.

Unlocking the smallest of three doors, he led them into a vestibule, which opened at once into a wide hall, lighted from above, and around which ran a corridor with other doors opening into vast suites of apartments. The chill of emptiness, and the desolation of silence, reigned everywhere. The floors were of marble, the walls were partly of stone and stucco, and the woodwork of a heavy order, but so garnished with white paint and gold arabesques that the natural formation could not be detected.

Ruth looked about with a little sensation of awe, and the aversion of youth to the chill loneliness of an uninhabited house. Mr. Barclay's critical gaze disapproved of the loading of so much fine timber with heavy coats of paint. The solicitor stood in mute and respectful admiration ; while Lillo was the only one of the party, except the old man with the keys, who was unconstrained. In truth, the place seemed familiar to him, doubtless because he had seen so many old palaces in his rambles.

They now ascended the broad staircase, and were ushered into a gallery, the heavy shutters of which had to be unbarred. This done, the golden sunlight streamed into the dusty apartment, lighting up the stately rows of pictures which hung upon the walls, revealing many the value of which was well known to connoisseurs.

" Here, monsieur," said the withered little solicitor, leading the way to a distant corner. " This is the very *vraisemblance* of the picture at your bazar.

Look! Am I not right in discovering the similitude ?"

Lillo laughingly acknowledged the truth of the
statement, though the picture was of an older youth,
and the costume that of mediæval days. Mr. Barclay
also saw it; and Ruth might have done so had she
not been struck with the strange actions of the old
key-bearer, who was shuffling about impatiently, but
at the same time watching the party with an intensity of observation for which she could not account.
At first his gaze had wandered from one to the other,
but at last it had rested exclusively on the painter;
and the crafty look had changed to open-eyed astonishment, and finally to fear, which increased as foot-
steps neared, and an old woman hobbled into the
gallery.

She was in the rough, woollen gown of the Italian
peasant, with the white *camicia* and red bodice;
around her withered old throat still clung the necklace of gold beads without which a peasant must be
poor indeed. Her gray hair, uncovered by cap or
tooaglia, was drawn straight back from her forehead,
beneath which glittered eyes of remarkable brightness. Though bent with rheumatism, she did not
walk feebly; and, judging from the rapidity of the
words addressed to the man with the keys, her mind
certainly was not as infirm as her body.

She seemed to be reproaching her companion for
some misdemeanor, as he moved uneasily away, and
sought to make her withdraw. But her impetuous
flow of language only increased; and, approaching the
visitors, she began another harangue in Italian of so

provincial a dialect that only M. Petitspains could understand even a few words.

"She is annoyed that Girolamo should have allowed us to enter to-day. She fears that the whole crowd in the gardens will wish to follow, and she rebukes him for his imprudence. I, however, will explain to her that we will say nothing to the others to suggest such a wish," went on monsieur, not noticing, as Ruth did, the sudden cessation of the old woman's voluble speech, and a sudden pallor and a quick movement. In another instant she had fallen, — not prone, not insensible, — but on her knees. They all sprang forward, but she pushed them violently aside, detaining only Lillo in a strong grasp, and gazing upon him with a look which combined astonishment, pleasure, and affection. Then, bursting into tears, she tossed her linen apron over her face, and sobbed aloud.

CHAPTER XV.

LEFT to herself a moment, for all the girls had gone
to dance, and the matrons were counting their gains,
Grace Alden drew her letter, with its American post-
mark, from her pocket, and sat down· to its perusal.
Though nothing of a beauty, and far less attractive
in manner than her bright young sister, Grace
Alden's physiognomy had good points, — a broad
brow, steady, well-opened eyes, a nose which might
have been smaller, and a mouth less generous ; but
her complexion — that charm so easily acquired in
these days of *rouge* and powder — was clear and rosy,
and when she smiled she displayed very even and
white teeth.   The lovely day, the delicious air, and,
above all, the possession of her letter, had put her
in a good humor ; and as she opened her red parasol
and fastened it in a convenient crevice, and drew her
skirts of creamy silk away from the inspection of
ants and caterpillars, — displaying thereby very pretty
silk stockings and equally pretty feet, — she was a
very fair sight to behold.   A smile of sweet satisfaction
was on her lips, a loving light in her eyes ; but, as she
read, the smile faded, the light was quenched, and
the small white hand crushed unconsciously the few
blossoms which it held into a shapeless mass, and,

before the letter was finished, the girl had swooned,
— fallen all in a heap among her silken fineries, with
her red parasol on top of her like a danger-signal.
How long she remained thus, she did not know or
care, for after a while consciousness returned, and
she managed to get upon her feet ; but at that moment, sailing down the path in stately and solitary
dignity, came Miss Marchbank.

"My dear Miss Alden!" she exclaimed, startled
at the pale face before her, but controlling the appearance of surprise, "you are not well. Has any
thing happened? Shall I go for Miss Alden?"

"No, thank you," responded Grace, "I beg you
will not alarm any one ; but if you can get a carriage
and send me home, I will be very grateful."

"But your sister or Miss Alden ought to be informed."

"Not at all," said Grace eagerly. "Why should
their pleasure be spoiled by my temporary illness?
Please oblige me, Miss Marchbank, by saying nothing of it till you get me off; but pray do that as
quickly as you can."

Miss Marchbank was a woman of decision.

"Certainly, my dear, certainly; I will do what I
can for you. Here is my bottle of salts, which I am
never without," and she unfastened her *vinaigrette*
from her girdle : "use it till I return;" and, re-seating
Grace very gently, she turned away, returning almost
immediately with a carriage, — as near as it could be
brought, — and Branly Potter as her aid. Useless
were Grace's remonstrances. Both of them supported
her, and both of them insisted upon returning with

her to the city. In vain she plead and besought; for
her one supreme wish was to be alone, to hide herself
and her agony. But, after all, it was better thus than
if her aunt or sister had been with her; for Miss
Marchbank, though a little fussy, was very kind.
But it seemed an age before the laughing voices and
falling waters and cadences of the music were left
behind, and another age before they were on the
high road for the city.

She did not attempt to speak; and her white face,
with its strained and tense expression of pain, made
it only too evident to her companions that conversation would be insupportable. To have her carried to
her apartment, send for a physician, and quietly un-
dress her charge, was Miss Marchbank's resolve; and
she executed it without delay, writing also a note to
Miss Alden, which Mr. Potter promised to deliver.

Grace submitted to all in silence. She knew that
it was useless to resist; but she knew too that her
illness was not to be dispelled by the customary
"limonado" which Italian doctors seemed to think
sufficient for all ailments, though she swallowed the
cooling draught, and submitted to a hot foot-bath.
But beneath her pillow lay the biting sting of her
disease, which she had hidden there for fear of May's
suspicious glance. To the dull pain which had succeeded the sharp agony, came now also the remorseful
thought, that, in her own misery, she had forgotten
her sister, and this was the evening of the masked
ball.

This thought did not come to her till long after
she had been put to bed, and in the darkened room

Miss Marchbank was sitting silently beside her. But now it was too late to do any thing. Mr. Potter had gone back to the *fête*, the day was nearly over. Her thoughts became clouded. She was again a child, wandering in green fields, listening to the birds, or she was tossing on the ocean. Scene after scene presented itself; and then a familiar voice called her, and she sat bolt upright, until Miss Marchbank's gentle force obliged her to recline again.

The day had fled with rapidity. Dance succeeded dance; and now long shadows lay upon the velvet turf. Every one was going. May Alden had been the centre of a gay group all the afternoon. Even Mrs. Gray had danced no more, and been no more the recipient of gallantries and adulation.. Her coquetry, her wit, her archness, her beauty, had won all the naval officers; and the lazy Mr. Morton had worked himself into the belief that May had bestowed her tenderest glances and brightest sallies upon him.

Whether there is a limit even to vanity and its successes, I leave for others to determine; but certainly May's brightness and gayety suddenly waned. She had entirely avoided her sister and Ruth. She had kept away from Miss Alden, who, indeed, was immersed in Mrs. Coit and the duchess; and she had adhered to Mrs. Gray with the determination of following her fancy to its utmost limit. But now, sitting at her leisure in the luxurious victoria, having resisted all her aunt's " becks and nods and wreathed smiles," she lapsed into a silence and revery so entirely in contrast to her former jubilant spirits, that Mr. Morton was puzzled to observe it. Mrs. Gray did not trouble herself to observe any thing. Her *vis à vis* was a new capture, a fresh sensation ; and she was enchanted to find him absorbed in her charms, to the neglect of all others.

The drive was necessarily slow. There were many vehicles before them, equally many behind ; and they had not reached the town where Mrs. Gray proposed to diverge, and stop at a small wayside *albergo.* Here they were to rest, change dresses, assume disguises, and, under cover of cloaks and mantles, return to the city in time for the ball.

The maids, with all necessary toilet appointments, had been sent early in the day to make proper arrangements. Mrs. Gray was going as Juliet, her cavalier as Romeo. May was to be a nun, and Mr. Morton a friar.

Had there been nothing equivocal in this freak, no spice of mischief, May would not have cared to take part in it ; but she retained still a childish love of daring to do what her elders condemned. Already there was in her mind a curious reversion of feeling towards her companions, and wonder at herself that she should find pleasure in their society. How could any one think them witty, wise, or intelligent ? Mrs. Gray's voice was shrill and discordant as a peacock's. Mr. Morton languished like a lackadaisical frog. Even the day seemed to have grown hot and dusty.

" Why so *triste ?* " asked Mr. Morton, attempting to be sympathetic.

. May disdained answering with any thing but a pout.

Just then a man on horseback pressed towards

them. It was hard work to get through the crowd, but he made out to do so; and May saw, with a little quiver of annoyance, that it was Branly Potter.

At this moment, Mrs. Gray ordered her coachman to turn out into the cross-road.

By this, May supposed they would avoid meeting Mr. Potter, whose salute she had purposely shunned.

What concern of his was it that they were not going directly to Florence? And yet here he was nearly side by side, turning into the cross-road too. A spy! purposely watching her, sent by Grace and Ruth, or possibly by Mr. Barclay. She remembered now that Mr. Barclay had said some trifling thing which made her suppose Ruth had told him her intention; and she knew Mr. Barclay disliked and disapproved of Mrs. Gray, and had avoided her all day. But what cared she for Mr. Barclay's likes or dislikes? He was always a man of whims and caprices. Had he chosen to take up Mrs. Gray, he would have found a score of apologies for her frivolities. She was not to be snubbed or scorned by Mr. Barclay, with all his old-fashioned prejudices. And she would have "a good time" for once; for, of course, she must sooner or later renounce Mrs. Gray, and yield herself again a slave to duty and propriety and aunt Althea.

Perhaps there was less regret in the alternative than she tried now to believe, though she strove to persuade herself that she was a victim. A pretty, piquante, pouting victim she was indeed, lifting her drooping lashes up to give Ned Morton a disdainful glance, and set him wondering in his lethargic way

what he had done to displease her and how he best
could propitiate the capricious damsel. Flowers, bon-
bons, — these were the only things he knew of which
would bring smiles, and these were not to be had
at the moment. A vague idea came that conversation might be made, if he only knew what to talk
about; but for the life of him nothing would come,
except, " I say, what stunning buttons these servants
have on their liveries!" and " I wonder now how far
we've gone," — to both of which brilliant comments
there was no response; and just as he had concluded
that he would ask what number gloves she wore,
and get up a bet on the winning horse at the next
race, the victoria stopped and Branly Potter rode
up.

May was herself again in an instant, — not a trace
of her recent sulkiness. She pretended great surprise at seeing Mr. Potter, tossed her bouquet and
fan to Mr. Morton, was out of the carriage and chat-
ting with Mrs. Gray and her cavalier before Mr. Morton had recovered from his surprise. They all went
into the small, sanded room which was the only parlor of the *osteria*, but Branly Potter came boldly up
to May and said, —

"I am sorry to summon you from so pleasant a
party, Miss Alden, but I am under bonds not to appear without you. If I could have captured you before
you started, I would have done so; but the crowd hin-
dered me."

" But I do not intend to be captured, if you please,
Mr. Potter, — thanking you all the same for your consideration," haughtily responded May.

"No, I suppose you would hardly allow the term; but, all the same, you must come home with me."

"*Must*," repeated May with even more hauteur: "I am not used to that expression either; but I suppose Ruth Morris and Grace have made a tool of you, Mr. Potter, and in a manner forced you to take up the *rôle* of dictator. Drop it, please, at once, and be your own natural self. I haven't the smallest intention of going home with you."

Branly Potter had a temper of his own as quick as May's, and he happened just now to be in no patient mood; for, in addition to her sauciness, Ned Morton was grinning with satisfaction at the encounter.

"Perhaps I am a little rough, Miss Alden, compared with your" — he was going to say "present companions," but he checked himself — "compared with" — He stumbled into something stupid about "hating to carry messages, etc.," and then declared it was stupidly warm and tiresome, and his horse needed looking after, but that he would be with her again in a moment; and May turned with a grimace to Ned Morton. But in a moment more Mrs. Gray came up and said, "What is all this about your sister, May? Mr. Potter says she is ill."

"Grace!" exclaimed May.

"Yes. He tells me he has come for you; he has gone to have his horse looked after, and wants me to send you back."

"I told him I would not go: it is all a subterfuge."

"Indeed, I am afraid it is true. He asked me to tell you, said he was always awkward and was afraid of frightening you, but that Miss Marchbank and he had to go home with your sister hours ago. It is too bad, isn't it?"

"I should say it was," put in the interesting and original Ned Morton. "It's a confounded nuisance, that's what it is, and that prig has invented the whole thing."

"Oh, no!" laughed Mrs. Gray. "He wouldn't have taken that trouble, would he, May?"

"I am sure I don't know," answered May gloomily.

"But I am sure of it," persisted the gallant Morton. "He just wants to have you all to himself on the drive home."

"I am afraid you judge him by yourself, Ned," said Mrs. Gray, still smiling sarcastically, and noticing that May had grown a little pale. "I don't imagine your sister would be the better for your return, May. You may as well have your fun out. An hour or two later will make no sort of difference. I dare say it's only a headache."

But May's fears, as well as her conscience, troubled her. Mrs. Gray's advice was cold and heartless. Already she had turned to see about dinner, and discuss the coming excitement; while her maid was taking up her shawls and looking after her fineries.

"Is Grace positively ill?" demanded May of Branly Potter when he returned.

"Positively; but I don't want you to be alarmed. She has had a letter or something, — at least Miss Marchbank thought so from some words she dropped just as she was coming to, you know."

"Coming to?"

"Yes: she had fainted once or twice."

"Good heavens! Mr. Potter, why did you not tell me at once? Come, don't wait a moment."

"Going, absolutely!" exclaimed Mrs. Gray. "What a sentimental child! — lose all this evening's pleasure because your sister has the blues or a fit of ill temper?"

"Yes, I am going," responded May, now quite serious. "I am sorry to disarrange your plans, but you will please pardon me; and if you would be so kind as to come too"— She hesitated as she saw Mrs. Gray's consternation.

"I! I! Indeed not. You surely cannot know what you ask. Fifine may go with you for propriety's sake, but you have Mr. Potter's escort: that is enough."

May knew very well it was not enough, that all her coterie in Florence would be shocked to see her driving in the evening with Mr. Potter; that it was not conventional, and that Mrs. Gray knew it was not. But how could she expect any thing else from Mrs. Gray, and had she not over and over again defended just this sort of independence? Oh, it was all very nice when her own feelings were not concerned, but now Mrs. Gray appeared to be utterly selfish and indifferent; and poor, poor Grace, what could be the matter?

Her thoughts were in much of a jumble; but presently she found herself in the victoria again, and alone with Fifine. Where was Branly Potter? Absolutely he had ridden off and left her!

It was dark when she reached the hotel, and Fifine was complaining in bad, but dramatic, French that madame was cruel to send them thus, that no money should tempt her to return, and that if mademoiselle would accept her services she would leave her erratic mistress on the moment. To all of which May made no reply. She was thinking, wishing, hoping, and praying, all at once, that nothing of real danger had happened to Grace.

When she entered, she was met by Ruth, who only whispered, —

"She is quiet now, but her fever is high. Miss Alden is with her. Miss Marchbank would not have left her, but she has to start for Genoa to-night; I am going to see her off, and will then return to you. Mr. Barclay will stay here, to be of assistance if necessary."

"But, Ruth, what is it? No one has told me."

"It is a nervous shock. We don't know the cause."

"Branly Potter says there was a letter."

"Did he? I don't think Miss Alden knows."

"Miss Marchbank said so."

"I will ask her, if you wish. The doctor allows no conversation. He says she must have perfect quiet, that there is just a possible danger of brain-fever."

"Ruth!" was all May could utter, and fell back in her chair.

"Yes, dear; it is very sad, and we all so soon to part. But Mr. Barclay will stay; and he is so very, very kind, and always knows just what to do."

Mr. Barclay came in at this moment, and hurried Ruth off; for Miss Marchbank had delayed her departure to oblige them, and now it was absolutely necessary to speed her on her going.

Tea was brought, and drank in silence ; Miss Alden coming in at the last moment, and giving May the merest shadow of a smile, drinking her tea and gliding off again without a word.

May never knew how that evening went. She remembered it as a dull blank, with now and then a picture of the garden party flashing and fading into a ghostly pantomime of masked figures. She knew that Ruth returned, and that Mr. Barclay said something kind to her, and that after awhile she fell asleep ; and then the morning came, and Miss Alden kissed her and said the danger was over, that Grace was sleeping beautifully, and if there should be no return of fever she should see her sister. Ruth, too, was sympathetic, and told her that Miss Marchbank had seen Grace crumple up a letter which was under her pillow, and that fearing it might be lost, or fall into wrong hands, she had dropped it in an empty vase standing near the bedside.

Bathing her swollen eyes, and rousing herself from her stupor, May rose from the chair where she had been all night, and followed Ruth to Grace's room. Ruth, too, had been up all night, alternating with Miss Alden in the watching.

Was it possible that a few hours' suffering could work such a change? May looked at Grace with wonder. White as an Easter lily, with great circles of shadow about her closed eyes, lay the sleeping girl. She was quiet now, but Ruth said her breathing had been like the convulsive sobbing of a frightened child.

CHAPTER XVI.

RUTH had gone from the room, Miss Alden was asleep on the lounge; and May still sat looking at her sister, when she remembered what Ruth had told her about a letter. Surely there could be no harm in her finding out just what had occasioned all this trouble. Her sisterly love overbore her sense of honor, and she carefully plucked from the vase the crumpled envelope with its American post-mark. Silently as she did it, the movement was seen; for at that moment Grace opened her eyes, and looked steadily at her. May in her agitation dropped the letter, and knelt beside her sister, regardless of all the caution she had received, crying, —

"Grace, darling, forgive me! But I must know what is the matter."

"Read it," said Grace languidly. "You may as well know. But don't criticise. Just let me get over it as best I can. And you had better tell aunt and Ruth. The worst is passed now. I shall be well again in a few days. Only I beg you will all try to forget and forgive, as I shall do."

May picked up the letter and read, —

"MY DEAR GRACE, — Your last letter reached me on the 1st; and its kind assurances of regard made me feel very grateful for your friendship, but very regretful that Fate had ever allowed me to be so presumptuous as to suppose that I could make you happy. The more I consider the difficulties that have surrounded me, the more convinced I am that we have both been unwise and hazardous in entering into an engagement which could only be productive of disappointment and vexation. True, I did at one time see this in a different light. I hoped for advancement, I trusted to rise; and in this hope and trust I made the offer of myself to you: for I knew well what a noble, generous spirit is yours, and I should have been a happy man indeed had I been able to secure you for my life-partner. But since then great changes have occurred. It is needless to enter into business details. You know I have worked like a slave, and with little or no remuneration beyond the meeting of my daily wants. You know, also, that I have others depending upon me. You cannot know or understand the complications of unfortunate investments, so I will not dwell on them: enough is it to say, that, harassed by toil and unceasing exertions, I have concluded that I will no longer indulge the hope of winning you. I am the further induced to do this by the offer of a situation in a large South-American house, which will require a residence in Porto Rico. It will be needless for you to remonstrate, as you may be tempted to do, because I have not given you the alternative of choice. I knew you too well to do so. I knew you were capable of any sacrifice; and I knew also, that, in view of your devoted attachment, I should be weak if I allowed myself to vacillate. I therefore write only to request that you will look at the whole transaction as I have done, as simply something forced upon us by circumstance, as a business matter, in fact, rather than one of sentiment. Be assured that I shall always esteem you as a most noble, generous, high-minded friend, a woman worthy of the best that the world can bestow, and one whom I shall always respect."

May had flung the letter down when she reached these words, with an angry and contemptuous cry; but Grace bade her pick it up again, and read a clip-

ping from ~ ~wspaper, which was attached.   It was
from a local newspaper of the town in which Mr.
Bainbridge's family resided, and read thus : —

"We hear with pleasure of the appointment of our promising
young townsman, Robert Bainbridge, to the consulship of Porto
Rico. This, in connection with his approaching marriage to the
wealthy widow of one of the firm whom he represents in that
distant city, is a matter deserving of our heartiest congratulations."

"The base traitor! the cowardly knave!" broke
from May's wrathful lips, as she again glanced over
the neatly written document, — in which there was
not an *i* without a dot, not a *t* uncrossed, not a word
misspelled, or a comma left out.

"Hush, dear!" said Grace.

"Indeed, I will not hush," said May.   "It's the
coldest, cruelest, most mercenary thing I ever read, —
not one word of regret, of remorse, or of pity.   He
is a mongrel, without the first faint tinge of gentlemanly blood in his veins.   If I were a man, I would
shoot him, only he'd not be worthy of an honorable
bullet."

"May! May!" implored Grace.

"I cannot help it, Grace.   I must give vent to my
feelings.   I have not half expressed my scorn and
indignation.   How did you ever love him?   How
could he ever have persuaded you to believe in him?
How were you so blind?"   But seeing her sister's
pallor and agitation checked her, and she exclaimed.
"But pray forgive me, Grace.   You are suffering,
and I am only adding to your pain.   I will go away

and storm by myself, if only you will promise to get well, and *let no one know you care.*"

Fortunately, at that moment, Ruth came back, and May had to see some people who had called. Among them was Mr. Potter, who was not especially gratified to find that his excuses for leaving her the previous evening were received with an apparent forgetfulness that there had been any need of excuse. Indeed, she seemed to be oblivious to every thing that had transpired, and was not even aroused to any interest in an account of the masked ball, and Mrs. Godfrey Gray's performance thereat, notwithstanding the sensation it had made, and the gossip which was already afloat.

"You are tired, I suppose," he ventured to say, when he found that she was not listening to a word, and was listlessly pulling her yesterday's bouquet to bits.

"Yes, I am tired," she repeated, "tired to death of every thing and everybody. Oh, don't be shocked at my rudeness ! — for I can be very rude, as you saw yesterday, — but Grace's illness has upset me. I am sick of all the nonsense and flummery of society. I want to go home, and forget that I have ever been abroad, learn to do something useful, and settle down."

"Just what I propose doing. Let us do it together."

"What !" said May, flashing her startled gaze upon him. "Why should you ? You have a thousand opportunities, where I have but one. A man seems an enviable being to me : he has the choice

of every thing, can mould his own destiny; while we
have to smile and simper till we secure a favorable
parti, or eat our hearts out with useless ambition,
and crush out every spark of individuality, to suit
the caprice of fashion and society."

Her companion smiled, and looked at her as if she
had suddenly been transformed, but was not altogether
displeased at this exhibition of novel points.

"And what of the favorable *parti:* if that succeeds,
does all go well?"

"Oh, charmingly in the eyes of the world!" this
with a fine scorn of manner.

His brow darkened, as he said, —

"Ah, you fashionable girls may sneer as you
like! It is the caprice of an idle moment. None
of you would marry simply for affection. You all
demand the *entourage* of fortune, in some shape or
other."

"Do we, indeed? and how about you of the
stronger sex? I suppose none of the gifts that daz-
zle have any charms for you. You are sublimely
above such weakness."

"We are getting absurd, Miss May. 'You're
another,' never convinces."

"No, certainly not. Let us have a truce. Mor-
alizing is not my style. Are you really going home,
Mr. Potter?"

"Really, yes; and to work."

"What sort?"

"I don't know."

"Don't be a literary man or an artist."

"Why not?"

"Oh, I hardly know! only there are so many, and it is so often an excuse for elegant idleness."

"Does it matter to you what I am?"

"No, I don't think it does."

"You are delightfully honest. Why do you undertake, then, to advise me?"

"From motives of general interest in the welfare of the world."

"How flattering!"

"Yes; it doesn't do to be too selfish. One must be wide in one's sympathies."

"Just now, I wish you were narrower."

She looked at him, and saw honest and genuine feeling in his face, and a positive fright seized her. Had he been Ned Morton, she would have been tempted, by her anger and grief at Grace's misfortune, to lead him on, and amuse herself at his expense by way of vicarious reprisal, — a girlish and absurd revenge, but none the less satisfactory; but Branly Potter inspired respect. He was not specially deferential, and he was often awkward, but he was manly, — and that goes farther than any thing else with some girls. But her faith in men had received a blow. Who could have suspected that Grace's lover would have proved so false? Had he not been all that one would suppose correct and proper and faithful, even if lacking in some attributes which win general admiration? She had called him "brother" Bainbridge because of his faultless appearance and rather religious aspect. If so grave and earnest a person could pursue such a crooked path, why might not others do the same? With quick perception of what might follow, if this personal talk went on, she turned about and tacked, as many a little craft finds it safer to do when the wind blows from a dangerous quarter. And Branly Potter allowed her to do as she wished. He was certainly in love; he acknowledged it, he knew it: but he was not so far gone as to put himself where he could not retreat, for he was by no means sure of this pretty, bewitching, but possibly capricious girl.

Mr. Barclay soon after entered, and asked if they had heard the news about Mr. Marsh the painter. They had not, and were glad of a turn in the tide of conversation.

"It is a charming little romance; but I shall have to begin at the beginning, if you are inclined to listen."

"Pray do," exclaimed May. "He has always interested me from the day he saved us from the waves off the Neck, Mr. Barclay; and he showed even then the stuff of a hero."

Branly Potter, not knowing what this allusion meant, was disposed to be contemptuous, but succeeded only in being jealous; he, however, listened to Mr. Barclay with patient politeness.

"Heroes are somewhat scarce now-a-days, and I don't know that being the subject of an accident of fortune or fate, as people term the chances and changes of this life, entitles one to the name of hero in any proper sense of its meaning; but certainly it is not a little unusual for a poor fisher-lad like Lillo Marsh to turn out the heir of a princely family and fortune, and unusual events certainly do cast a glow of romance around the most ordinary of mortals. But let me begin my story in my own way.

"The Romanos, as you may be aware, are as old, if not older, than the Medicis, and as proud of their native city as any of the Florentines, but in a way far different. It was their province to do the harder, coarser work for their contemporaries. Instead of interesting themselves in *cinque cento* architecture and the revival of learning, they toiled simply to amass the wealth, which, after all, was the moving force of the new growth. They were known as hardy, brawny, rough men; having commercial relations not only with their fellow Tuscans, but with the Genoese and Pisans. They disdained no personal effort to secure success, and many of them became masters of vessels and traders with foreign ports. But, with the force of this strong animal nature, they were also men of violent passions, and were known to be quarrelsome and headstrong even in their own families. True as this was of the Romanos of the twelfth or thirteenth centuries, it remained true of them down to the later period, when, with fortunes wasted and estates ravaged by Northern enemies, they had little left of their ancient magnificence. The Romanos of the present have dwindled down to a mere handful. Nicolo, the Count Romano, head of the family, and owner of the villa where our garden party was held, is an old, disappointed, and sorrow-stricken man. He had one son, a wild, lawless fellow; and one daughter, a young shrinking creature, afraid of her very shadow. On these two children all his hopes and happiness depended; and yet, so inconsistent can a man be, he had done nothing to insure either their obedience or respect. He neglected their education, he allowed every indulgence, and yet, when their wishes clashed with his, saw no reason why they should be unsubmissive. The usual result followed. The son ran away from home and became a sailor. Returning by stealth to see his sister, he countenanced her in an attachment for one of his comrades, — an ordinary seaman like himself,— to whom she was married secretly, which, on the count's discovery, led to a dreadful quarrel that caused the daughter's death. She left a child, however, to whom the count became deeply attached, and who was cared for by an old family servant until it was three or four years old, when the father claimed it; and the uncle stole it, or rather had it conveyed to the ship on which they both were employed. The count never knew what became of the child. His son never returned, neither did his son-in-law, whom, by the way, he had never acknowledged. Grief and disease wore upon him; and, like a vulture eager for its prey before its victim's death, a distant relative began a series of law-suits which embarrassed the estates, though they did not succeed in depriving the count of his patrimony.

"You will not now be surprised at the finale of my tale.

"At the *fête* in the Romano Gardens, M. Petits-pains, a solictor interested in Count Nicolo's affairs, saw a remarkable resemblance in a little picture painted by Lillo Marsh to one in the Romano gallery, which led to a comparison, and finally to the greater discovery by the servants in a resemblance of both pictures to Lillo himself, and his identification as the Count Nicolo's grandson.

"The wife of Girolamo, the steward, had been the nurse of Lillo's mother and of Lillo himself. She was overcome with surprise and remorse, and nothing could convince her of the possibility of mistake. She had connived at the child's removal from his grandfather in revenge for the mother's death, but had suffered deeply in consequence; for, never hearing any thing more of him, she had supposed that the usual fate of sea-going people had befallen them all, — the father, the uncle, and the child. Undoubtedly the uncle was lost at sea, and the father also, but not in the voyage which conveyed the child to its American grandparents."

"And how did the Count Nicolo accept this, and what proof does Mr. Marsh bring?" asked Branly Potter.

"The count was eager to have the story substantiated," went on Mr. Barclay; "as eager as Mr. Marsh was reluctant. But M. Petitspains, with deft, lawyer-like penetration, gained from Lillo so much that was conclusive, that there seemed really no reason to doubt."

"But why was the count so willing, and Mr. Marsh so unwilling?" asked May.

"The count is in his dotage. Past errors, past failures, have weakened him, and made him long for a strong arm to lean upon, besides the better inclination to make reparation, if that be possible. With Lillo there is the manly disinclination to appear an adventurer, or to take undue advantage of what might possibly be only a romantic similarity. Besides, he is all American, self-made, democratic, with no wish to wear a title, or make himself conspicuous."

"And what will he do?"

"He is going home for papers which may decisively prove what is now only conjectured."

"Home? To America?"

"Yes. The count is impatient with the restless eagerness of age, so he has promised to go at once. He will take the same steamer, probably, that Ruth and Mrs. Vedder cross in, so that he may return as speedily as possible."

"And then?"

"I really can tell you nothing more, but I suppose in due course of time he will be the Count Romano."

CHAPTER XVII.

WHEN Mr. Marsh found himself undergoing close
and repeated questionings from M. Petitspains, and
the recipient of embraces and caresses from the aged
crone in the Romano picture-gallery, he felt himself an actor in what might prove to be more than
a comedy. But when that same evening, he had
parted from his friends, and had been conducted into
the presence of Count Nicolo, with only Mr. Barclay
and M. Petitspains as audience, it seemed to him
a broad farce. That he — a simple-minded American citizen, a dauber of paints, an unknown fisher-lad
— should be a supposed aspirant to Italian nobility,
was too absurd. He felt himself, as I have said,
an actor, playing an unexpected part in a surprising
drama ; and though there was enough reality in all
that had transpired, and enough connection with
that which had been always a dream to him, — viz.,
his days of infancy, — he now found himself most
reluctantly forced to accept the truth, and comply
with the count's request to return to the States and
collect every vestige of paper which might have
any power to prove his identity.

He found the count as Mr. Barclay described him,.
— an old, sorrowful man, living in an out of the way

part of Florence, unvisited, forgotten by the gay
world, absorbed in the one only thing which interested him, — simply the defence of his property,
which, little comfort as it yielded him, was yet a something which aroused the only remains of his old spirit ;
a something which he would keep, if to retain it was
only to withhold it from the clutches of the ravening
aggressor who assailed it. The new hope which the
discovery of his possible and probable heir aroused
was as marrow to his bones and warmth to his veins.
His whole being was stimulated. To have the aid
of a young, fresh, vigorous spirit in the warfare he
was waging; to make the possession of his property an impossibility to his enemy in the future, as
well as in the present, — was even more than he could
have hoped. With tremulous eagerness, he was confident of success ; and he welcomed Lillo with senile
tenderness that would have touched the young man's
heart could he have forgotten that this same man's
anger and wretched failure of parental duty had been
the cause of his mother's misfortunes.

Their meeting was peculiar. Lillo did not speak
Italian with ease, Count Nicolo knew no English ;
but M. Petitspains was an enthusiastic interpreter.

By the glimmering light of candles, in the gloomy
apartment, might be seen the remarkable family
likeness between the grandfather and grandson ; but
it seemed to be purely physical, for in the young
man's steadfast gaze there was none of the older
man's vacillating weakness. Mr. Barclay noticed
the almost contemptuous indifference of Lillo when
M. Petitspains enlarged and dilated upon the mag-

nificence of being a Romano, and the questioning disappointment which crept into the old man's countenance at the negative part which Lillo took in the discussion.

The candles flamed and flared. The lawyer presented every point of the necessary legalities, and with rapid pen wrote out remarks, directions, explanations; his little wizened face shining with acuteness. On his left sat the white-haired count, wrapped in some sort of a loose cloak, which, from its braids and frogs, seemed a remnant of military service. In his delicate white hand, with its signet ring, was held a metal snuff-box, from which he carefully took a pinch at odd intervals. His gaze was fastened with intensity upon the young painter, who, after the cordial recognition vouchsafed him, had drawn somewhat into the shadow of some overhanging drapery, and leaned carelessly upon the carved back of a *prie-dieu.*

Lillo's fine features were just a little flushed, and his foot tapped the polished floor uneasily. The ordeal was not agreeable to him, and it was with great reluctance that he assented to the propositions urged. He had not intended an immediate return to America, and it interfered with his professional plans so to do; but when his grandfather clasped his hands, and wept, he could not have refused, if only from motives of pity. But besides the pity, and independently of all other considerations, there was now the desired opportunity of making certain the proofs of a legal marriage between his father and mother, with-
.out which he would never ask Ruth Morris to be his

wife. To be sure, he had in an unguarded moment given her an inkling of his admiration, and had been made glad by the sweet confidence with which that inkling had been received ; but he would not have felt himself justified in asking her to accept a name to which, perhaps, he had no right.

"You will go then and return as speedily as possible?" urged monsieur.

Lillo nodded.

"And you will accept your aged relative's offer of a permanent home as his only son and heir?"

"Pardon, I cannot promise that."

"Why not? why not? Every advantage is to accrue, — the estates, the title, the political honor, the" —

"None of which I care for," interrupted Lillo.

The lawyer glared upon him, so great was his astonishment.

"You forget that I have a profession," said Lillo.

"But that need not interfere."

"I have made my own career ; I am satisfied : why should I burden myself with all these empty honors and unwelcome privileges?"

"Because you are a Romano," said the lawyer decisively, with a wave of his hand.

"Because I am but half a Romano, left to fight my own battle with the world, disowned, discarded, neglected, forgotten," said Lillo indignantly.

"Pardon me, that is not truth : your grandfather loved you ; you were taken from him ; he would have nourished you as the apple of his eye."

"As he did my mother, perhaps," said Lillo satirically.

"Ah, young man!" pleaded the little lawyer, "you little know the keenness of a parent's disappointment when a child marries wilfully, secretly, out of her station. But let that pass : her wrongs have been atoned for by years of acute remorse and humiliation. Accept, I beg you, this grandparent's contrition. Look at him ; see his eager hope : would you cloud it ?"

"I have no wish to add to his sorrows," replied Lillo, forced to answer.

"Then give him the satisfaction he so desires."

"I promise nothing," said Lillo again, rising from his leaning attitude and preparing to depart, "nothing that may harass my future movements. You will please make my" (here he hesitated) "my grandfather — if that is the title the Count Nicolo prefers me to use — understand how much I thank him for his proposal and warmth of recognition, and assure him that I shall either bring or send him the papers I possess. I will do that, but I will bind myself to nothing more." He drew himself up with some hauteur, and the old count looked from one to the other with pleading inquiry. M. Petitspains was much disconcerted, but strove to maintain a smiling aspect.

"I will trust to your better nature, your generosity. You cannot be so cruel as to disappoint this aged parent! This has come upon you too suddenly. You have really had no time to consider ; and you will better appreciate the brilliancy of position, wealth, family, an ancient name, when you find how the world regards this opportunity. Ah, young man, I have no fear but that all will come around as we wish! Every thing happens to those who wait. This time next year, no one in Italy will be so much sought after, no one better known for his fine prospects, than the young Count Lillo Romano, grandson and heir of the Count Nicolo." His beaming smile and as- sured tones revived hope in the aged count, who rose, and, as Lillo departed, placed upon his reluctant hand the signet ring from his own finger.

"I feel like a thankless prodigal son, who prefers the husks and the swine from sheer choice," said Lillo to Mr. Barclay as they separated.

It was indeed wonderful how quickly the story got about, and how soon congratulations came pouring in. Between the day of his leaving and that of the *fête*, a week had hardly elapsed; and yet numerous cards were left, and carriages rolled away from the studio, to Bianca's delight, who saw in this attention a recognition of her lodger's importance which might bring her in an increase of *franchi*.

How the news spread, Lillo did not know, but he shrewdly suspected M. Petitspains had a hand in it. He had little time to speculate, however, on this or any other question: the arrangement of his affairs, the finishing of pictures already ordered, and the preparation for his journey, took up all his time.

CHAPTER XVIII.

At the last moment of the steamer's sailing, in which Mrs. Vedder and Ruth were to leave, they were surprised by the appearance of her son. He came aboard in haste, and showed no especial pleasure in so doing; for, in truth, he had been forced to this by a quarrel with his elder brother and a failure of funds. But he seemed to be more resigned to his fate when he discovered that his mother had so young and pretty a companion in her travels, and he soon made it apparent that he intended to assume every cousinly right. But Ruth was far from responsive. At a first glance she had conceived an aversion difficult to conceal, and a nearer acquaintance froze her into an icicle of reserve, which increased Mr. Vedder's ill-humor.

Lillo Marsh was also on the same steamer, under no new name or title. But Ruth was conscious of but one presence, and that was Mrs. Vedder's.

I do not know whether the ocean malady has been analyzed in these analyzing days, but I am confident that no aspiring, elevating emotions are ascribed to it. Ruth found it absolutely degrading. She felt herself indulging all sorts of regrets. She wished she had never seen her aunt, never heard of her cousins, never left Mr. Barclay.

In the pauses of intense misery her ears were filled with Mrs. Vedder's complaints of the way the world treated her, particularly the little world of exclusive people journeying to their republican homes with a fresh stock of aristocratic ideas. "Snubbing," as Mrs. Vedder expressed it, was dealt out in large measure. She could not understand why she was the object of so much indifference. What had she done or left undone?

The poor woman had not a particle of tact, and intruded herself on people without knowing how repugnant she was to them. Neither could she comprehend why her beloved Charley was not regarded with admiring eyes. Was he not outwardly all that a gentleman need be?

And why did not Ruth like him? What other girl but would be pleased with his attention? To be sure, he was a little frisky, and sometimes made mistakes.

Ruth listened to her aunt's complaints as she listened to the throb of the engine, and the rush of the waves,— with the apathy of despair.

Should she ever behold her native land, she would never again trust herself off of *terra firma.*

One day she seemed stronger, and the stewardess urged her to leave her berth. Muffled in wraps, and attended by Mrs. Vedder, she did so. It was the first sight of her which had gladdened Lillo's eyes since their departure. He noticed keenly her pallor, her listlessness, and the fatigue of Mrs. Vedder's presence. With delicacy he sought to divert her; but she scarcely brightened, her depression re-acting upon himself. It seemed to him that he must have been mistaken in those vague but happy imaginings in which he had indulged. Even the day was an uncertain one, — the sky full of gray clouds, the sun glancing out only at intervals. No one spoke to them. Mrs. Vedder's voice intimidated those who might have approached the interesting languid young invalid; and Mr. Vedder's cigar-smoke made an impregnable halo about them. It was impossible that the conversation should be any thing better than the merest commonplace; and yet it was with a quick perception of jealous regard that Lillo saw Charley Vedder assume the proprietary right to be Ruth's guardian and escort, and strive to make his trifling words carry an accent of meaning wholly lost on Ruth.

Poor Ruth was sadly homesick, and the mere mention of Mr. Barclay brought tears to her eyes.

Uneasy and discomposed, Lillo wondered if, after all, the absurd reports — absurd until now — concerning Mr. Barclay and his young ward had any foundation.

Was it altogether impossible that their strong affection for each other had taken a different coloring? Why should he have supposed as entirely a matter of course that the love of which he was so conscious should be returned? Had not many a young girl given similar recognition of an unconcealed passion, and then acted in the most deliberate and contradic· tory manner. Even granting that she was free from the guile of coquetry, might she not have been mistaken in her own feelings?

Every lover can thus torment himself. It is but a phase of the tender passion, that such doubts should ebb and flow. And it was not an unreasonable supposition for an imaginative person to hold, that Mr. Barclay should have reared and educated a charming young girl with the intention of making her his wife, — a wife of his own modelling. He knew that this view was held by many. But why, then, should Mr. Barclay have allowed Ruth to leave him even for a few months? Perhaps the separation was to be a test. Perhaps he was generous enough to wish her to see the world for herself, unbiassed by his presence or advice; and perhaps, too, she was only just now appreciating how very much she cared for him. Lillo's thoughts ran in this current all that day. So long as Ruth staid on deck, he remained beside her, loath to give her into Charley Vedder's keeping; for, in addition to the cigar-smoke, Mr. Vedder had made frequent visits to the steamer's bar. But Ruth's mood was one of such utter indifference, that, had there been an opportunity for serious conversation, Lillo would not have seized it; for moods can be as unconquerable as barriers of stone. The day grew darker, the wind higher, and Mr. Vedder found stimulants even more necessary than before. Indeed, so unsteady had his nerves become, that Lillo was obliged to persuade him to seek the retirement of his berth; but he was not a youth accustomed to yield to persuasion which conflicted with his own views. No, he would not go, and he would persist in maudlin attentions to Ruth, who at last roused to the true condition of her cousin rose hastily for the purpose of going to the cabin. How she rose, and how both young men advanced with her, and the one in eager haste to baffle the other sprang before in such a way as to confuse the heated brain of his companion, can hardly be told: enough that one of them plunged down the narrow companion-way, striking his head in his fall, and lying senseless.

There was instant stir and commotion. The surgeon was summoned, and a crowd of excited, questioning people gathered around.

Lillo hurried Ruth to her state-room, and returned to his unfortunate acquaintance. The surgeon was applying remedies, and there did not seem to be much harm done. But Mrs. Vedder was frantic in her accusations. In vain the cooler heads tried to calm her. " Hush! hush!" they said. But she began to weep, and amid her sobs asserted that the young painter had been the cause of the fall. It seemed absurd to notice her, but Lillo essayed to stem the reproachful torrent of her speech. She would not listen to him. Nothing and no one could convince her that she was mistaken ; not even Ruth could change her: so after that Lillo kept away from her as she desired. This affair did not increase the Vedders' popularity. Mr. Vedder remained in seclusion the rest of the voyage, and Mrs. Vedder maintained her anger. Ruth forbore any further defence of Lillo, and the journey came soon to an end, — heavy fogs making it still more dreary. Her great-uncle, Mr. Boggs, met them on landing, and was profuse in his welcome. His studs were larger than ever, and his voice even more resonant.

"Glad to see you, Miss Morris, glad to see you with your aunt. She's the proper person for you to be with. Never did like the idea of your livin' on a man who was neither kith nor kin to you. Hope you ain't too fine a lady through his foolish notions. Goin' to be somethin' and do somethin' now, ain't you?"

Ruth opened her large eyes and looked at him as she might have done when she was the little friendless girl of years before. Her present desolation nearly equalled that of those long-forgotten days.

"Now, Cauldwell," interposed Mrs. Vedder, "don't be too aggravatin' just as I've reached my native land. The stars and stripes make me feel good-natured, and I don't want to be riled. Get my things through the custom-house, and let Charley and Ruth come on with me. Charley's not well, and Ruth's had an awful sea-sick time. We'll go to the Fifth Avenue and get a good dinner, and take the evening train straight to Berryville. See here," and her voice dropped to a whisper, "there's a lot of lace sewed inside the trimming of one of my wrappers; take care that they don't find it out. And I've got lots of gloves and things that haven't been worn, that they'll want to charge duty on; but it's none of the Government's business: I am not a smuggler, and they've no right to suspect me. The custom-house is a mean, miserable concern, anyway."

While Mr. Vedder harangued her brother, and the luggage was being inspected, Lillo drew near to bid Ruth good-by. He had necessarily kept aloof,—for Mrs. Vedder's unreasoning aversion and his own self-respect obliged him to,— but he was none the less determined to know Ruth's whereabouts and plans, even if, as he feared, there might be little chance of his ever having any share in them.

She was standing in all the confusion of the wharf, looking absently toward the bay and the far-away vessels. Her color rose as Lillo approached and offered his arm.

"Let us get a little out of the crowd," he said, drawing her away from the bustling and pushing people. "Our rather unsatisfactory journey has prevented me from asking you where you are going, and how long you will remain with your aunt: may I not know?"

"Certainly, as far as I can know myself. But truly I am much confused. Mr. Boggs has just now suggested that I must 'be something and do something:' what would you advise?"

Lillo looked amused as he said, "Is it worth while considering what such a man thinks?"

"Oh," said Ruth, "I don't think he is alone in his views: everybody is expected to be something or do something extraordinary now-a-days. I am afraid my guardian has hardly prepared me to meet the expectations of society."

"Society is a tremendous humbug. But how long are you to remain with these people?"

"I really don't know," said Ruth ruefully. "If I had known that Mr. Vedder was to return with his mother" — She stopped short.

"Does he annoy you in a way that I can help?" asked her companion, blazing up.

"Oh, no, no!" she cried, fearful of these two coming in conflict again; "and I hope you will forgive the rudeness you have suffered from them."

"That's a trifling matter; but may I not hear from you? I am on my way to Codtown, as you know, and expect to return by next week's steamer."

"So soon?"

"Yes; there will be nothing to detain me, and my newly found relative will be impatient. Mr. Barclay will want to hear all about you. May I not visit Berryville, if that is where you are going, so that I can report?"

"Of course," replied Ruth, unconscious of the little bitterness with which her companion spoke, for she was thinking how desolate she would be. So long as he had been near, she had been sure of some one who understood her and sympathized with her. She looked up at him now with a glance, which, had he been in a more hopeful state of mind, would have carried enlightenment. He mistook its tenderness for regret at her separation from Mr. Barclay.

"And the Aldens, too, — you will have some message for them?" he went on, wishing to prolong the conversation, yet jealous and unsatisfied with its turn.

"Yes. I must write at once to May. Poor Grace will not care much. You know that her engagement is broken?"

"I heard so. Does she care?"

The little mocking tone did not escape Ruth.

"She is wretched."

"Is it possible? I supposed good little girls obeyed their parents and guardians, and had no feeling in these matters. Miss Alden, I presume, believing the young man too poor, forbade his addresses."

"You are mistaken," said Ruth gravely.

At this moment, Mr. Boggs and Mrs. Vedder, having superintended the opening of numerous boxes, drew near, and at the same moment Charley Vedder appeared with a hack ; and Lillo released Ruth's hand from his arm. He looked at her with a certain questioning intentness, which made the color again flush her pale cheeks, and tint even her pretty little ears, in which there were no rings.

"You will come see me," she said earnestly. "I want to hear all that romantic story of yours, your own version of it, and whether you are going to be Count Romano ; and besides, I shall feel quite a stranger in my native land."

"You will miss Mr. Barclay," said Lillo ; adding, "If you wish me to come, I will certainly do so."

Then Mrs. Vedder, who had stood by rather awkwardly, with a very nonchalant nod, put out her hand, and said, —

"I believe, Mr. Marsh, I was mistaken on the steamer. I was all riled up and disturbed by that accident. Charley says I was a fool to act so. You must come and see us in Berryville ; we are all goin' there soon. Ain't this custom-house business a bother ? But you ain't got the traps we have. Now, just look at Ruth : she's as pretty as a picture to-day. That's all because she's on dry land. The ocean don't agree with her, nor with me either. Isn't the weather hot here in New York ? I'm all wrapped up in my sealskin, so they shouldn't charge duty on it. Well, good-by. Don't forget to come and see us."

Ruth got into the carriage with a dull, desolate feeling that she had made some great mistake. Every thing had suffered a sea-change. She had been so happy in the last few months, had so thoroughly enjoyed her youth, her liberty, her friends, — and, above all, the new and exquisite sensations which had come like the first sweet breath of summer, the mere shadow of a hope as evanescent as the perfume of wild-flowers, a something intangible and yet joyful, a something which she could not translate, for which speech had no words. And now where was it?

Not long was she allowed to indulge in revery. An earnest discussion had arisen as to what should be ordered for dinner, and Mrs. Vedder had loudly inveighed against the cookery of the Cunard steamers.

"Oh, dear me!" she said. "We must have a real good spread. It is late for shad, I suppose. June shad ain't good for much. Ruth's looking as thin as one now! I suppose strawberries are plenty. Oh, how hungry I am, and how glad to get away from all those foreign fixin's! Cauldwell, I advise you never to go abroad."

"I never mean to: America is good enough for me," said Mr. Boggs, clearing his throat as if for a speech, and addressing his sister as from a rostrum, with a wave of his hand, on which glittered a huge carbuncle.

"I suppose," he continued, "you saw much of the deplorable effects of dram-drinking in those towns and villages where grapes are raised."

Ruth thought with a shuddder of his nephew's habits, and feared lest a personal reproof might be coming; but Mr. Boggs's words were but the preface to a long address on the follies of the day. He liked to hear himself talk, and did not expect replies. But Mrs. Vedder also liked to talk, and had no intention of letting him have all his own way. Was she not fresh from scenes that his eyes had never beheld, and had she not met people of much more importance than Mr. Boggs had any conception of?

But the bad pavement over which they were passing made Mr. Boggs's elocution jerky, and the rusty springs of the hack deprived his expressions of grace; besides, the blocked and tangled mass of vehicles, with swearing drivers, made it necessary for both of them to shout: so after a while conversation was abandoned, and they drove on in silence, leaving Ruth to her desolate meditations.

"Here we are at last!" exclaimed Mrs. Vedder, as the carriage stopped before the gleaming white front of the Fifth-avenue Hotel. "Now for a good dinner!"

CHAPTER XIX.

"A note from Miss Alden, sir; the man waits for a reply," said Mr. Barclay's servant, presenting the billet on a silver salver.

Mr. Barclay was at his writing-table this warm morning, with a heap of correspondence before him. He tore open Miss Alden's note and read: "Can you come to me for an hour's talk this afternoon? I need your advice."

"Certainly. I will be with you at four P.M. We can drive afterwards, if you wish," was his reply.

He had staid in Florence solely on Miss Alden's account, as her niece's illness had prevented her from leaving when all their American and English friends had departed; but he was finding it very irksome. The Protestant schools were closed; the Duchess of Stickingham was on her way home; Mrs. Coit had gone to Switzerland; and Mr. Barclay, without Ruth or Miss Marchbank, found the days too long for him. He missed his young ward sadly; and, as the possibility of losing her altogether was thereby suggested to him, there came unbidden the query, whether, in spite of all reasons against such a step which he had always argued so plausibly, he should not secure himself against such a loss. Yes, in his loneliness and ill-health and depression, he had allowed himself to look at their relation from the vulgar point of view which he had so condemned, and really was thinking seriously if he had not better make Ruth his wife. To be sure, he did not deceive himself with any absurd idea of being in love again. A man never really could be that but once in his life, and his past was an unusually sacred one, too sacred to be even thought of in connection with this present plan, which, after all, was perhaps more for Ruth's benefit than his own. But, though he had no such love to offer, he was sure that no one's society was so necessary to him as that of Ruth's. Had he not trained and trimmed and guided her young life entirely to his liking? Had he not instilled his own views, principles, and opinions, even to such an extreme that he had actually seen the need of her viewing the world for a while through her own eyes, as an educational advantage? And who could be more sweetly devoted to his comfort than Ruth? Ah, how much he missed her pretty ways, her attention, her docility! How much he missed their talks and walks and readings? How silent and empty the rooms were, how vacant his time! And who could understand her so well, who could make her so happy, who knew her every wish and thought? Surely no one but himself.

And yet, there was the possibility that even now she might be making new ties, new friendships, which, if they did not sever, might weaken old ties. For Ruth was young, and Mr. Barclay remembered with a sudden uneasiness that novelty and change sometimes worked wonders with young people. Of one thing he was certain : she had no thought unknown to him, she had no friendships made under his eye that he need fear Even her personal attributes were presented to him with strange force and persistence as he sat thinking these thoughts, with his pen in his hand, and his note-paper before him. Her sweet face rose before him like a vision ; and he almost heard her soft footfall, and smelt the faint fragrance of her fineries. As he dawdled over his letters, he imagined her by his side, questioning, criticising, examining, as had been her wont, and as he had allowed. She was a very lovely girl, a rare refinement in her by nature, and the daughter of a man he had loved. Why should he not follow this impulse? Would there, could there be but one answer if he did? Ah, again came that vague uneasiness as to what change might have already been begun in her !

Drawing a fresh sheet from a quire, and dipping his pen leisurely in the ink, he began writing.

"MY DEAR RUTH, — It is with a strange feeling of surprise that I find myself compelled to consider why I allowed you to leave me."

No, that was not what he wanted to say : so he began over again.

"MY DEAR RUTH, — Since your departure, I find myself a strange and lonely being. All Florence is changed. Everybody except the Aldens has gone. Grace is yet very weak, and her aunt very uneasy about her ; while May is as fresh as a rose, and vexed with impatience to be off. I cannot leave my old friend to the untender mercies of innkeepers and servants, therefore I linger. But a constant undercurrent of wonder at myself for letting you leave me is ebbing and flowing through all these lonely days. I did not appreciate my dependence upon you, and, in truth, have come to look at our relative positions in a very remarkable way. I believe I am growing old, Ruth, — not so much outwardly as inwardly, — which is a very curious admission for me to make just now to you, meditating, as I do, the asking of the greatest favor a man can ask or a woman can grant. But you and I have always been very honest to each other, and to tell you any flattering falsehood would be as foreign to my nature as to yours. Old I am, and clinging more to the idea of home and established ways : it is this which has been bringing me around to the conviction that I must cease to be your guardian. I have positively fought against this idea, mainly because it was the common one of the stupid people who think all friendships between man and woman must culminate in matrimony, but also because it seemed ungenerous to offer you so little and ask so much. But here I am asking it, after all, — and why ? Because I see no other way of keeping you all to myself."

The little silver travelling-clock here rang out three clear notes ; and Mr. Barclay, remembering a necessary errand before going to Miss Alden, as well as the need of dressing, was forced to lay aside his pen for a more convenient season. There was no haste required, and he wanted to put his ideas very deliberately on paper. So he rose and began his toilet. It was past four when he reached Miss Alden's, and found her waiting for him.

"The girls are out, most opportunely," she said, as she greeted him.

"What! not Grace? I thought she was yet too ill."

"For any lengthened exertion yet, she is. But May has urged her into making an attempt. They took the maid, and Branly Potter was to drive them. But I must go home, Frank. These girls have kept me now in a perpetual worry for so long that I have reached the limit of my patience. Never, never again shall I be induced to chaperone marriageable girls: it is too great a responsibility. My brother has relied too much upon me. May's freaks of independence, her intimacy with Mrs. Gray, and her wilful opposition to my views have been most harassing; while Grace's engagement terminated, as I knew it would, in disaster, — not that I supposed the man would do quite what he did, but I knew no good could come of the affair."

"Is she getting over it?"

"Yes, I think she is. Our difference of opinion previous to the *éclaircissement* has prevented me from being in her confidence; but I see that her natural pride is asserting itself. She never mentions the man's name."

"Naturally," said Mr. Barclay.

"Oh, yes! I trust such folly will never be repeated. But I sent for you, Frank, to have a business talk, and I must not allow myself to digress. Here is a letter from my brother that has troubled me greatly, and I can't quite make it out. He has lost heavily in recent speculations, but I fail to see why it should affect me. Suppose you read it and explain: a third person can always do better than an interested party."

Miss Alden handed Mr. Barclay the letter, and

took up her crochet. Her needle flew in and out of the fleecy wool, and the diamonds on her slender fingers flashed with each movement. Her soft, rich black silk and creamy lace became her well; but her face looked worn and thin, and her eyes were somewhat dim, as if they had recently shed tears.

Mr. Barclay read in silence, but rose hastily as he ended, and stood before the window.

"Well, what do you make of this strange document, Frank, which to me was so perplexing?" asked Miss Alden anxiously.

Mr. Barclay came back from the window with heightened color.

"It does not contain good news," he said quietly. But something in his tone made Miss Alden's work slip from her fingers; seeing which, he took her hand very gently and drew it to his lips.

"What is it, Frank? what is it that you have discovered?" she asked; and her voice trembled.

"Be courageous, my dear friend; there are many things worse than the loss of money in this world."

"Oh, no, no!" she cried; "not to those who have no power of making it. Nothing but crime and sin *can* be worse."

"The loss of those we love," he began gently, remembering the blight upon his own life; but she quickly broke in —

"Those losses Heaven consoles; sorrow carries its own balm; but money — Oh, it is simply what we cannot do without! But how does my poor brother stand? Is he penniless?"

"I fear he is."

"And I? how will it affect me?"

"I am afraid" —

"Oh, there you must be mistaken, Frank! My brother may be involved, but it cannot do me much harm. To be sure, I must help him as far as I can; but — Why do you look so at me?"

"Is it possible you do not know?"

"No; I see no cause" —

"For hope that any thing remains." He completed her sentence, as a surgeon might, with incisive firmness, plunge in his scalpel.

"Frank!"

"My dear friend, do not deceive yourself. Your brother has used your funds as well as his own."

She rose now in her excitement, and her eyes flashed with a strange light; but in a moment more she had dropped into her chair, and was sobbing violently.

Mr. Barclay went for water, and found a *carafe* on the sideboard, and a glass, into which he poured a few drops from the little flask his own invalidism necessitated carrying; but already Miss Alden had conquered her hysteria, and was fanning herself.

"Forgive my outburst, I beg of you," she said feebly. "I could not bring myself to believe *that* was the truth; but I see now it must be as you say. What shall I do? what shall I do? Alas! here come the girls. Let us keep them ignorant a little longer."

"By all means," quickly responded Mr. Barclay, admiring her quick repossession of herself, and her equally brave desire to bear her trouble alone. "But remember I am every way at your service." He had not time to say more; for, like a summer breeze, May burst laughing in, and Grace followed, leaning on Branly Potter, and looking still like an Easter lily.

"We have bought all the shops out, auntie," cried May, "for I knew this was my last chance when I saw how well Grace bore the fatigue; there is no earthly excuse now why she should remain in Florence. I tried to inveigle Mr. Potter to wager that we would return when he does; but he had no faith in my betting-book, — nor in me, either, I am afraid." But catching a very expressive glance from her now confessed lover, she stopped and looked from one to the other.

"Something is the matter," she said decidedly, and with a little sniff of her pretty nose, as if she smelt something in the air.

"Matter enough," said Mr. Barclay, gallantly hastening to assist Grace to a chair and a footstool and a fan, and any thing and every thing which would cover Miss Alden's emotion. "You are too giddy, May, for a good nurse; I shall have to take Grace under my wing."

"With all my heart," answered May, waving her hands in a fresh pair of palest primrose *gants de Suède.* "As soon as you please, I will resign; only I hope she will not be the torment of your existence as she is of mine, with her proud determination to give up every wish and whim of her own, and become a perfect saint. Saints always were my abhorrence, and Grace is fast becoming one: so take her, Mr. Barclay, and welcome."

Poor Grace smiled faintly, and looked appealingly to Mr. Barclay, saying, —

"It's all because I wouldn't be extravagant and buy a pair of amber bracelets for these wretchedly thin wrists of mine, and would make her take the money for some tortoise-shell things which she wants to give away. An easy way to procure saintliness, is it not?"

"Oh, the motive is quite equal to many that have gained niches in the chapels! We don't measure the deed," answered Mr. Barclay, wondering why the talk would run on money, and pitying Miss Alden deeply. He was touched, too, with the new, sweet expression of Grace's face. She looked wan and weary, and no longer had the bright girlishness of May; but there was a look of calm serenity which indicated that she had conquered in the trial to which she had been subjected, and would hereafter be equal to the duties her life might impose, with perhaps an added power of sympathy with the wants and woes of humanity, which her own pain had taught her.

Mr. Barclay thought he had never seen her looking lovelier; and it pained him to think what was before these girls who had not known even the restrictions of small means. All their lives they had lived in luxury; not in wanton wastefulness or in pompous show, but in the delightful ease of gratified desires, as pure and healthful and refined as education and culture inspire. To what now might they be hurrying? — to privation, toil, care, want. It made him chilly as he sat there with Miss Alden's hopeless, sad glance meeting his in dumb anguish. She had taken up her crochet; but the needle seemed to catch in the wool, her fingers were so tremulous: and in the pauses of May's lively rattle he caught the sound of one or two sighs which were almost sobs. Poor woman, what a crushing grief this was to her! For, besides the loss of money, both he and she knew that there was loss of honor. He would not go till he could assure her of his sympathy and aid, and beg her to keep the worst of the tidings from these innocent girls. There was no need of their knowing all.

It was late before Branly Potter ceased making *les beaux yeux* to May, and she to him, — for if ever two people were to outsiders confessedly "in love," and yet unwilling to acknowledge it, these were; and for May, Mr. Barclay had little apprehensiveness. Her very happiness was a shield; not even poverty could sting her with its usual venom. But for the aunt, whose pride was intense, and whose locks were even grayer than his own; and for the girl whose recent acute experience of sorrow rendered her as a bruised reed, — Mr. Barclay was full of pity. So he staid on. But he gained no chance to express himself that evening; for after awhile Miss Alden, unable to bear the strain of suppressed feeling, excused herself, and as she left the room seemed to have become shrunk and bent under the burden of her woe.

CHAPTER XX.

MR. BARCLAY went to his rooms with almost as much depression as Miss Alden displayed. His sympathetic nature was disturbed, and he was deeply concerned about these friends. He saw nothing before them, no way out of their trouble. What could they do? and how should he help them? He was translating some hymns for the use of the schools, and he sat down to his work with the uncomfortable feeling that it was hardly difficult enough to absorb him, that as a man he might be doing more; but his habits were too fixed now to change, and, as far as money went, there was no need for him to do more. But he knew that, had he been a business-man, something would have suggested itself by which he could have aided these unfortunate women. Miss Alden was too proud, he knew, to easily accept favors which she would never be able to repay; and yet she was entirely unfitted by her age and manner of life for arduous exertion of any sort. He cast about for any method whereby she could aid herself, and put aside as utterly impracticable every thing that was suggested. The customary self-sustaining work of middle-aged people was the keeping of schools, boarding-houses, and accounts, or sewing. All these might do for women of tougher fibre ; but for his friend they seemed as absurd as engineering or any of the pursuits of men. Why, he did not stop to define. And as for the girls, poor tender young things, how his heart ached for them ! It quite absorbed him, and the letter he meant for Ruth was put aside as of secondary importance, something that could be attended to when his thoughts were less painfully occupied. It seemed too selfish to be considering his own affairs, when these friends of his were overtaken by disaster.

Just then Branly Potter came in ; and Mr. Barclay thought it best to give him some hint of the state of Miss Alden's affairs, wondering what effect it would have. The young fellow seemed positively elated by it, and confessed that he had been holding off from any communication with May's aunt because May would not let him speak; but now she must give way. He would not only speak, but he would insist upon immediate marriage ; as, no matter how poor he might be, they were poorer, and together they could bear the brunt of unkind fortune.

Mr. Barclay smiled in spite of himself at Branly's eagerness and quick solution of his part of the problem, and then he sighed to think how quickly poor Miss Alden would be obliged to succumb and yield her favorite ideas of prudence, etc. But Mr. Potter succeeded in cheering him, and imparted some of his own hopeful spirit ; and together they walked over to Miss Alden's rooms, and found the girls alone, reading and sewing, their aunt not having risen.

"Aunt is not at all well," said Grace, putting down

her book as she welcomed the two men, and May laid aside her sewing.

"I was afraid she would be affected by the painful news she received yesterday," said Mr. Barclay, as Branly Potter drew May into the recess of a curtained window.

Grace looked startled.

"Has she not told you? Is it possible you do not know?" he asked hurriedly.

"No; she has told me nothing. She seems feverish and dull. I am afraid we have staid here too long; our maid tells me there is much illness about. What is it, Mr. Barclay, that troubles aunt?"

"Oh, if she has said nothing, it will be as well to wait! I was rash; but I supposed, of course, you knew."

"Oh, pray, Mr. Barclay, tell me all! I can bear any thing now, — any thing. Is any one ill?"

"Ah, dear child, you do not know what you ask!" said Mr. Barclay, looking pitifully at this slender, dark-eyed young thing, who had so recently been struck with so cruel a blow, and who seemed to have grown so much older and wiser than her years.

"No one is ill," he continued. "But there is an entanglement in your aunt's and your father's business affairs — a great loss — much embarrassment," he stumbled on, hardly knowing what he was saying; when she suddenly interrupted him, putting one of her pretty hands on his arm with a quick gesture, saying, —

"Is that all? and do you fear telling me *that?*"

"To be sure: it's deplorable, dreadful."

"Not at all, unless there has been something fraudulent;" and then she stopped, with a sudden flush of color. The supposition took away her breath, and it was in a whisper she said, "*That* only can make loss of money the bitter thing you think it."

He waived her questioning look, and said, —

"You are brave indeed, dear Grace. But remember you know nothing of hardship. It is my fear for you that makes me think so much of the mere loss of money. You have been so delicately reared, and know nothing of the trials of adversity."

"But I know where to look for guidance," she answered reverently.

Then Mr. Barclay asked to see her aunt, and she went to find out if he could be received.

Meanwhile, Branly Potter had urged his suit with May, and made her acknowledge that it was now time for him to speak to her aunt, whose acquiescence he hoped to obtain. But it had taken many words and much persuasion, for she felt that it was positively taking an undue advantage of her aunt to gain her consent while under the depressing influence of evil tidings; but the young man was accustomed to have his own way, and as soon as Mr. Barclay reappeared he was also allowed an interview. He found Miss Alden supported by pillows in an easy-chair; but there was the flush of fever on her cheeks, and its glitter in her eyes. By great effort she had risen to receive her old friend; and, notwithstanding all his kind assurances, she had not grown calm. When Branly, after a few hurried expressions of sympathy, made known his errand, she quickly responded, —

"You find me *hors de combat*, Mr. Potter. I appreciate your affection for my neice, but I am no
longer capable of exercising calm judgment in the
matter. I have always regarded marriage as excellent and desirable if the parties to it were of. equal
birth, education, and fortune, with a strong leaning
towards the surplus being in the masculine hands;
but my point of view was from the comfortable ranks
of those who possess competence. I find myself
deprived now of the very means of existence. My
nieces are equally destitute. My friend Mr. Barclay
is our only dependence. He promises to take us
home at his own cost, though of course my jewels
will recompense him. If, knowing all this, you still
persist in asking my permission to marry May, you
are either a — a fool — or a very high-minded
man."

"I will take the latter, if you please," said Branly,
laughing, in spite of the gravity of the discussion, and
pressing Miss Alden's hot hand. "I love May very
much, and I flatter myself that she cares a little for
me, — at all events, she has promised to, — and I don't
see that we can do better than join forces at once;
for, if I have the right to protect her, I can also assist
you, my dear Miss Alden."

Miss Alden put her hand over her eyes. "It does
increase one's faith in human nature to see such an
exhibition of kindness, but common prudence demands that I should ask you if you can do this without an utter sacrifice of all your plans and projects."

"My dear Miss Alden, all my plans and projects
centre in your niece."

"Ah, well, it is a mystery to me! But I suppose we are not all able to fathom mysteries."

And then Mr. Potter withdrew, very well satisfied with this conclusion.

So it came about, that, after many conferences and much discussion, there was a hasty departure from Florence and a rapid journey to England; and Mr. Barclay had to have passports *viséd*, and luggage forwarded, and make preparation for the quiet little ceremony which they concluded to have performed in London. It was rather rapid work; and, in addition, Miss Alden's condition was alarming. She rallied from the first prostration; but at times her brain appeared to be affected, and fits of silence were followed by intervals of spasmodic talking, which were more painful to hear than the silence was to endure: for the theme was invariably of bold projects and plans which her listeners could not but think the fantasies of mental disorder.

Grace's devotion to her aunt was noticeable. She was far from strong, but all her energy of character manifested itself. To be sure, she had the quiet and patient sympathy of all, but Mr. Barclay remarked that Miss Alden turned to Grace for more complete understanding. Was it any wonder that he found himself admiring her gentle womanliness and self-sacrifice, and that even her countenance had an increase of beauty for him?

"You have certainly the gift of sympathy, Grace," he said to her one day, after she had been more than usually taxed to divert her aunt.

"Do you think so?" she said, smiling in that half-

sad way which had unconsciously become a habit.
" Is it any thing uncommon ? "

" It is very rare, and is seldom a birthright : one
has to gain it through suffering.   But all sufferers
do not possess it : they rather hug their own pains to
themselves, and forget all about other people."

" That seems to me a poor and trivial relief.   What
is the adage about a trouble shared ? "

" You have proved its truth.   But, Grace, you are
too young for so much wisdom."

She shook her head.

" We must find some way for you to forget.   The
time has not arrived for you to need so much philosophy.   You must not mistake a little breeze for a
great blow."

Again she shook her head, as she said, " What I
want is work, Mr. Barclay.   When we get home, will
you help me find it ? "

" Certainly," he said gravely, wondering what she
could do.

" Next to religion and philosophy comes work, as
a panacea for our many ills."

" What can you possibly know about it ? "

" Oh, one can know intuitively a great deal without absolute experience !   I have done a great deal
of thinking lately."

" More than has been good for you, I fear.   But
may I ask what sort of work you desire ? "

" It puzzles me a little.   I am not a skilful needle-
woman, and I am afraid I don't know enough about
mathematics to teach in schools ; but I think I might
get writing or copying to do."

Mr. Barclay here remembered his own work of late, and the bright thought struck him that it would be well to transfer it to her hands.

"Are you fond of translating?" he asked.

"I can read French and German with some ease," she replied modestly.

"And Italian?"

"Not so well."

"I want some help in a hymnal I am preparing, — in fact, if you can render some of the verses into prose, together we might make them jingle, — and perhaps it would be as well for you to begin with such work before undertaking any thing which would bring you in contact with strangers, who would necessarily be more exacting."

A bright look of gratitude made Grace's eyes glisten.

"This is extremely kind. I will begin as soon as we have a quiet moment, and at least try what I can do. Really, Mr. Barclay, you have been our haven of refuge in this storm."

At this Mr. Barclay politely demurred, attributing all to the happy accident of their being together. They were now in London, and making haste to have May's marriage over in time to take the steamer home. But Miss Alden, at the last moment, had taken a freak to postpone it; declaring they had been too precipitate, and that such unseemly haste was not dignified. Notwithstanding Mr. Potter's family had all concurred, and that a younger brother was to be best man, she shut herself up, and declined to have any part in the proceedings. In vain Mr. Barclay remonstrated, and Grace argued, and May wept : there seemed to be really no way out of the dilemma but to take their own course, regardless of her disapprobation. But this was a most disagreeable thing to do ; for no outsider could detect in Miss Alden's irreproachable appearance and manner the distraught condition of her mind, and her nieces' love and respect for her were undiminished. Thus several weeks elapsed, as May was inclined to wait, hoping for a change ; but at last there was no alternative, and so after interviews with the American authorities and legal representatives, and clerical dignitaries, the little party, minus Miss Alden, drove to St. George's and had the ceremony performed.

It was a dull day, and the drizzle did not lend a cheerful aspect to the wedding. Mr. Barclay gave the bride away ; and the bride herself was teary and pale, but not more so than her bridesmaid, who, however, strove to do her part courageously. There were few lookers-on, but that they did not mind ; and, as soon as the service was concluded, Branly Potter hurried May off to catch a train which was to take them to Scotland, for he was determined to have a little honeymoon which should be as bright as he could make it.

Thus Grace and Mr. Barclay were daily together. The translating had progressed favorably, Grace proving herself more capable than he could have supposed ; and as Miss Alden preferred to be much alone, maintaining a proud disapprobation, they were necessarily dependent upon each other for society.

Who does not know the power of propinquity?

Neither would have admitted for a moment that there was any thing but the coolest, calmest friendship between them. Both had their own sad memories into which they withdrew as into the shadow of cathedral aisles; and yet, in these retreats they found less and less gloom. The afternoon light from ruby panes shone not with a richer glow than did the mellow radiance which was more and more surely revealing the depths of these two hearts each to the other.

With a pang of remorse, the elder was the first to discover that he no longer lived in the past, and measured every happiness by the sorrow of his youth. He felt himself a traitor to the dear companion of early days, and would have torn himself away from this sweet-faced, gentle girl as from an evil iufluence, had not all the heroism of his manhood demanded that he should not desert her.

This may seem absurd in the face of his written, but unsent, letter to Ruth; but a totally different reason for his proposal to Ruth had urged him to that action, — one which he fancied far less recreant to the beloved object of his early affections; and he smiled, as he tore it up, to think how purely a matter of benefit to Ruth, and convenience to himself, that idea had been. And yet it was painful for him to admit the truth; so painful, that Grace feared she had in some way lost his confidence and approbation. And, in her anxiety on this account, it first became evident to her how surely his untiring kindness and gentleness of character were effacing the memory of that sad attachment of hers for a man, who, though he had proved himself unworthy, yet remained enshrined as a broken image might retain its place on an altar deserted of its worshippers.

Ah, poor weak and blind children of a tender mother ! Nature knows no unmotherly preferences : as she commands, we obey ; thinking ourselves wise, profound, so above the common herd, that even our affections have a finer and firmer texture, — one that will withstand time, silence, distrust, and death itself.

CHAPTER XXI.

PERHAPS nothing is more depressing and mortify-
ing than to find that which one has supposed to be
almost an heroic action entirely deprived of its best
element, to have our poetry reduced to common
prose. And yet this conviction is just what pressed
upon Ruth, as she paced her close hotel-room the
night of her arrival in New York. Her aunt, now
that she was on her native shore, and having her son
with her, was in a most satisfied and happy condition of mind, and appeared to. Ruth not only not to
need her, but to find her just a little unsociable and
inflexible. For, elated with having made a successful
voyage, and free from the critical and uncongenial
persons she had met, Mrs. Vedder had loudly protested her gladness at the dinner-table, and had even
suggested, but quite contrary to Ruth's wishes, a trip
to a watering-place before settling down at home.

It had been a day of remarkable loveliness and
early June freshness. Even the city felt its charm ;
for as yet there had been little of the intense heat
which bakes and burns, and makes New York a terror by night and by day.

The balconies and court-yards, the restaurant windows and the parks, were smiling with flowers.

Heaps of them, loosely strewn or trimly set in baskets, and tied and wired in bouquets, were on all the street-corners, compelling, by their sweetness, the banishment of evil odors; and on the table in her room Ruth had found a choice bunch without card or name attached. So delicate an attention had not come from the Vedders; and poor Ruth put her face down in the blossoms, and wet them with her tears. Her sacrifice of inclination had lost all purpose and merit. She was tired, disappointed, and disheartened. Her pompous uncle reminded her of the sad days of her childhood in this great, noisy city; and the thought of close association with him and his still more repugnant nephew became abhorrent. How should she escape? Must she be tied to these people until Mr. Barclay should release her? Was there no way out of this enforced bondage, none the less enthralling that she had forged the bonds herself? She could not sleep. The dinner upon which Mrs. Vedder had so felicitated herself, had hardly been tasted; and the evening had only been gotten through by going to the theatre, where Charley Vedder found some pretty actresses who were more responsive than Ruth, and towards whom Ruth felt almost grateful for securing his attention. Morning came at last, but brought no relief to the exhausted, dejected girl. Mrs. Vedder was even in higher spirits than on the previous day, and had a new programme made out, which included much shopping, visiting, and many excursions; for she was honestly desirous of entertaining Ruth in her own way, and had not the faintest conception that

there could be any other which would be more agreeable. Mr. Boggs harangued again from the depths
of the newspaper, but principally on political matters
and side issues of small moment to any uninterested
in local affairs. He had an overbearing way of deliv-
ering the slightest opinion; and both his nephew
and sister made no attempt to thwart him, though
their irritation was visible. He objected to every
proposal, was urgent to have his nephew enter into
some business arrangement which was repugnant to
the luxurious young man, and finally told his sister
that she must attend to her affairs, as his own were
of paramount importance and called him home. To
this there was no remonstrance. But he did not go
until he had again made Ruth wince by unfeeling
allusions to her father, and his own regret that she
should have been brought up by so unpractical a man
as Mr. Barclay; for, he added, —

"I've no sort of idea your accomplishments are of
any financial value."

"I don't know," said Ruth, smiling a sad sort of
smile, "having never tested them in that way;" but
quite sure that her guardian was guilty in the light
of Mr. Boggs's accusations.

"But you may have to, you know," said Mr. Boggs,
resuming what might better be called a monologue
than a conversation. "You may have to. Your
father didn't leave a cent; your grandfather doesn't
know you, and, if he did, would just as likely leave
his fortune to the Lenox Library. He's nothing but
an old bookworm. Now, if I'd had a hand in the
care of you, you'd have been at Vassar or some-

where else, instead of dawdling over Europe; and by this time you could have had a good situation in the public schools. My influence would have procured that. But I did my best. I warned Mr. Barclay, and I offered to do my share. He was too proud and stuck-up to listen to me; and, if ever you suffer, it'll not be my fault. Has he made provision for you, in case he marries? or does he mean to marry you?"

This question capped the climax.

They were sitting in the public parlor, — Mrs. Vedder gazing out of the window at the throng in the street; Charley with his back to the empty fireplace, twisting his thin mustache, and watching Ruth as she leaned back in the cushions of a sofa, with a book in her lap. She was tired and pale, — almost as white as her muslin draperies, with their falls of creamy lace, — but her only sign of uneasiness had been in a little nervous movement of 'her hands. Now the color poured into her face. She looked at Mr. Boggs with an expression in which were blended indignation and contempt; but, meeting his self-confident and impertinent gaze, she regained her composure, and said very quietly, —

"I am not in the habit of discussing my private affairs in this manner, Mr. Boggs; nor do I think your interest in me warrants any inquiry of the sort. You forget that we are comparative strangers."

Mr. Boggs glared, Charley Vedder drew in a half-suppressed whistle, and Mrs. Vedder turned from the window to see what was going on within. The scowl on her brother's face, and Ruth's returned paleness, would have warned any one else; but she was too obtuse, and instantly asked what was the matter.

"Matter enough," growled Mr. Boggs. "A decent question deserves a decent answer; but I'm not fine enough for this elegant piece of goods you've got hold of, Mrs. Vedder."

"O Cauldwell!" ejaculated his sister, "don't be cross so soon; you're forever finding fault with Jim and Charley, but you might let Ruth alone. —Come, Ruth, don't mind him: he is always preaching. Let's go out and shop. I want lots of things, and it's ever so much easier to buy things here than where they jabber French at you."

She rose and trailed one of her new French garments after her, in which she was as dazzling as the Queen of Sheba; and Ruth followed, glad of the chance to escape, but in no mood for the doubtful pleasure promised.

The day had grown very warm, with the sudden fiery heat which comes like a simoom; and, though Mrs. Vedder took a cab as she went about from place to place, Ruth became more and more wearied. The city was entirely new to her, and many of its ways contrasted singularly with her foreign experiences; none more so than the tardiness or indifference manifested in the shops.

But Mrs. Vedder was thoroughly happy. She chaffed the clerks, joked with their superiors, and tumbled about the fineries as remorselessly as if they were her own; and, when at the end of her purchases, sighed that she had no more money to spend, or wants to gratify. After an ice at a restaurant, they drove about the town, despite the glare from the heated pavements. With Mrs. Vedder as *cicerone*, it was no wonder that Ruth became hopelessly mixed as to localities ; and she had only a confused sense of row upon row of tall and narrow buildings, incongruous architecture, and showy equipages, mingled with the painful remembrance of the corner drug-shop where she had procured her father's last bottle of medicine, which was doubly enforced by Mrs. Vedder's pointing out the dingy boarding-house from which her poor father had been carried to his last resting-place. Had Ruth been of the sternest stuff, she could hardly have steeled herself to bear two such blows as she received that day from her well-meaning, but callous, relatives, without giving evidence of it. As it was, she became ill enough to excuse herself from any more immediate expeditions, and shut herself in her room for at least twenty-four hours, — hours of lonely self-reproach and regret, and a dull sense of resistance.

The heat had not abated, and the incessant roar of the surging multitude about the hotel made her long for quiet. Not even a letter had come to cheer her, and Mr. Vedder had made this the topic of frequent jest, — striving to pierce the thick armor of a reserve which she had found it necessary to wear in his presence. He was the type of man she most disliked, — frivolous, insincere, sensual, and selfish, and yet attracted to her by one of those peculiar and inexplicable attachments which have no foundation in any congruity of nature, and seem to be merely wanton freaks. Why he persisted in his attentions, she could not conceive. He loudly admired the powdered and painted damsels of the ballet; was as quick to perceive the fine points of a handsome woman as of a fast horse, and in much the same terms; and, in short, had no sense of appreciation of any thing delicate or sensitive. Ruth did not think of herself as I have put it, but she knew she had nothing in common with Mr. Vedder, — no point of approach in any one way; and yet he, in these few days, had striven to *pose* as her lover.

If any thing had been needed to complete her unhappiness, this accomplished it; and, without coming to any definite conclusion, she was casting about for a way of escape. She could not bring herself to speak to her aunt, whose satisfaction at her son's regard for Ruth made her supremely happy, and who was purposely delaying her departure from the city, "that Charley might have more of a chance."

She had no intimate friends in town, and no desire to seek their advice (notwithstanding one has said very wisely, "Men choose a course of action, women an adviser") in any case; for an instant, the thought of her unknown grandfather flashed across her mind, to be quickly put aside. But help was nearer than she thought.

CHAPTER XXII.

NEW YORK is thought to be too crude and new,
too barren of old historic mould, to bear upon its
exterior any of the clinging ivy of romance. Com-
merce has its grip upon much that might have been
retained to suggest that past which is not wholly
devoid of dignity, and which had a delicate flavor
which is fast disappearing under the rank growth of
excessive wealth. But, in spite of its mercantile advancement, there are some quarters of the city which
are more interesting to the student of human nature
than might be supposed possible. One of these is
situated between the two extremes of business and
fashion. It is comparatively quiet and unassuming;
but it has some points of elegance and picturesque-
ness dear to its denizens, and wears upon its face an
expression of ease and contentment which comes
from a sense of superiority to the vulgar haste with
which the towering tenements in the upper part of
the city rear themselves. Just beyond this pleasant
quarter are abodes of vice and misery, and perhaps
because of their close proximity stands one of the
oldest churches in the town, — a structure suggestive
of mediæval architecture, with its castellated Nor-
man towers and oaken doors; a church that was once

the resort of the wealthy, but which now opens its pews principally to the poor. Faithfully and regularly are its services maintained, without any of the modern arts with which people are lured to their duty, but with a simplicity and earnestness which commend themselves to the humble and God-fearing worshipper.

Not far from the church, in one of the side streets which diverge from this region, is the mission-house of the old church, — a place where its charities are dispensed, and from which proceed other Christian industries. It is under no ecclesiastical rule other than that of the parish rector, nor is it obligatory that its affairs shall be administered by a sisterhood; though its active work and good organization are undoubtedly due to the same spirit of self-abnegation and Christian love which animate the sisterhoods. It is a centre of influence for good, physically, morally, and spiritually, combining as it does a lodging-house for the church's homeless ones; an infirmary for its sick; a dispensary for the ailing; a meeting-place for its workers; and rest, refreshment, advice, as well as food and clothing, for the needy.

On this warm summer morning St. Armand's had been unusually well attended. A few families of distinction still cling to it, and many short sojourners in the neighborhood find it a welcome retreat. All these and more had shared in the services, as well as strangers from the near hotels; among them, our little, disappointed Ruth, who, hearing it mentioned, had found her way to it alone, without the irksome attendance of her cousin. She had walked the whole

distance down the glaring avenue, with the hot sun
in her eyes, and was glad to get within the sombre
coolness of St. Armand's; but the services had
soothed her, and she had lingered till nearly all the
congregation had dispersed, when, rising suddenly, a
faintness came over her which obliged her to resume
her seat.

"Are you not well?" said an even-toned voice in
her ear; and, looking up, she saw a gentlewoman in
garments of black, but with the rigid simplicity of a
Quaker's dress. The face within the small poke-
bonnet was so sympathetic that Ruth would have
been glad to respond, but her voice failed her: she
could only gasp "water," and then the darkness of
unconsciousness overpowered her.

When she recovered, she was in the open air, supported by the lady, and having stimulants proffered
her by the sexton. Quickly rallying, she made an attempt to walk, and would have summoned a cab; but
the lady was urgent to have her remain until stronger,
and begged that she might accompany her to the
mission-house.

"It is but a short walk, and the effort may revive
you. Let me have my way, and do something for
you. I am known as the Sister Camilla, and it is
my vocation to aid the sick and suffering."

The calm voice, in which there was a ring of resemblance to that of some one of her own friends, and
the persuasive manner, carried the point. Ruth took
her new friend's arm, and walked away.

"This is my first Sunday in New York since I
was a little child," she explained; "and I did not

realize the heat of the day, in coming so far. I am Miss Morris."

"Of Morristown?" questioned Sister Camilla.

"No, of New York. But I have been abroad so long with my guardian, Mr. Barclay, that I am almost an alien."

"I know a Mr. Barclay of Boston. Is he not related to Miss Alden?"

"Oh," joyfully exclaimed Ruth, "it is the same one! No, he is not related to Miss Alden, but we are all friends. Oh, this is charming!"

"Indeed it is," responded the quiet sister, regarding her young companion with admiration; "for now I can claim you for more than a moment's rest. I should like to hear about the schools in Italy, for which Mr. Barclay has done so much."

"And I shall be so glad to have something to tell Mr. Barclay about you."

"Not about me, but my work," said Sister Camilla. "And here we are at the mission-house. You will dine with me now, and let me be assured that your faintness was but temporary. May I send any word for you to your friends?"

"Oh, I have none!" came forth from Ruth, with an ingenuous earnestness that made Sister Camilla pause in surprise and pain.

"What *do* you mean, my child?" she asked.

Whether it was due to an overburdened mind, or the strange, quaint unworldliness of the *religieuse*, and her simple directness, and the peaceful atmosphere of her quiet, darkened apartment, acting upon an imaginative nature, Ruth could not have defined;

but, in another moment, she was opening her griefs to Sister Camilla as to a confessor. To no one else could she have so spoken, and to no one better qualified to listen. She did not speak of the one thing even yet hidden to herself, — the vague and tender longing of her heart, — but she spoke of her utter disappointment, her dissatisfaction, her wasted effort; she told how she had really longed to be useful to her aunt, but how entirely impossible it was; and then she touched lightly upon the new and repugnant situation in which Mr. Vedder's attentions had placed her.

"Clearly, this is a case for me," said Sister Camilla, smiling, as Ruth paused in her impassioned speech, and pressed her hand held out so cordially.

"Oh, can you help me? Can you suggest to me what I shall do? You must be so wise, so clear-sighted," cried Ruth.

"Do you think you could endure to share what I can offer, — for a while?" said Sister Camilla.

"Endure! Why, this seems peace and heaven itself, compared to what is before me! Let me share your work too : it is what I have longed to do."

"But the Vedders, — how will you explain? Must I do it for you?"

"No; I can be brave. They will be angry enough, but that will not hurt them. I will tell my aunt that this is just what I need. She is generous enough to yield, not because she will understand, but because she has doubted me from the first. Poor woman, she was wise enough to see that we had no affinity!"

"And her son?"

"I cannot imagine how he may regard it," and Ruth drew herself up proudly.

"Is he capable of revenge?"

"I do not know. He is both weak and wicked."

"An undesirable compound. But how do you know that you will like my monotonous toil, my meagre hospitality?"

"Something assures me of peace here," answered Ruth, glancing at the chaste and simple neatness of the room, and the calm exterior of her companion.

"Can you put aside these pretty garments?" said the sister, touching Ruth's gauzy habiliments, which glittered with beads of iridescent hue; "for of course they would be superfluous here."

"Gladly;" and she thought, but did not say, "They are symbols of a false happiness, while yours indicate a useful life and higher aspirations."

"Come with me, then, and see our rooms for the sick people. Perhaps they may intimidate you."

She opened the door, and led Ruth to where the narrow cots in their white draperies stood, — some empty, some bearing pale-faced invalids. Every thing was neat and spotless; but it was the abode of suffering, and the cross upon the wall was the token of its only hope.

"You cannot alarm me," said Ruth, as she watched the pale faces brighten at the sister's approach, and heard her words of cheer.

"Then, if you are resolute, we will take counsel here," said Sister Camilla, opening another door, disclosing a small oratory. In silence they knelt on the cushions before a reading-desk which held a Bible and a Book of Common Prayer, and in silence they arose, feeling no need of speech. The compact was made.

After that they had a genuine love-feast. A note had been despatched to Mrs. Vedder; and Ruth, recovering some of her vivacity, talked brightly of her travels, of their mutual friends, of books and music. Sister Camilla had no depressing austerity of demeanor: she was cheerful, even gay, with a fund of anecdote, and quickness of repartee. The dining-table was spread on a vine-covered piazza, where flowers bloomed, and birds in cages sang. It opened into a little, narrow city garden, trimly set with box, but making a spot of greenery most pleasant to the eye, despite the brick walls surrounding it.

Ruth could scarcely understand her own rise of spirits. Her faintness had gone entirely, and Sister Camilla's companionship enabled her to be herself again, — something she had not been during all the Vedder period. Unconsciously with them she withheld herself, spoke in commonplaces, ventured no deep thoughts, was guarded at all points, as one must be with coarse or even common natures, unless they wish their sanctities trampled upon. Now she spoke of sweet and serious things long treasured in her mind, and found in Sister Camilla a responsiveness and understanding that warmed and exalted her.

But this peace was rudely broken. St. Armand's bell had begun to summon them to afternoon prayers, — the day was waning, — when, with loud and impetuous haste, Mrs. Vedder burst in upon them.

"What is all this nonsense, Ruth? Why did you

frighten me half out of my wits sending me word you were sick? Who is your friend?" (this in a stage-whisper). "A nun, to be sure. None of your nuns for me: I've seen enough of them in Europe. Come, I want you to go to Central Park with me. I haven't been able to get my nap, and my head aches. Come along. Charley will meet us, and to-morrow we must be off for Saratoga."

"I find that Sister Camilla is a friend of Mr. Barclay's, aunt Abby," said Ruth. "She has been most kind to me. I was quite ill in church this morning."

Sister Camilla had risen at once, and welcomed Mrs. Vedder, who chose to be very distant, in a childish, undignified way that she once in a while assumed when displeased.

"Oh, indeed! Well, I thought you were foolish to come so far down-town. I've got a carriage at the door: a ride will do you good."

Ruth knew that the storm had to be met; perhaps it would be better to break the news to her aunt gently, and without disturbing Sister Camilla: so she said she would go; "to return as soon as I can," she whispered to her new friend.

"What is that you were saying to that woman?" Mrs. Vedder asked, as soon as they were in the carriage. "I don't like her looks. What does she dress up in that way for? Who is she, anyhow? And what possessed you to dine there instead of at the hotel, where you can get any thing you want that's to be had for money."

Ruth despaired of making Mrs. Vedder, whose religious feelings were very crude, comprehend her

new plan or Sister Camilla: so she wisely forebore
an explanation, but, in as direct a way as she could,
told her aunt that Sister Camilla had invited her to
make her a visit, and she had accepted.

"What! stay in that dismal hole this hot summer
weather? You're crazy, Ruth; you're out of your
senses!"

"No, aunt Abby, I prefer it to Saratoga."

"Nonsense, nonsense!"

"But I have quite made up my mind."

Then Mrs. Vedder stormed, and became more and
more angry. She had lost all the humility with which
her foreign disappointments had invested her; and
she boldly told Ruth that she believed she was pin-
ing for Mr. Barclay, and that Charley was a great
deal more suitable; that she ought to be kinder to
him, and not treat him as if he were the scum of the
earth. It was the old story of the lioness and her
whelp. She forgot every thing but her own griev-
ance; and the crowd of amusement-seekers in the
Park, that Sunday afternoon, turned their startled
gaze upon the occupants of the landau, where a red
and voluble woman sat beside a pale and delicate girl,
who received the storm of words in silence. But this
phase of the situation wore off by the time they
reached the hotel; and Mrs. Vedder, whose moods were
very variable, became tearful and penitent. But Ruth
was not to be shaken. With quiet determination,
she packed and locked her trunks, wrote her letters,
and made her preparations. She pitied her aunt, but
her conviction that she had made a grievous mistake
in thinking that she could be conducive to her happiness remained the same.

They parted the next day, kindly, even affection-
ately, — for all the quarrel; Charley only maintaining a sullen scorn. Several letters for Ruth were
in his pocket. He took them out, and burned them,
one by one, in the gaslight of the smoking-room.
Mrs. Vedder was quite sure Ruth would soon join
her at Berryville.

CHAPTER XXIII.

SARATOGA is a social vortex, which gathers in all sorts and conditions of men, from the gravest to the gayest, — the clergyman and the gambler being led thither by as contrary roads as can well be conceived; and it would be an endless task to attempt to delineate the mixed motives which propel the crowd towards its refreshing waters.

It was not therefore surprising that the two men of my story most interested in a certain charming young woman should have met in Saratoga, under circumstances far from pleasing to either. One was perplexed, uncertain, and desponding, as the more sensitive, artistic nature is so apt to be when the world's jar and confusion disturb its delicate balance. The other was vexed, snarling, and sore at the deprivation of any thing which his selfishness craved. Neither would have approached the other, had they not been in a measure forced to do so by meeting at a public table, and the angry one being desirous of getting a chance to wreak his wrath to its fullest extent. To Lillo's annoyance, the story of his life had gone before him. He had been to Codtown, was returning, and had stopped at Saratoga to find a man with whom he had business relations.

Before he knew it, he was a centre of attraction. Cards were showered upon him, introductions sought, invitations given, and a bevy of pretty girls making him the target of their bright attacks.

"The Count Romano" they insisted upon calling him, with true republican distaste for the plain "Mr." But it was as Mr. Marsh that he responded.

"Find yourself quite a lion, don't you?" said Charley Vedder, between the puffs of his cigar, as the two strolled towards one of the springs, after a brief allusion to Miss Morris, in which Charley managed to convey an impression that she was to rejoin them shortly.

"Oh, any thing serves as a subject for gossip in this warm weather," said Lillo absently.

"Have you been interviewed by the newspaper men?"

"Not yet."

. "They know how to do it in a devilish under-handed way."

"It's rather hard lines to earn one's living by that sort of rubbish," said the painter, in the same nonchalant manner with which the talk had begun.

"Then you've no objection to furnishing the beggars with their means of subsistence?"

"I am not anxious to do it," said the other, and turned to join an acquaintance.

"I'll give them a few points," muttered Vedder, casting a glance fraught with malice after the artist, who was now the centre of a group of men whom Vedder knew only as people of social worth and standing, but who would have none of him. The opportunity was not slow in coming. A reporter, with his roll of yellow paper, was on the piazza of the hotel, taking notes, as Vedder returned. A cigar and a glass of whiskey soon established harmonious relations between them, and the catechism which followed enabled Charley to do what he wished without much mental effort.

The following morning Mr. Vedder was absent from the breakfast-table when Lillo appeared. He thus lost half his sport at seeing the latter turn over the pages of a morning journal, glance down a certain column, crush the paper suddenly, and thrust it aside; while the veins of his temples swelled, and the angry flash of his eyes betokened a storm. Rising impetuously, he left his breakfast half eaten, and sought the open air. Who had thus dared to make his affairs the subject of so much idle talk, was as nothing compared with what he read between the lines. The innuendoes, the hints which made his blood boil, were of Ruth; and the climax was capped by an insinuation that the artist's rival was by no means his junior. Of course there were no names, and there was a misty veil of sentiment concealing facts; so that the whole read more as an emanation from the writer's brain than a veritable history. But Lillo saw it all, and it burned into his brain like caustic. His hot, Italian blood was in a ferment, and yet he scorned himself for his anger. Why should he rave at the wretched scribbling of this penny-a-liner? He flung himself into the crowd on its way to some boat-races, and strove to forget the insult. Had his passion for Ruth needed any stimulus, it received it now. Her grace, sweetness, and companionable qualities were not of an order to inspire furious ardor ; but a Cleopatra might have been satisfied with the sudden blaze that rose in his breast, and made her seem the only necessary acquisition to his happiness. What would success, fame, the fulfilment of his wishes be without her ? Apples of Sodom, indeed ! He wanted nothing of his Romano relative ; but, if the title would win her, he would take it. He had the necessary proofs of his rights ; but, unless she so ordered, they should never be presented. And then came the chilling doubt of Mr. Barclay's prior claim. Why might not a man fight for the object of his affections as in primitive times ? Why couldn't he seize her and ride like young Lochinvar ? Must he stand idly by and let that gray-haired " dotard " mildly take as his due all her wealth of young affection ? And then he reverted to the newspaper's cut-and-dried phrases, in which he was alluded to as a disappointed aspirant, etc. Who could have done it ? A rollicking set of men drove past him, and Charley Vedder gave him a familiar nod. Then came like a flash the few words of the day before. Could it be possible that this fool had been amusing himself in so contemptible a manner ? and if he had, how could he punish him ? He was impervious to slights, or the ordinary way in which gentlemen rebuked each other. Nothing but a sound thrashing would make an impression on him. The temptation to give it increased as he went on ; his fists clinched involuntarily, and the desire to whip the scoundrel was so strong that he found himself following the man to the stand where a good view was to be had of the boats.

A gleaming, pretty sheet of water, on which the dazzling sun was pouring his hottest rays; crowds of gayly dressed women in pleasure-boats, in carriages, on foot; men of all ages, with the ribbons of their favorites in their button-holes, laughing, cheering, betting; and the long line of rowers bared to the waist, bending to their oars, as they sent their skiffs over the water with electric rapidity, — this was the scene before him. But he was in no mood to enjoy it. A pretty throng of girls saluted him.

"Who will win?" "Which do you think has the best chance?" "Be on our side, do!" "See, there's Harry Holton; what splendid muscle!" "Did you ever see the equal of this abroad?" These were the words flying about his ears, when he heard a strange, cracking sound. The boats had flashed past: it could not come from them. The hub-bub of voices increased as each one strove to exalt his favorite; but the laughter rose to a shrill shriek, for now, not only was the cracking heard, but there came a great crash, and down went half of the stand whereon stood so merry a throng of human beings. The light jest, the lively banter, merged into groans and screams. Dense confusion ensued. Those not on the structure crowded about to succor those who were. Men and women fought frantically to push their way in and out, displaying the usual selfishness of fear. It was a time of wildest disorder, and the little squad of country police were at their wit's end to know what to do.

Lillo had been one of the first to notice the sway-
ing of the light structure, as well as to hear the
cracking sound, and had leaped quickly aside, grasp-
ing as he did so the girl nearest him, and pushing
several others towards the steps. These were then
in no danger, but it had been impossible to save
more ; and though the water was by no means deep,
nor the stand very high, there were many who might
be seriously injured. He had dashed therefore into
the water, and with the alertness of one accustomed
to it was soon relieving others, and giving orders to
the clumsy but well-intentioned countrymen about
him, who were only too glad to be directed. In the
exercise of this authority he was obliged to divest
himself of as much of his clothing as he could tear
off, and plunge into deeper water. He found the
current strong, but not strong enough to warrant a
curious, dragging sensation which now thwarted his
movements, and which, striking out to rid himself of,
he became conscious was the grasp of a man.

This meant death, unless he could get free. Vainly
he struggled to see who was thus clutching him with
drowning desperation. The more he strove, the
more frantic and fast became the other's grasp. But
now their positions changed ; for Lillo, with the art of
a practised swimmer, made a movement which threw
the man beneath him, and then both sank. But, as
the clear water bubbled over them, he saw Charley
Vedder's distorted features.

For an instant a fiendish joy took possession of
him ; but in another he was aware not only of his own
danger, but also of the necessity for a cool and calm

effort that should save them both. He was so used to the water, that many of his movements were involuntary; and, indeed, now there seemed to be two distinct and separate lines of thought flashing along the electric wires of his nerves. With one he maintained his composure, his presence of mind, and unimpassioned action. With the other he was absorbed in that retrospection which is so common to crises like this.

As they sank, he remembered that he had a common case-knife in his pocket; and, though he was fast losing strength, he managed to get it out, and cut away the clothing in Vedder's grasp. In a moment more he had risen to the surface, free. With one long inspiration of the pure air, and a glance at his whereabouts, he dove for Vedder, but in doing so struck an unseen rock. Stunned, bewildered, but half-conscious, he tried to grapple for his late companion. He had a frantic desire now to save him: it seemed to him an awful necessity, that he must do it or be guilty of his death; and again he struggled and sought, but all in vain. Nothing but mud and pebbles met his touch; and with a weary, hopeless prostration he let himself go, thick darkness shutting him out of life and light and happiness.

CHAPTER XXIV.

ON the second floor of one of those cheap and convenient London lodging-houses, in a room which is but sparely furnished, sits Miss Alden, knitting. Her face looks worn and anxious, and she seems to be impatient for the coming of some one for whom she is waiting, as she turns towards the door whenever a passing vehicle jars its loosely hung hinges. But she has not long to wait, as the small travelling clock has hardly struck six when Grace enters alone. She is tired and agitated, and falls listlessly into a seat as her aunt's knitting stops, and a scrutinizing glance asks as plainly as words for information. But Grace apparently forgets her aunt's presence: she leans wearily back, takes off her gloves, pushes the hair from her temples, and seems lost in thought.

"Well, was your walk pleasant?" queries Miss Alden.

Grace starts, and says, "Oh, yes, about as usual!"

"Why did not Mr. Barclay come for his cup of tea?"

"He has friends at his hotel, he wanted to meet" — And Grace falters under the still keen and scrutinizing glance.

"Has any thing happened?"

"How, when, where?" vaguely asks Grace.

"Between you two," comes out the frank reply.

"Why do you ask, Aunt Althea? What should, what could happen?"

"Much," is the brief answer.

Grace looks up, and meets the same unswerving glance. Her aunt is quite well now, but her temper is less under control than it used to be. They are waiting for the rather tardy bride and groom, who have staid in the lake region half the summer, and they are expecting to return with them to America; and, meanwhile, the translating of which I have spoken has been completed.

"You are keeping something from me, Grace," resumes her aunt.

"Why do you think so?"

"From your manner. You know very well what I expect to hear."

"Is. it not quite natural that I should dislike to disappoint you?"

"Grace!" almost screams her aunt, "have you refused Mr. Barclay?"

"I have," comes resolutely but painfully forth from the girl's compressed lips.

"I will not believe it," says her aunt, rising and coming towards her: "you are not such an utter fool." She even puts her hand on her niece's shoulder, as if to see whether she is really in the flesh and speaking sense.

"I am quite what you call me, if doing as I have determines it," Grace answers.

"Oh, oh, oh!" moans Miss Alden, "you surely do not know your own mind; you cannot justify this in any one way. Why, I thought you had entirely forgotten that wretched creature who was so base, so dishonorable! It is positively weak and wicked in you, Grace, to cling to him: he may be married by this time. I hope he is."

"I hope so, too," is the quiet response.

"What? do you know what you say? Are you in your right mind?"

"I trust so, aunt."

"Then what under the sun has made you act thus? I have been hoping so much that every thing was working around to the desirable conclusion I had promised myself. It has been evident enough that you two were absorbed in each other, and I did think you were becoming rational enough to look at life in a common-sense way. Where would you find a man to be a truer friend than Mr. Barclay?"

"Nowhere," Grace says, in that same wearied, quiet, acquiescent tone which so irritates her aunt.

"Then why don't you explain?"

"I cannot hope to, aunt: you and I have never quite understood each other."

"Oh, I beg to differ," says Miss Alden impatiently. "I have always understood *you* as being unpractical and unwise in the extreme, led by your feelings rather than by your judgment."

"Perhaps so," again replies the girl, wondering if it would do any good to tell her aunt that she too has a very well-defined opinion as to her relative's lack of sympathy.

"But I never supposed you were quite such a fool as this," continues Miss Alden.

Grace does not seem to care in the least for her aunt's reproaches, which sting the more.

" It is so ungrateful of you, besides, to refuse a man twice your age, — one who has done so much for us, who is so chivalric, so kind," — Miss Alden is now weeping — "one whom I have known and respected so long, and he too so long devoted to the memory of his first wife, who was a lovely woman, an angel indeed."

Grace winces.

" I cannot understand it," continues Miss Alden, who suddenly dries her tears and bluntly queries, "Are you in love with any one else ? "

But Grace rises now, and her listlessness is exchanged for a dash of her old spirit and fire.

" That is my affair, if you please, aunt ; and do let us cease this useless discussion. Mr. Barclay has asked me to marry him, and I have declined the honor : that is all."

" Indeed, it is not all. How are we to live ? What will you do ? You forget our humiliating position."

" I forget nothing," says Grace proudly, wearied with conflicting emotions within and without. "Helpless as I am, unfitted as I am for my own maintenance, I would rather die than marry any one simply for a support."

The girl spoke with so much earnestness and dignity, that for a moment her aunt was subdued, but her old habits of thought regained the ascendency.

" Ah, that is all very well in theory, but not in practice ! "

"I hope I may live long enough to prove its truth in both," responded Grace, leaving the room.

When she returned, her eyes were red with weeping; but the housemaid was bringing in the tea, and she sat herself down to pour it out. The postman's whistle was heard soon after, and the letters for a while served to divert Miss Alden's attention. But she returned to the charge immediately after, for one of the envelopes contained a brief and hurried note from Mr. Barclay, bidding her good-by, and telling her that he had left a sufficient sum at his banker's at her disposal until Mr. and Mrs. Potter's return, when he supposed some other and more permanent arrangement for her comfort could be decided upon. There was no allusion to Grace, and no intimation of where he was going, and she read it in blank despair.

But it was useless to question Grace. The girl's reticence was complete; and, though she was evidently unhappy, she showed a self-command which Miss Alden could not but admire.

The next day Grace was gone for so long a time that again her aunt was on the tip-toe of expectation. It was very wearisome for this once active woman to sit alone in the dull lodging-house, pondering her unhappy fate, her disappointments, her misfortune. Set aside from all the busy currents of a world that she had so long enjoyed, and to know that all her influence with her nieces had been as naught, it was more than wearisome. And yet, so strangely do we all adapt ourselves to an altered course, that she gazed from her window with a languid interest in the children playing in the street, and found herself wondering what would be the next scene in their domestic drama.

"Here I am at last," cried Grace, entering with her arms full of bundles, assuming a gayety she did not feel, and striving to amuse her very much vexed and injured companion, who had been silent and *distraite* in her presence since the evening previous. "Here I am, and you cannot guess what I have here, or whom I have met!"

Miss Alden made no response. She had not been nursing her wrath in all these long, silent hours for nothing, nor was she to be easily appeased. Grace tossed her bundles on the table, saying, —

"I was looking for the office of the Decorative Art Society, when my good genius led me to inquire for the Duchess of Stickingham. A pompous old butler nearly annihilated me for supposing her to be in town so late in the season. But when I assured him that I knew she did occasionally come to town, and that she would very much regret not meeting an American friend, he yielded to my persuasions, let me in, and actually brought me wine and biscuits in a grand, old library, which was dim and dark and mysterious as any haunted chamber. Of course I had to wait and wait, but I knew the duchess would come; for she had told me in Florence that she made it a point to be in the city on Tuesdays if she were near enough to do so. And at last she came, was as sweet and kind and interested as if we had always known each other. It was a great relief to me, for I knew the old butler had been nervous about admitting me, and had kept strict guard on my movements;

giving me the slight refreshment as much for an excuse to be in and out of the room, as for my comfort.
Well, the short and long of it is, that I can get all
the work I want ; and here are crewels and silks and
canvas enough to keep me busy till May comes, and
long after, if you prefer London to New York."

Grace stopped for want of breath. Her aunt drew
herself up in a stiffly dignified and disdainful manner.

" It is bad enough that we are paupers, without
making the world aware of it. I cannot commend
this sort of beggary."

Grace did not retort : she knew that her aunt was
smarting under a sense of injury; but she was hurt
too, and could not trust herself to argue. She took
off her hat, opened her work-basket, and began to
embroider. But it was difficult not to let the tears
impearl the design. The false view her aunt took
of her honest effort to be independent and self-sustaining did not encourage her to make the explanation she knew was due to her relative. And other
reasons also made that difficult. She was not sure
that she could ably defend the attitude she had
assumed towards Mr. Barclay. Sometimes she re-
proached herself as bitterly as her aunt could do; and
then, again, she neither repented nor was willing
to have any one suppose that she did.

The hours seemed to drag themselves along. Her
work was difficult, for she had the disadvantage of
inexperience to contend with, although she had been
well supplied with patterns, and received many useful
hints ; but these were not equal to the practised skill
required. To be sure, the duchess had given her the

privilege of instruction in the classes at the Kensington school; but she was at so great a distance, and would be so obliged to leave her aunt alone, that she could but infrequently avail herself of these opportunities.

It was a dreary time, but she worked on courageously; although the bitter feeling that she was misunderstood, and under her aunt's displeasure, was not cheering.

Miss Alden's correspondence seemed to have wonderfully increased. She spent hours at her little table with pen and ink, and seemed so absorbed that Grace hardly knew what to make of it. She had always held a ready pen, but as soon as her reverses overwhelmed her had declared her intention of cutting loose from society, and had left all her letters unanswered.

One day she looked up at Grace with a quizzical smile and a trace of her old good-humor, saying, —

"How much will you get for that piece of work, child?"

Her niece had become so used to her indifference in this direction, that, for a minute or two, she was at a loss how to account for so unusual a remark; and she was slow in answering.

"About twenty shillings, I suppose; nearly five dollars, you know."

"Humph! that's little enough."

"Yes; but you see," Grace went on to explain, "I will do better after a while. They can't pay me quite as much as my time is worth yet;" and then, seeing the undiminished look of interest on her aunt's countenance, she proceeded at further length. "My next order will bring me more, as it is for marking house-linen for the duchess; and such lovely linen as it is, too, — heavy as satin damask, and so fine. Ah! it is a nice thing to be able to possess beautiful " — But here she stopped, checking her sudden flow of confidence as she saw her aunt's brow darkening.

"For goodness' sake, Grace, don't remind me of that absurd freak of yours in going to the duchess. She doubtless looks upon you as a polite species of beggar, or a representative of American audacity."

"I don't agree with you. She is large-minded enough to respect the wish to make one's industry remunerative; indeed, she told me very kindly that she admired the step I had taken."

"Polite humbug! You know well enough she wouldn't put you on her visiting-list."

"I really don't know. It would, of course, be a mere form if she did, when all my time must be given to turning an honest penny. Poor people have no leisure for visits; it is one of the hardships of their life. But, either way, the duchess is no sham, and she shows her honest interest in working-women."

"Working-women!" repeated Miss Alden scornfully. "Yes, I suppose that is what we are."

"It is good Saxon, I believe," said Grace, smiling, and drawing a long silken thread through her pretty fingers, which had learned to move more swiftly and accurately than she had ever supposed they could do; "but, dear aunt, you needn't include yourself, unless you propose to do a little dressmaking, which I fear may soon become necessary."

"No dressmaking for me!" exclaimed Miss Alden, holding up her hand with a deprecating gesture. "I'd scrub first; and I may as well confess first as last, Grace, that I have earned a little money." With what shy pride this was said, and how painfully Miss Alden blushed as Grace's merry laugh pealed out! She hadn't laughed in so long a time that it fairly frightened Miss Alden.

"Hush, child, hush! It is no laughing matter, I assure you. Look! here is a check you will have to get cashed for me. I couldn't endure the thought of touching Mr. Barclay's money after your cruel treatment of him; and so I set my wits to work, and wrote to several literary friends, who have secured me the post of foreign correspondent to a newspaper at home."

"You, aunt Althea!"

"Yes: why not I?"

Grace couldn't speak; her work had slipped from her grasp, her spools and scissors were falling, — she was completely dumbfounded.

With a curious blending of pride and humility, and an abject sort of submissiveness, Miss Alden, drumming on the table nervously with a paper-cutter, went on, "I know it seems absurd; but what is it, after all, but relegating to pen and ink the power of speech with which we entertain others? And *that* I have done all my life. I have a fund of experience to draw upon which will last some time. To be sure, I am not in active connection with the usual sources of supply of newspaper correspondents; but with the aid of foreign journals and reviews I may be able to continue to please" (she could not get out the word "employers") "my — ah — the people for whom I write. And, Grace, I want you to see if you can get me a free admission to the Museum; for of course, with the aid of the resources of the British Museum, I can make my letters quite readable."

Grace had lost much of her girlish impulsiveness, but it was not all gone; and she sprang from her chair, courtesied profoundly before her aunt's little table, and seizing her hand pressed it to her lips.

"Grace, don't be so ridiculous!" said her aunt, drawing away her hand, and giving her a little slap with the paper-cutter. "Sit down and behave yourself."

"How can I?" exclaimed Grace. "Oh, isn't this richness!" She was quoting Mr. Squeers, but Miss Alden did not recognize the authority.

"Richness! No, indeed: the pay is hardly better than yours."

"It is a triumph, nevertheless," said Grace, wiping her eyes, for she had laughed till the tears came; "and I congratulate you with all my heart. Let me see, the duchess will be just the one to get me a ticket for the Museum."

"Then I will do without it," promptly replied Miss Alden.

"Oh, no, you won't!" said Grace, looking out the window. "Why, what is this? A brougham, men in livery, a splendid pair of bays!"

"Do stop your nonsense," said Miss Alden. But that moment the housemaid handed in a note, which Grace read.

"The duchess has placed her carriage at our disposal for a drive, aunt : will you go?"

"Are you quite certain there is no error?"

"Quite. It is a friendly little note. She is not in town, you know, and says she will take it kindly if we will exercise the horses. The air will do you good."

"Well, I suppose I must," answered Miss Alden resignedly. "You may get my bonnet."

CHAPTER XXV.

WHEN Mr. Barclay received from Grace Alden her grateful, but none the less decided, refusal of his offer of marriage, he was completely and humiliatingly surprised; as much so as a younger or more self-confident man might have been. He could not understand it; and, with more precipitation than was common to him, he rushed off to the Continent again, eager to get away from surroundings that embarrassed him. All his friends knew that he had espoused Miss Alden's cause, and had been, as she said, chivalric in his kindness; and he wanted to escape from their inquiries. Ruth had written him of her failure of intention, and had told him how entirely she was satisfied to remain with Sister Camilla till he should command otherwise. She had no wish to do any thing in opposition to his wishes, but she confessed that she would be glad to assist Sister Camilla in her work, and live for a while with some more distinct object in view than amusement or even cultivation; and he saw no reason to refuse. In fact, he knew it would be good and useful employment. He had a high estimation of the sisterhood to which Miss Camilla Deforest belonged, and on the whole he would prefer not to have Ruth with him until he

had become used to his disappointment; for, of
course, he had been very absurd, very ridiculous, and
wholly mistaken, just as Ruth had been, and it was
by no means an agreeable thing to have to acknowledge it. Yes, Ruth could get along without him;
but how about this other young creature, for whom
he had conceived so tender a regard, but who had
cast him off, not disdainfully, not contemptuously,
but alas, quite firmly? Did she know her own mind?
Was it not possible that her painful experience of
one man's faithlessness had led her to doubt all?
Perhaps he had not waited long enough; he had been
in too much haste, and in his suddenness had put an
end to her sweet confidence and trust in him as an
adviser. Why had he not exercised more patience,
and been better satisfied with those long, quiet hours
in which this girl's true and tender, though resolute,
nature had been as open to his contemplation as the
field flowers are to the sun? And why, too, had
never a doubt that he would win her crossed his
mind? Were girls of the present so different from
those of the past? Ah, he had been too sure, he
had forgotten his age!

These were not pleasant thoughts, and Mr. Barclay found himself quite moody and morose. He
missed Ruth: she had been his occupation, he had
lived quite out of his grief in her. But there was no
desire to repeat that unsent note. No one must ever
know of that: it had been a momentary folly. After
a while he would go home, and Ruth should return to
him, and be the head of his house, the stay of his old
age. But, meanwhile, what should he do with him-

self? He was in Switzerland, whither he had gone
so hurriedly; and a letter from Branly Potter, long
detained because of his uncertain movements, informed him that Branly, having received an excellent
offer in Colorado, was to sail, with his wife, the last
of August, but that Miss Alden had decided to remain in England for the winter. This puzzled him
still more. How could he go home and leave Grace
alone with her aunt in a foreign city? What if she
had severed the bond that held him, was he not still
her friend? Nettled, vexed, disappointed, hurt, he
had yet enough magnanimity to forget his own
trouble when he thought of hers. Hers was to be a
fight with fortune, single-handed, and without other
weapons than merely youth and courage. Ah, hers
was a sad experience for one so young! and since
Miss Alden's mental disturbance he felt her to be
very unreliable. The more he thought, the more perplexed he became. He could not thrust himself
upon these lonely women as a dictator, nor could he
even open his purse to Grace with the hope that she
would use it now: indeed, he knew she would not;
and yet how was suffering—absolute, positive suffering—to be averted?

It was now the last of August. The weather was
uncertain. It was too late to be lingering in the
mountains, and he had invitations for the autumn at
English country-houses. But Mr. Barclay was no
sportsman. He had liked to carry a gun about with
him when wandering; but none of the keen zest of
killing, or the fine fury of the chase, ever possessed
him. However, a man could do as he pleased in those

houses which opened their hospitable doors so sys-
tematically to large parties of people, and their libra-
ries fortunately equalled their stables, in most cases.

So he concluded to accept one, at least, of the
invitations, though he knew it would cost him considerable annoyance; but that had to be met sooner
or later.

As the train whizzed along which was carrying
him to Paris, a few days later, he suddenly made up
his mind to another and an entirely different course.
He would not go to the country; he would do something more effective, even if it was quixotic. Staid
and tranquil as was his usual demeanor, his eye began
to flash, and his cheek to burn, at the scheme which
now presented itself. But of this scheme it will not
now be necessary to say more than that it gave Mr.
Barclay considerable exercise of ingenuity. While
he was leaning back on the cushions of the railway-
carriage, with all his customary luxurious appointments about him, he remembered that he had not
looked at a newspaper for weeks, that in his absorp-
tion he had even neglected to write to Ruth, and that
her letters had been few and far between, and also in
one of her latest she had mentioned the intense heat
of New York as being something terrible, worse than
any thing she had imagined.

Now, with a pang of remorse, he wondered if
she had been ill; but of course in that case Miss
Deforest would have forwarded intelligence. No,
Ruth was young and vigorous, though so fair and
slender. And yet he was a little uneasy, just
enough so to make him wish he had been less neg-

lectful. Taking up an Italian journal shortly after, he saw the death of Count Romano, which set him wondering whether the young American painter would change his mind and assume the title and fortune that belonged to him.

Arriving in Paris, he lost no time in getting on to Calais, and from thence to London; but here, tired and travel-worn as he was, instead of going to the Langham, his usual comfortable resort, he made a cabman drive him to a little inn of the East End where nobody who was anybody ever went; and, so far from registering at his banker's, he took good care to avoid it, leaving most of his luggage at the railway-station, and carrying only what was barely necessary for his immediate wants. But even at this inn he did not stay long. Evidently Mr. Barclay was getting more and more capricious.

CHAPTER XXVI.

"I HAVE been here at least three weeks, and as yet have seen nothing of the homes of your poor people, Sister Camilla. You make me too much of a guest," remonstrated Ruth one morning, when the July sun was pouring down torrid beams upon the blistering earth. "Every day you go and come on your errands; while I sit here in this cool and darkened room, doing nothing worth speaking of. Why cannot I go with you to-day?"

Sister Camilla paused as she replied. She was just going out, and her hand was on the door. "I have feared you were unequal to it; but you are not doing nothing when you regulate my accounts, and give little Dora music-lessons, and look over my linen, and prepare my basket of supplies."

"But I don't feel as if that were any thing, when I see you going and coming, night and day, in and out among those who are suffering. Let me go with you occasionally, now, — to-day, — as a beginning."

Miss Deforest assented reluctantly. She had not wished Ruth to see all that she saw, and was accustomed to; but Ruth's desire was sincere, and she allowed herself to be persuaded.

It did not take long to reach the quarter where her

ministrations led her. The poor and the rich have often only a few layers of brick between them, however wide the spiritual distinction. The heat made it hardly possible for the aged and infants to remain within doors : they swarmed on the door-steps, under awnings, and wherever air and shade could be found. But there were many who could not do this; and Ruth's heart ached when they mounted up rickety stairs to the stifling bedrooms, where wan and weary people were struggling with fatal illness, or children, too weak to move, turned their glassy gaze upon the visitors.

Sister Camilla saw that Ruth was growing faint and pale, and made her errands shorter on this account; but not until she had been a messenger of aid and strength to many. To one she gave medicine, to another wholesome advice, to all that needed it food, and sometimes money ; but, to each and all, words of sympathy and hope, which drew forth thanks, and occasionally the merest shadow of a smile.

"How do you stand it ?" said Ruth, as they turned their steps homewards. "It was too much for me, I confess ; but *you*, — it is your life."

"Yes, it is my life," said Sister Camilla gravely, "chosen deliberately."

"It can never be mine," said Ruth hopelessly. "I am beginning to think myself a failure every way."

"You must not do that. Take it more patiently. You are very young yet."

"But is it not true that only women who have had some trouble, some great sorrow or disappointment, ever give themselves up to a life of renunciation ?"

She spoke as if thinking aloud, and the color rushed to her face as she became conscious that her companion regarded her with a quizzical little smile.

"Oh, forgive me!" she cried. "I was debating the question in my own mind. I was not intending to question *you.*"

Sister Camilla seized her little hand, and squeezed it.

"I understand," she said. "You, like all the rest of the world, think only a *man* can drive a woman to good works."

"I did not put it that way," said Ruth, blushing again.

"No, but you mean it. You think a lover is a necessary adjunct to a woman's happiness ; and that, if he prove false, she may then turn her attention to something else : well, I admit that to be a very moving force among women, and rightly. Nothing is sweeter and lovelier or more ennobling, than a tender and true affection ; but it does not come to all. Many live and die without it. Look at our professional women, — authors, artists, editors, teachers, nurses, physicians. Are they all heart-broken people ? "

"Oh, no ! of course not ; at least I suppose not, " faltered Ruth, who by this time had sunk into a bamboo chair in the little parlor of the mission-house, and was waving a palm-leaf fan.

"You have started me on one my hobbies," said Sister Camilla, "and I will have to give you a little sketch of my own career, by way of illustration, if you care to hear it."

"If I care," repeated Ruth reproachfully; "you know I shall be delighted."

"Take this lemonade, then, and don't look so utterly dejected. Ah, Ruth, that far-away expression of your eyes tells me a tale!"

Ruth's color came and went again.

"It is only the heat," she said, but Miss Deforest knew better.

"No matter, dear, that will all come right, — 'so he be brave, so he be true.' Well, to go on about my indifferent self. When I had emerged from a very lively and untrammelled girlhood, I had what may be called a very keen intuition that marriage was not to be my portion. I was not pretty to begin with, nor had I any other 'attractions' in the way of wealth or wit ; and, though I tried very hard to believe I was talented, my genius never seemed to be properly appreciated by other people."

Ruth laughed.

"Now, that was the very hardest thing I had to bear, though I can laugh with you about it easily enough ; for no matter what people say about usefulness, those who can entertain others by the least show of any one talent are much more highly regarded than the poor hum-drum, useful people."

"Oh ! there it seems to me you must be mistaken," put in Ruth.

"No, I am not," said her companion emphatically. "See what a fuss is made over a good picture or a successful novel if it is by a woman. But who hears of the humble one, she who in a quiet home exercises as much financial ability as a railroad king, and makes of that home a haven of peace for some weary man, and nurtures his children for lives of industry and

self-respect? No one. But let a woman have a
voice like a bird, something that she hardly has to
make an effort to use, — I don't speak of the artificial
cultivation of it demanded now-a-days, — and her
name is known through all the civilized world. But
I only say this to prove the truth of my assertion
about usefulness not being so much appreciated as
talent. Well, as I have said, here I was with youth,
health, strength, no prospect of marriage, no genius :
what was I to do? My grandmother died; I was an
orphan, and she had indulged me greatly. Her death
opened my eyes to the selfish vanity that possessed
me. Could I not do something for somebody? I
asked myself in those days of sorrow. I had been
indifferent to religious duties; but I now went to
church, and gradually became convinced that in the
faithful performance of Christian duties there was a
higher peace than in the pursuit of any pleasure. I
studied nursing, and found it an excellent means of
helping others. One thing led to another, and here I
am, — heart whole, happy, and pledged, as you see
me, to a life which is my choice." She paused, and
just then there was a peal of thunder, and in a few
moments more a driving shower obliged them to close
the windows; but not until Ruth's quick ear caught,
above the sound of wind and rain, the hoarse cry of
a new's-boy shouting an "extra." It jarred upon
the quiet of the room and the even tones of Sister
Camilla's voice, and they both listened as the sound
drew nearer. "Boat-races !" "Saratoga !" "Accident !" — "Hark ! what is it?" said Ruth. — "Lives
lost !" came again the cry, now beaten down by

the blast, and again rising above the sweeping gale.

"I will send out for a newspaper," said Sister Camilla. "I am afraid the morning visits have been too much for you, Ruth; or are you timid when it lightens?"

"I don't know," faltered Ruth. "I feel oppressed, alarmed; what does that dreadful cry reiterate?"

"Oh, it is nothing! We never mind those sensational things: the least occurrence serves as a pretext to issue an 'extra.' Ah, here comes Mary with a paper, wet with rain!" and she held its dripping sheet away from her, reading aloud as she did so, —

"An accident on Saratoga Lake; the breaking down of a platform; men, women, and children precipitated into the lake. Daring conduct of a young artist. Fears that his life may be lost. Drowning of Mr." — Sister Camilla stopped suddenly, and looked at Ruth.

"Go on," she said, but growing steadily whiter. "What are the names?"

"There are only two mentioned," said Sister Camilla, putting down the paper; "no one that we know, probably. At least, only one is familiar to me; and you are ill, and had better not look at the details."

"I must," said Ruth, seizing the paper and glancing hurriedly at it. "Mr. Marsh and Mr. Vedder;" both names stood prominently before her as she repeated them aloud. "Which is drowned? or are both?" she asked in a pitiful, beseeching voice.

"It is not known yet; these things are always

exaggerated," said Sister Camilla, in the way that people try to soften dread tidings.

"I am so confused," murmured Ruth. "There must be some mistake: he was to return to Italy. Perhaps it is some one else."

"Yes, perhaps," said Sister Camilla, equally confused, for she knew nothing of Mr. Marsh; and, though Ruth had spoken of Charley Vedder, she could not imagine that any thing happening to him would cause quite such intensity of anguish as was now apparent. But she had no time to consider, for Ruth was falling unconscious beside her, as white as her dress, and as motionless.

The storm had subsided when the young girl had recovered sufficiently to be carried to her room, but she looked as did the flowers in the garden when the gale was over. She tried to rise, but her strength was gone; and all the long hours of the night were spent in a wakefulness which alarmed Sister Camilla. She could not close her eyes without visions of terror and pain; and the faces of the old and young she had seen the day before were confused with those of her former companions.

"I must go to Mrs. Vedder," she said to Sister Camilla, after a day or two spent in this silent, prostrate way.

"It is impossible!" was the answer. "Besides, she has left Saratoga."

"You have heard from her?"

"I telegraphed for information."

"Please tell me all," urged Ruth.

Sister Camilla looked steadily at her for a few moments, and then said, —

"Yes, I will tell you; for suspense is always harder to bear than definite news, however ill they may be. Charley Vedder was drowned. Mrs. Vedder was taken home by Mr. Boggs. The accident was not as severe as at first supposed, for his was the only life lost; the other people were more or less injured."

To her surprise Ruth simply said, "Thank God!" and turned away her face.

"Surely you do not thank God that the man's life was lost," said Sister Camilla in her bewilderment.

Ruth shuddered and grasped her hand; with a burst of tears she sobbed, —

"I did not think of him — forgive me — I had forgotten him. I was so grateful — that no one else" — She stopped convulsively.

"No one else!" repeated Sister Camilla thoughtfully. "Were you interested in any one else?"

"Yes," said Ruth between her sobs. "But I am so sorry for poor Mrs. Vedder. Poor, poor aunt Abby, whose heart must be broken! And now I can do her no worse harm than to let her see me. She will never forgive me."

Sister Camilla, like a wise woman, forbore questions. It was much of an emigma to her; but she knew that this outburst of violent grief was better than the quiet, pent-up stillness and suffering of the last few days. Ruth sobbed till exhaustion and sleep followed; and, when this phase of her illness was reached, Sister Camilla knew that recovery would follow.

She was not mistaken. Ruth slept like a tired child, — once in a while sighing softly, and waking to weep; but re-assured at finding the calm, tranquil face of Sister Camilla beside her, or bending with a motherly tenderness to offer the nourishment of beef-tea or jelly.

"I do not deserve this," she said once, after an ice had been given her. "Your poor people should have these good things, and you; but not I who have proved my weakness and miserable insufficiency."

"Tut, tut; none of us are of brass or iron, child. And you have not had a mother's nurture; any one can see that at a glance," was the reply.

"What *do* you mean, Sister Camilla?" asked Ruth, brightening a little.

"Just that, my dear," said the sister roguishly. "Men are very good in their way, but not at bringing up young women. How little Mr. Barclay knows of girls, is proved by you. Why, he hasn't the shadow of a doubt but that you are as giddy and gay at this moment as the flies that are whirling in the sunshine!"

"He knows I am with you," said Ruth, remonstrating.

Sister Camilla laughed. "I accept the implied trust, but all the same consider myself justified in my assertion. What mother would have left a tender young creature like you to meet such possibilities and probabilities as you have done? Ah, it was like a man!"

"Now, Sister Camilla, you shall not abuse Mr. Barclay: he is the dearest, kindest of men," said Ruth.

"Of course; but he went out of his sphere in undertaking your education and bringing up."

Ruth saw by the twinkle in Sister Camilla's eye

that she wanted a tilt; but again the heavy weariness of sadness overcame her, and she answered faintly, —

"He could not have saved me this."

"Oh, yes, he could!" said the sister, "at least in a measure. 'Make doors upon a woman's wit, and it will out of the window; shut that, 'twill out at the key-hole; close that, and it will fly with the smoke from the chimney.' That means we are good at contriving and baffling destiny, which men are not. But now tell me where would you most like to go, — to the mountains or the sea?"

"Oh, to neither!"

"Now, that is selfish, my dear: you cannot get strong in this hot city."

"Well, what does it matter? I am of no use."

"No, I know it; but you can be by getting well."

"To whom?"

"To me, to yourself, to Mr. Barclay, and perhaps to some one else in the vague, indefinite future."

Ruth turned away.

"I am quite in earnest," proceeded Sister Camilla. "Some of my poor people are going away, thanks to the 'Fresh-air fund;' the rest are to be under the care of Sister Anne till I return: for I must have an outing, you know."

"Ah, if it is for you, I will go anywhere!" responded Ruth.

"Well, it is for me as well as for you: change is absolutely necessary. Where would you rather go?"

Ruth was still a moment. Her thoughts flew back to the childish pleasures of days spent with May and Grace Alden after her father's death; she remembered the glittering sands, the light-house, the long roll of the waves, the rocks, the salt smell of marshy land; and it seemed as if a breath of that air would indeed put new life in her.

"To the sea," she said.

"And so be it," answered Sister Camilla. And then she put a package of letters before Ruth, — one from Scotland, one from London, and one from the Engadine.

Ruth turned them over. "Are these all?" she asked.

"Yes, all."

Ruth sighed.

CHAPTER XXVII.

HERE stands the old brown house which has been looking out to sea these long, long years, in the face of fogs and driving storms, over the glittering sands, out to the line where sky and ocean meet, waiting for the ship to come in which shall bring to it life and happiness. It looks no older, no more weather-worn, than it used to look when a merry boy went whistling through its doors, or old Abner Marsh sat in the sunshine mending his nets; and it seems still to be a picturesque part of the land or water scape. Its doors and windows rattle at the passing gust, and here and there it has been propped or strengthened by a heavy beam, which, with a little red paint and a few tiles, are all its modern improvements. But its ship has come in, — as our ships so often do, without our knowing it. For from the chimney curls a thin thread of blue smoke, and in the sitting-room is the customary litter of an artist's working-room. No frescoes and dadoes here, no brasses and bronzes and tapestries, to delight the artistic eye; nothing but an easel, some mahl-sticks, sketches, stretchers, and canvas. The floor is still one of bare boards; but the open shutters of the windows let in the sunshine and the broad sweep of the distant sea, which is so much rest to the eye, so suggestive to the mind.

It is meant to be a place for work, and not one of ease or amusement ; but its owner touches neither paint nor pencil. He is recovering from something worse than illness, — a fit of disdain, of bitter self-reproach, of dissatisfaction with all the world. Why had he not staid always in this little old brown house and been contented ? Why had fame or fortune tempted him, and what had they brought him that he should have been lured to listen for a moment to their siren voices ? Never again would he swerve from his allegiance to art. And then that horrid day at Saratoga hung still like a black cloud between him and his brightest dreams.

He had been rescued by a boat, when so far exhausted by the blow on his head, and his efforts to evade the clutch of a drowning man, that it had been several days before he could rush from the scene of horror to the quiet of the one spot on the earth which had for him no painful suggestions. For with his recollections of Italy came the remembrance of Ruth ; and she to whom he had poured out his story in page after page of burning words, she to whom he had left his fate, the decision of his career, the choice of a titled name, had disdained even to reply.

What wonder, then, that his work stands undone, and that the days crawl on in their slow length, leaving him to his lethargy.

The visitors at the Neck have all gone, the houses are closed, the sands are deserted. The days are getting shorter, the gales are beginning. So Lillo now ventures abroad. He has become thin and worn and haggard from so much thought and so little exercise. He stops a little, as with his oars and fishing-lines he makes his way to a boat; but he has resolved to shake off this deadly oppression, and be himself again.

If he could have saved that miserable life, which had been almost in his hands, he would have been better satisfied. Often that despairing, dreadful glance comes to him; and often his own hateful wish for revenge, rises like a ghost in his memory. And how wasted was all that passion! spent on a girl who had given him one or two tender smiles, who had made him the whim of the moment. Was she, indeed, so fair and false as to wilfully deceive him? or had he been so weakly presumptuous and mistaken? He knew little of women; they were more or less mysteries to him, as they are to so many men. But if she had cared ever so little, would she not have answered his letter? Where was her grace? where her courtesy? Could the letter have miscarried? Not likely; but, whether it had or not, he should never know. For, of course, she would be Mrs. Barclay some time or other; that was more than likely, as the miserable scribbler had insinuated. It must have been apparent to everybody but himself. And what a dreadful waste of time was all this questioning, surmising, and useless, vain speculation! So he fights his despondency, and goes out to wage war with the elements.

It is a bleak, wild day, and he notes the white curling foam of the breakers tossing high against the

rocks.   Nature is unsympathetic only to those who
do not love her.   For those who do, she has always
an undertone that responds to the mood one is in.
The sun may shine upon one's sorrow, but it does
not gladden : it is only the smiling mask which
makes the world believe that death and decay are forgotten.   The gray sky, the tossing waves, the gloom,
were in keeping with Lillo's turn of thought ; and it
was with keen desire for a contest that he loosened
his boat, and sent her flying.   At least, the air of
heaven was his, and its saltness gave him strength.
His good right arm had power to breast the waves.
And what better life need a man ask than this wild
freedom ?   Perish dreams !   Let them fade, — given
this strong actuality of life and force.

But, as he pulled valiantly against the strong current, new thoughts came to him.   Ruth had been
his personification of all that was lovely in womanhood.   Why should he forget her because of her
apparent disdain ?   He became convinced that he
had erred.   She was as true, as gentle, as perfect and
fair a flower as ever, whether she loved him or not ;
and he vowed that nothing should expel her image.
To be more worthy of her, more capable of trusting
her, and so of trusting all women, was the higher
and nobler way of solving his difficulties.   It was
puerile to be jealous and doubting.   Time would yet
give him the opportunity to make all clear between
them.   And, meanwhile, he would work.   The resolve
brightened his mental horizon ; but, around and about
him, sky and sea were uniting towards denser gloom.

He had gone farther than he knew, and Seal

Island was before him. It was a barren little spot
still, with only its few shrubs and a hut which served
as a shelter for fishermen ; and, as he guided his craft
among its rocks, he was surprised to see another
small boat drawn upon its beach, for the fog was
rolling in, and to any one unaccustomed to these
waters, a return to the mainland would be a difficult,
if not a dangerous, thing. To warn any unwary traveller seemed to be only ordinary civility, for the
boat was one of the sort hired by guests. So Lillo
shouted, "boat ahoy !" at the top of his lungs. For
a while there was no answer ; but presently from a
far corner came a slim, straight, black-robed figure,
more like a Florentine nun than a Codtown visitor.
In her hand was a book, and on her head was a
small poke-bonnet, and so absorbed was she in her
near-sighted reading, and slow strolling, that she
neither heard nor saw what was before her. Lillo
moored his boat, sprang from it, and, with accustomed grace, doffed his cap, and stood in her path
before she discovered him. Then with a startled
smile she closed her book, and gave him a calm and
cool salutation.

"Are you aware, madam," said he, "that it is
already hardly possible for you to return to the mainland ? And may I ask who has been so stupid as to
bring you here such a day ?"

"You may ask, but I am not certain that I shall
answer," said the lady ; "seeing that it will oblige
me to exonerate all the men at the Neck, who
warned me of my foolishness. But, really," and she
glanced hastily at the forbidding sky, "I had not

been aware that the fog was driving in at this rate, I was so interested in my book; but this is bad, isn't it?" and she turned towards the path which led to the hut, as if to get something she had left there.

"Pardon me, if you are alone, pray get into my boat at once, and I will take you back. Is it possible you rowed here by yourself? Few ladies attempt it."

"Ah, that is just what made me try it. But I am not alone. Could you manage to carry two of us?"

"If you are quick," answered Lillo, going back to where his craft was now tossing restlessly. "A bad bargain," he muttered, as he peered into the thickening distance. "Just like a woman! I've half a mind to make her stay where she is, as a lesson."

He bent to loosen the knot which secured the other boat, but decided that it would be better not to strive to manage a tow, and re-tied it again; when a hand was laid lightly on his sleeve, and a remembered voice thrilled him with its sweetness.

"Is it possible that this is you?"

He was instantly erect, himself in every fibre.

"Miss Morris!" was all he said, but his eyes devoured her.

"She is pale, she is thin, she has been ill and suffering. Am I in a dream?" he asked himself. But again her sweet voice spoke.

"This is Miss Deforest, Mr. Marsh,—or am I to say Count Romano?—and she tells me we have no time to lose, that you think there is some danger. We had no idea we were so venturesome; at least, I trusted to Sister Camilla's excellent seamanship."

She stopped confused at his intent gaze, and at

the strange situation. She was dressed in a dark brown cloth, faced and hooded with velvet; and her hair was coiled under a cap of the same, with a snowy sea-bird's wing fastened with a glittering aigrette of curious stones. At her feet were the cushions and shawls which they had brought from the boat to the hut. He saw her as if she were a picture, and not a living reality; and his own voice sounded strange and far away as he replied, —

"There is not a moment to lose. Indeed, I am not sure but that discretion would advise your remaining here till the fog lifts. The wind seems to be rising; if so, it would be hard pulling, but safer than to risk this. — What is your opinion, Miss Deforest ? "

Sister Camilla saw his uncertainty had arisen at sight of Miss Morris. She saw, also, that the embarrassment of these two must have been caused by more than was now apparent; and as she peered into the fog she said, —

"I don't fancy the prospect before us, either way; but, if you will be good enough to share our captivity, I shall be less anxious than if we are left to our own responsibility."

He seized the chance, flung his oars back into the boat, and drew her high and dry out of the waves.

"Now, I suppose we must return to the hut, if we wish to keep off this penetrating moisture," said Sister Camilla, somewhat relieved to see that on neither countenance was there any thing more than constraint, and that even this was fast disappearing from Ruth's.

Lillo took the wraps and cushions in his keeping, saying rather brusquely as he did so, " I thought all visitors in this part of the world knew more than to trust wind or weather to-day ; and, indeed, I cannot imagine what brought you here. I have been told that all the houses are closed for the season."

" So they are, — at least, all but the one we are in," answered Miss Deforest; "and when a wilful child who has been ill expresses a wish, it is wise to grant it, don't you think so ? "

" Have you been ill ? " said Lillo, turning to Ruth, who lagged behind, and wondering if she had known that he was in this neighborhood too.

" Yes ; and I had so pleasant a remembrance of happy days spent here long ago, that I wanted to see the Neck once more. I did not know — at least I 'was not sure — that this was where you used to live."

Unhappy speech ! it turned his hope to bitterness. He stalked on moodily, pushed into the hut, threw down the cushions, and went out again, saying he would soon return.

" Who is this, Ruth ? and what is the matter with him ? " asked Miss Deforest. " He is an Adonis in the rough, is he not ? "

" Have I not told you his story ? " responded Ruth. " O Sister Camilla, he is angry with me; but why, I do not know."

" Oh, is he the young count whose history is so romantic ? "

" The same, but " —

" You said so little that I had to imagine much.

But here he comes with fire-wood : that is thoughtful and practical. I like him, dear."

"Hush!" said Ruth, smiling.

In a few minutes there was a light blaze dancing in the rude fireplace; and, though the little hut was bare and smoky, there was a homely comfort in the warmth.

"Now for my provisions!" said Sister Camilla, opening a basket and displaying a well-stocked larder.

"You had better be frugal: there is no knowing how long you may have to stay here," said Lillo.

"Oh, you only want to frighten us!"

"Indeed, no ; it is possible that night may add to your discomfort."

"That is not a pleasant suggestion."

"Necessarily, truth is apt to be unpleasant."

"Now, there I differ with you. But I thought I heard oars : could anybody be coming for us?"

"I will go and see."

"Pardon me, let me look out; you stay with Miss Morris. — I will return in a moment, Ruth."

Sister Camilla pushed open the door and vanished.

Lillo took a long look at Ruth. She did not raise her eyes, but it seemed to her he must hear her heart beat.

"I must say one word," he hurriedly murmured: "did you get my letter?"

"What letter?" she asked, in a surprise that it would have taken a clever actress to feign.

"One that I mailed to you two days after leaving New York. I addressed it to Mrs. Vedder's care, at the Fifth-avenue Hotel."

"I never received it."

There was no mistaking those words nor the simple directness of her gaze; but Sister Camilla this moment entered, saying, "I was wrong: there is no boat, it was the beating of the waves. We are indeed stranded: the fog is worse than ever."

CHAPTER XXVIII.

THERE was nothing to do but wait for the fog to lessen, and Sister Camilla buried herself in her book. Lillo stirred up the driftwood fire; and Ruth, perched on an upturned box, sat dreamily watching him, a faint flush of color in her cheeks, and a gladness in her eyes that Miss Deforest had never seen in them before. The girl seemed to be so contented with the peace of the present moment that she made no effort at conversation; but at last, as Lillo suffered the fire to rest, and began tracing with a stick in the soft, white ashes, — an old habit of his, — she gathered her wandering wits together, and said, —

"I have never heard the conclusion of your story. Are you going to Italy? and will you assume the title which belongs to you, Mr. Marsh?"

"You know, then, that my grandfather is dead?" he quickly returned.

"I saw the death announced," she replied.

"And any thing else?"

"Nothing of consequence."

He looked narrowly at her as he said, "The newspapers cannot let people alone: why they meddle with personal concerns so much, I am at a loss to understand; for me they are the most trivial of matters."

"I hope you do not resent a friendly interest," Ruth said gently.

"Indeed not," was the quick reply, with an equally quick look of gratitude. "No, I am not going to Italy, unless," and then he checked himself, glanced at Sister Camilla, who was reading intently, and said in a low tone, "unless you send me there."

Ruth's eyes dropped; but he at once resumed more audibly, "My grandfather's death makes the position now much more difficult, for the lawyers tell me that the informalities of my papers, — which are nevertheless genuine, — and the legal differences of the two countries, would involve long-continued litigation, which would be a great bore to me; the game not being worth the candle. My Italian cousin, who is next of kin, will probably regard me as an amiable lunatic for giving up what he thinks so much to him so easily. But what do I want of a title?"

Sister Camilla now laid down her book and drew near. Ruth's delighted sympathy and appreciation, and the young artist's enthusiastic disdain, were charming to her: so she purposely said, —

"Is not a title considered by all respectable and ambitious Americans the proper handle to one's name? I am afraid, Mr. Marsh, you are not up to the times."

"I am not up to society's shams, Miss Deforest. If titles are emblems of honor, let those who have them keep them: my crest is a painter's brush. You know it is said, I forget by whom, that those who now wear coats-of-arms were wearing coats without arms a short time ago."

Miss Deforest laughed; but Ruth said softly, —

"You forget, though, that you have the right to some family distinction."

"No, I do not consider it a right in one sense; for I think I owe more to the poor old fisher-folk who cared for me, than to the proud family who cast me off, and made my poor mother suffer." He rose as he spoke, and his tall young figure seemed to touch the top of the hut.

"Then you wilfully renounce the pomps and vanities offered you?" said Miss Deforest.

"Yes, wilfully. Whatever I can do to make a name for myself will be a better satisfaction than the empty honors of the Romanos. But I must go now and see to our prospect for getting home to-night," and he left the hut.

"What a delightful young democrat!" said Sister Camilla mischievously, watching Ruth's expressive face. "He does not seem to consider for a moment what a feather in his cap a title would be, nor how the girls would dote on it."

Ruth's lip curled, and a proud satisfaction in her young hero could not be concealed.

"He has the right spirit. I am so glad he thinks the title unnecessary."

"Why, what difference does it make to you, dear?"

"Oh, none particularly!" faltered Ruth, conscious that Sister Camilla was laughing in her sleeve; "but I like to hear noble sentiments expressed."

"Especially by one so graceful, so gifted, so manly."

Ruth looked up. "I did not say so."

"But I do."

"Are you jesting, or in earnest?"

"In sober earnest.   He is admirable.   And to think that we found him in this desert spot, — a *chevalier sans peur et sans reproche,* — this suits my idea of romance!"

Ruth still was not sure she understood Sister Camilla's banter, nor did she altogether like the looking at Lillo as a mere hero of romance.   To her he was a very real embodiment of the bravest, manliest sentiments; besides, she was pondering what he meant by saying he would not go to Italy unless she sent him there.

Sister Camilla gathered her skirts about her, and sat down at Ruth's feet.   "Forgive me," she whispered, "I never can resist a little teasing.   I will say no more, after I have told you that you are looking like a new creature."

Ruth bent down and kissed her.   The door of the hut now blew open, and they could see the gulls flying, the white-caps tossing, and the fog breaking.

"We have wind enough now," said Lillo, coming in.   "Will you venture home?"

"If you will take Miss Morris in your boat," said Sister Camilla, "and not otherwise.   For, though I can pull a strong oar, I should not like to risk such a stiff breeze as this, with more than myself as passenger."

"Very well," said Lillo; "as you please."

They were soon embarked, glad not to have the discomfort of a night on Seal Island; and, though the low band of yellow light in the west bespoke the need of haste, the short day drawing to its close did not intimidate them.

It was indeed hard pulling for a while, and there was enough to do to manage their boats; but, as they neared the shore and shoal water, Lillo leaned over his oars and said, —

"Have you any conception of all the miserable doubt I have been in these past few months, Ruth?"

"No," she answered. "I thought you did not care, — that you had forgotten every thing."

"Then you *did* wonder a little why I neither wrote nor came?"

"Yes."

She did not tell him how she had suffered, nor did he ask her more. He was satisfied to be near her, to look at her sweet face, to note the tender outline of her features, — more delicate than when in stronger health, — and to breathe the same atmosphere. He was so happy that he could hardly believe himself to be the gloomy, morose, dissatisfied creature of the morning. He leaped to the shore in time to take Miss Deforest's oars and secure her boat; then they walked up the sands in the dim light, the wind blowing the drifting clouds about, and a few stars peeping here and there in the dark space. As they approached the house where Miss Deforest was lodging, a ruddy light streamed from the doorway; and the lounging men on the step moved off uneasily under Lillo's sharp rebuke to them for allowing ladies to go on the water alone in such rough weather, — though their inattention had given him such unlooked-for happiness.

"You will stay a while longer at the Neck, I suppose, Miss Deforest," said Lillo as they separated.

"Long enough to visit your studio, if you will allow us to-morrow," she replied.

He laughed at the idea of calling his old house a studio, but promised to show them any of his studies that they cared to see.

People in love are not supposed to be so material as to suffer the commonplace pangs of hunger, but Lillo's man of all work was kept busy that evening over his kitchen-fire; and when he raked out its embers, it was with some dismay that he heard orders for breakfast which would oblige him to be stirring early, having exhausted all his resources on the evening meal. He had so long had his own leisurely way, that it was also a surprise to him to have to put the whole house in as trim shape as a ship's cabin, and to see his master trailing in heaps of woodland treasures which he had gone miles to gather in the early morning. The shells and seaweed which adorned the small sitting-room had to yield precedence to masses of crysanthemums, in white, yellow, and red; but the man smiled knowingly, when, later in the day, two ladies made their appearance.

"So this is your den," said Ruth, "the place of poetic visions," as she glanced at the low walls, the bare boards, and the quaint, stiff, straight chairs.

"Oh, no! not my den; these are my ancestral halls," said Lillo, laughing, "the palace of the Marsh-Romano."

"It would not be a bad idea to link the two names," said Miss Deforest. "It, in a way, establishes your right to relinquish the title, or not, as you please."

"That shall be as Ruth chooses," he would have liked to respond, but he had to check himself. The reversion from the exultant frame of mind which had been his had set in, and he was now again in suspense.

"Look," he said, as he threw open the wooden shutters; "the title to this is one that no one can dispute."

The broad blue expanse of water lay calm in the autumnal sunshine, dotted here and there with the white sails of the fishing-smacks. Ruth seated herself near the window, and gazed in silent abstraction.

Meanwhile, Lillo drew out his sketches and studies for Miss Deforest's inspection, saying, as he did so, —

"They are hardly worth looking at. I have done no good work for months, but I shall begin in earnest as soon as I have secured a studio in New York."

"I am glad you intend to do that. This may do very well as a place to dream in, but every artist needs the friction of active city life; besides, your work requires good, living models."

"Yes, seclusion will not answer; one must be in the world. — By the by, Miss Morris" (he did not dare to say "Ruth" before Miss Deforest), "what has become of all our little Italian world of friends? Where are the Aldens and Mr. Barclay?"

"Surely you've heard of the Aldens' loss of fortune," answered Ruth.

"Not a word."

" Nor May's marriage ? "

" No ; to Branly Potter, I suppose, as a matter of course."

" Yes. I should have thought he would have written."

" Oh, when a fellow's happy, he forgets his friends ! I am glad, however, to hear of his good luck. Do you know what he is about ? "

" He is going to Colorado. Their steamer was due some days ago, but I am afraid I have missed seeing May. We have wandered about so, that letters have miscarried, or not been forwarded ; and my illness made me negligent about writing."

" And Miss Grace, — where is she ? "

" With her aunt in. London. She writes that she is very busy. She has found a good friend in the Duchess of Stickingham. You remember her. What a contrast she was to Mrs. Coit ! Grace is determined to maintain herself, and has resisted all May's inducements to go with her to the West. She and her aunt are almost penniless. Indeed, I don't know what they would have done, had it not been for my guardian."

" And is Mr. Barclay well ? Does he soon return ? "

" Ah, that I cannot answer ! He has been very mysterious lately. He must be well, for he has been to Switzerland ; but whether I am to join him abroad, or he is to return, I really do not know."

Lillo received this answer with another chill of anxiety and impatience. He knew that Miss Deforest was to leave the Neck on the morrow, and the prospect of more uncertainty was unendurable.

It was well that Mr. Barclay could not hear his mental apostrophe. Miss Deforest now arose from looking over a portfolio, and suggested a walk; but Ruth seemed quite contented to remain where she was. She had not paid much attention to the studies and sketches : she was thinking of the old Italian gardens and palace, and contrasting them with the little brown house she was in, and wondering whether it was quite right, after all, to throw off the burden of ancestral honors, and be contented to toil obscurely on, as Lillo proposed to do. To be sure, here was peace and primeval simplicity ; but might not the other career be better, wider, larger, more suited to his talents ? Could not his influence be made more conducive to the good of others ? She was quite lost in these abstractions, as she arose dreamily to do her companion's bidding.

Lillo misconstrued her absence of mind immediately as a lack of interest, and he too became moody. There seemed to be less sunshine in the day, as they all emerged from the house. But the good sister had her surmises ; and, as they neared the sands, she turned quickly away, and said she must go home to pack, leaving her young friends to themselves. It was the opportunity Lillo had coveted, but his lips seemed sealed. The ocean, in its limitless expanse, was suggestive of the futurity before him. He too had his thoughts of Ruth, and her sweet womanhood, as momentous, as conflicting, as her views of his career.

There was a thrill of deep emotion in his voice, when he at last found courage to speak.

"Ruth," was all he said.

She turned towards him at once, but seeing his excitement, became, as women will, all eagerness to avert an issue.

"How bright and clear the view is to-day! Who would have supposed yesterday, that the sun would ever shine again, and where do the fogs come from so suddenly? It must be a dreadfully dangerous coast. An old woman on the beach, the other day, told me she had lost her father, her husband, and three sons, all by the sea. And yet we think it so beautiful, forgetting its cruel hunger, its deadly enmity."

"Ruth, I must speak to you."

"Yes," she sort of gasped.

"You know I love you."

She did not say "yes" again, but her face lost its look of alarm for one of tender sadness. Love comes as a great and solemn trust to a girl of her nature. She listened intently as he went on, now rapidly, now slowly, — watching her as he spoke, and wondering if she understood him.

"You must have known this long ago. I would have spoken before. The letter I wrote you contained the expression of it, but that never reached you; and the withholding of an answer made me desperate. I am not worthy of you, but no one is. I would strive to be, if you would let me. Am I mistaken in daring to hope that you care a little for me?"

She could not speak yet, the joy and the pain were too exquisite; but he saw her lips parting with the words that trembled to escape.

"I must speak the whole truth now, and tell you

that I have tried to live without you. When no answer came, I was wounded, and it added to the doubt I have had all along; for, you know, it is thought by so many " — But here he stopped, unwilling to put his doubts in shape.

"Yes, I know," said Ruth, made calmer by this allusion.

"But it is not true, Ruth. Tell me so, for I cannot live without you. All my interest even in my profession has died within me; only you can waken it. Do speak to me, Ruth!"

His tones had varied from the simplest, manliest utterance to the passionate pleading which intense feeling only could impart, and Ruth felt so shaken by it that she could scarcely command her voice. She had thought of him as always so strong and joyous; but she rallied her forces and whispered, —

"What shall I say? That I, too, have tried living without you, and found it impossible."

He could not take her in his arms as he would have liked to do, but he grasped her hands as if she might possibly escape him.

"And you are not in any way bound?"

"No. Mr. Barclay has never demanded what the world expected, nor do I think my gratitude could have gone so far."

"Then you have no absurd heroics to overcome. You will be my wife?"

"I will," came slowly and softly, but firmly, from her now smiling lips; and once again, as when a boy, Lillo felt as if the earth were air, and he had wings.

They never knew how that day spent itself. There

was so much to say, so much that remained unsaid ; but Ruth managed to make known the failure of all her aims, and her utter inability to be or do any thing remarkable, which all the more satisfied her lover, as giving him the larger share of her affections.

They strolled till again the stars were twinkling as on the night before, here and there in wind-swept spaces, and the fishing-boats were coming in over the tossing waves.   Long lines of light darted from the cottage windows where busy women were making suppers ready for the hungry toilers of the sea, and the voices of little children trilled out shrill welcomes to the deep bass of fathers' and brothers' voices. There was a homely warmth and gladness even on this chill, windy coast, and it found a response in the happiness of these two young hearts full of their new, deep joy.

Sister Camilla met Ruth with a playful reproof that needed no defence, for she knew intuitively what had happened.   Hers was no ascetic soul narrowed to the small groove of one set of duties.   She could feel for those who were happy as well as for those who sorrowed, which is sometimes the more difficult task.

Lillo concluded to turn the key in the door of his little house on the sands, and go with his friends to the city.   It was rather late in the season, but he had now a new impetus towards climbing the ladder of fame, which, if not synonymous with that of fortune, ought to be ; and there was much to be done in the way of establishing himself for the winter's work.

As yet there could be no immediate hope of marriage, for besides Mr. Barclay's approbation, of which he was by no means sure, in view of any such preparations, Mr. Barclay's purse would also be an important factor, — a truth, however, not so apparent to him as to Ruth.

CHAPTER XXIX.

It is a cold, cheerless day in London; and Grace Alden cannot help comparing its inclemency with the bright, soft airs of Italy, or the abundant sunshine of her American home. She is the more inclined to do this because of her loneliness and sadness at having to part with her buoyant young sister, who came upon herself and her aunt with the suddenness of a cyclone one morning, and expected them to at once take leave of the Old World for the New, and join fortunes with her and her young husband. This Miss Alden would not do. No amount of persuasion or argument could induce her to leave London now that she had tasted the sweets of independence, in the shape of checks for her foreign letters; and least of all would she go to the horrid West, the frontier, the place of barbarisms, the uncivilized chaos of society. Branly Potter urged that its new life, its freshness, were just what she needed, and that nowhere else could she be so entirely respected for herself alone as in their new home. He was to hold some responsible position connected with the mines, and felt amply able to assist Grace and Miss Alden in any effort they might wish to make. But Miss Alden was invincible. No new country for her, "Bet-

ter fifty years of Europe than a cycle of Cathay,"
though this Western Cathay was a much worse place
to her imagination than the Eastern one, a place of
dreary uncouthness and disorder, sterile of refine-
ments. So Mr. and Mrs. Potter had begged and urged
in vain, and had at last said "good-by" reluctantly;
for they felt convinced that sooner or later Miss Alden must yield, and it would be so much pleasanter to
have Grace go with them at once than to be worried
about her until she joined them. Grace, of course,
had to make the best of her aunt's decision, though
better than any one else did she know what it meant,
— steady toil, hard fare, and small pay. She looks
around her now at the faded carpet, the cheap furniture, the battered fire-irons, and the dull fire. Her
work is beside her; so is a clever book that has found
its way to her through the kindness of some friends
(for friends had found them out, in spite of themselves),
but she has no time to read. She looks at it long-
ingly, but takes up her needle resolutely, thinking
what pleasure it would have been to go with May to
that far away West, where with new courage and
hope she could have helped to make her sister's
little home a happy one. And she smiles with a sad
sort of contempt at her own forlornness, and her
aunt's preference for this dingy drudging to the
plunge into the more primitive conditions of Western
life. What indeed could be more absurd than their
weak struggle to be ladies and working-women combined? This is her way of regarding her aunt's
high-flown notions. She knows better, she knows
that nothing she does in the way of work can render

her less a lady than she has always been ; but, for all
that, she prefers to say she is not one, that she has
descended to a lower social scale, and is contented.
This is partly the result of her aunt's long-continued
conversations, partly the effect of all her trouble ; for,
with all her courage and determination, hardship has
worn upon her. It is a trial to get up early these
dark mornings, and do what she can before their fire
is lighted, and breakfast brought in ; and it is a still
greater one to go out for the petty marketing which
her small pelf obliges her to do rather than trust to
her avaricious landlady. She thinks it would not
have been hard to do any of these things if she had
been brought up to them, — these small economies
or the sacrifice of ease ; but she remembers only
too well the luxury of her American home, where,
with no mother and an indulgent father, there had
been as lavish outlay as in many foreign palaces.

Miss Alden breaks in upon her meditations with a
question which answers itself concerning the postman. The letters are a never-failing excitement ; and
they have just been brought in by the poor, hard-
working little housemaid, for whom Grace has more
fellow-feeling than she ever had for any of the maids
in her father's fine house. Instantly both are absorbed in their correspondence. Only those who
have few interests know the value of letters. Busy,
active people find no time for them ; gay, worldly
people think them a bore ; and even the studious and
reflecting would rather not be forced to attend to
them. Letters seem to have had their day ; the
constant influx of news in the journals and maga-

zines, from all quarters of the world, having taken their place. The sprightliness, the grace, the charm of letters are no longer appreciated, except by those who pay for them. But this is not the case with Miss Alden and her niece. Both are glad to forget their surroundings, and hear of the sayings and doings of their friends; and frequent travelling has made letters a necessity. Miss Alden goes through her pile first, and is about gathering them together for re-perusal, when she sees something in Grace's manner that attracts her attention. The girl has apparently forgotten the letters, though but a few minutes before absorbed in them, and is gazing into the half-burnt coals of the fire as if she saw a wraith.

"Grace!" calls her aunt.

"Yes."

"What is the news? who have you heard from?"

"Several people." This is spoken so mechanically that Miss Alden's ire is aroused.

"That is rather vague."

"Yes," is still the abstracted answer, and Grace still peers into the dull fire.

"Who are they?"

"Oh, one and another!—the Browns, Miss Perkins, Lily Everett."

"They are of no consequence," says Miss Alden impatiently. "I wonder you keep up with them."

No answer.

Grace is wondering if her fate is always to meet her in a letter, as far as she can form any thought at all; but she struggles to be unconcerned and indifferent, and succeeds, for directly Miss Alden asks the meaning of the note with the duchess's crest.

"Oh, that is an invitation!" answers Grace, now crushing the other letters into her work-basket. "The duchess wishes us to spend a few days with her."

"No; you don't say so?"

"Yes; here, read it." She is quite alert now.

Miss Alden devours the gracious request, written in the large, flowing style she likes so well. It is in the third person, and was probably penned by her Highness's secretary or governess; but that is no matter. It pleases Miss Alden, who, to Grace's surprise, begins to think of ways and means immediately.

"It is uncommonly kind. I don't see that we can refuse. I wonder if my velvet dress is in proper shape."

"Why, aunt, will you really go?"

"I think I ought to, she has been so kind, so attentive. Just think of all the fruit and flowers and game we have had lately."

"Yes, she has been kind; but I am not so sure that all those gifts came from one source: we have other friends, you know."

"None who would so go out of their way to do us a kindness: no, no one but" — And she checked herself, for she now never mentioned Mr. Barclay.

"But surely you forget how difficult it will be. There's the cost of the journey, some necessary outlay besides, and — Why, we haven't enough even to tip the servants."

"A very vulgar thing to do, in my opinion. Yes, I dare say " — this is said with a sigh — " that I shall have to spend a little more than is prudent; but I must go, if only for your sake, child." And Miss Alden glances in the looking-glass in an inquiring way, as if to see whether society will discover her attempt to keep up with it on lessened resources.

" Oh, don't count me in, please ! " says Grace : " I have too much to do."

" Nonsense ! lose such a chance as this, — 'twould be absurd ! "

" My wardrobe would forbid it, if nothing else did. I cannot appear in the necessary freshness. My silks are old-fashioned, and my evening dresses all in disorder from being boxed so long ; and as for gloves, I am on my last pair now."

"Why, how careless you must be, Grace ! *My* things are all as good as ever. My brocade and my satin are older than my velvet, but the three are all very handsome, even if rather antiquated in style ; but I would rather have them that way than be taken for *nouveau riche* by my splendor."

Grace leans back in her chair, and laughs softly to herself.

" It is *nouveau pauvre* with us, as your words betray. Poor dear aunt, don't cheat yourself into thinking there will be any possible pleasure in this attempt ! I cannot go."

" O Grace, don't thwart me in every thing ! "

" I'm sorry, but it is impossible."

" Now, don't you suppose all sorts of people go to these places ? Literary persons never have any

money.   Look at Carlyle and his wife, — poor as
church-mice always."

Miss Alden already felt herself of the guild of
authors, as may be perceived.

" They never appeared in gay society, so far as I
know," said Grace.   " They would have scorned to,
with their hatred of shams."

Miss Alden saw the mistake of her illustration.

"Well, it was Carlyle's business to preach, mine is
to entertain; it is necessary, therefore, that I endeavor to see something which will serve my purpose."

"I quite agree with you, if it is feasible."

" Then you will go too?"

" Ah, that is not necessary!   Really, I cannot.
Don't ask me to.   Look at all this work.   It will
take me till Christmas to finish it."

Miss Alden went into another room to look over
her fineries.   She did not know that almost all of
Grace's had been sold, and she hoped by dint of
coaxing yet to accomplish her end.   Grace seized
the opportunity while her aunt was out to again
look at her letters.   One was from Ruth, full of her
new happiness.   This alone was unexpected, for
Grace had had a theory of her own in regard to
Ruth, which this letter completely upset; and the
other was from her father's business-agent, enclos-
ing a draft for a respectable sum, and a statement
which overpowered all the other news.   It was to
this effect: All Mr. Alden's affairs had been settled in such a manner, through the kindness of a
friend, that Mr. Alden himself would be able to re-

sume business, and had gone to California with that intention; and that later, if Miss Alden and her aunt would join him, he should be glad to have them do so.

The one thing that checked Grace's gladness at reading this was the uncertainty as to whom the friend, the financial friend, might be. Her thoughts were in a whirl. Was their misery soon to be ended? Was her father really free from all reproach? It had come upon her so suddenly that it seemed unreal. Her father seldom wrote to her. She hardly knew his friends, — brokers, bankers, men of money; hard men, as she supposed, not likely to do any greatly unselfish deed, men who laughed at sentiment, and thought generosity a weakness. Could any of these have changed his nature, and, in violation of his training, become a benefactor? No, it was not possible. It was all out of order, incomprehensible. She would wait for further intelligence before throwing this bomb in Miss Alden's way. The news might prove untrue. It was hard to believe, even if true, and no good could be gained by disturbing her aunt. In her heart of hearts, she believed there was but one man in all the world capable of doing so noble a deed; and a great tide of shame and regret rushed over her as she thought of him. Where was he? Why had he been so quick to take her at her word?

She pretended to be very much absorbed in her work when Miss Alden came into the room again, but her hand trembled so that her stitches went wrong.

Miss Alden was full of the new project.

" I find, my dear" (she did not often now-a-days say to her niece "my dear") "that I am in better trim than I supposed. My evening attire is all that a woman of my age needs, — substantial, dignified, almost elegant. If I could be as sure of my morning gowns, I would be quite satisfied. What do you suppose, Grace, is *en regle* for breakfast dress? Would my plain black silk answer?"

" I don't know. I suppose so. All the shopwomen wear black silk. I mean the fine shopwomen who preside over the small-fry."

" Grace !"

Grace looked up smilingly, quite unconscious of the vexation she had caused.

" I wish you would be serious. For pity's sake, don't associate me with such people."

" I beg your pardon, but really some of them are fine-looking women."

" *Canaille*, all of them. What they do or don't do does not interest me. Have they the faintest idea of harmony or artistic fitness in dress?"

" They have but feeble appreciation of either, very likely, though they sometimes light on what is becoming. Now I think of it, I believe their black silks are all given to them by the firms who employ them."

" Why will you persist in talking about them?"

Grace laughed. She was really wild with suppressed excitement.

" I know what I will do, aunt. I will go to some celebrated establishment, Redfern's perhaps, and ask them just what would be the proper thing for you.

They will expect an order, of course, but no matter; I'll just mention the duchess, and they'll send you any thing you want to look at."

"Grace!"

"Yes, it's polite stealing of their ideas; but to keep up with society, one mustn't be too particular. We can find out that way just what is worn, and then hire some poor little sewing-woman to copy."

"I do not know what has gotten into you. This sounds like Mrs. Godfrey Gray. Do behave yourself."

Grace tossed away her work and went to the window, saying, —

"I believe I'll go out, I need exercise. My head throbs."

"I should think it might, if folly ever causes headache; and please get me some note-paper. I must write our acceptance.

"Not mine."

"Oh, you may change your mind. Fresh air is wonderfully beneficial."

She was gone only a half hour, long enough to calm and collect herself, and consider whether she had not better inform her aunt of the news. It seemed so selfish to keep it to herself, even if it were unreliable; for she was not at all disposed to accept it as a certainty after so much harassing trouble and doubt and wearing anxiety. When she returned, she found her aunt in conversation with a gentleman who was in the shadow of their cheap, stuffy curtains, nor did she at first recognize Mr. Barclay.

CHAPTER XXX.

YOUNG people exact far more sympathy in their love-affairs than do their elders; for when a person of maturity risks all in a venture of the affections, and loses, it is looked upon as a mistake which age and experience should have prevented. No one thinks it a very deep wound, probably because the person of maturity has learned the art of hiding the pain, and does not bemoan his fate as a younger man would do in similar circumstances.

Mr. Barclay had not been without his share of trials, and had learned philosophy; but he suffered nevertheless. The loss of his wife had been an intense sorrow, out of which he had come unimbittered, though broken in health and spirits. Time (scene-painter, as well as scene-shifter) had brushed his healing wing over the past, and mellowed its pictures into a dreamy distance, a poetic vision which was not without a certain charm for a contemplative nature. This new stroke was a fresh, keen, cutting one, a disappointment that bade fair to sour him; the more apt since he had so buried himself in London that no friend had been able to find him.

·He had gone about from one suite of rooms to another, finding fault upon trifling pretexts, dissatis-

fied, ill at ease, not staying long enough in one place
to discover whether it suited him or not, and at last
settling down in an obscure quarter where his servant could hardly make him comfortable.

But he was not to be moved again. It was no small
matter for one so accustomed to space and ease,
and a large way of living, to relinquish his usual
habits ; but he had a purpose in doing it, from which
he was not to be deterred by any personal inconven-
ience. He became much addicted to long and solitary walks, and equally given to silence and medita-
tion. He looked thin and altered, even much older.
The people who noticed him thought him in ill-health,
and would have recommended Nice or Mentone
rather than the approaching dull, dreary, English
winter, if he had encouraged their confidence, which
he did not do. They were not friends. They had
only seen him in the street or at church, but his
appearance attracted them.

Although with so pre-occupied an air, he seemed
always looking for some one, expecting some one ; but
this was only apparent to close observers. Others
thought him a very dignified, gentlemanly, sad sort
of a man, rather at a loss for something to do. But
these observations came from the very few with whom
he had to have some contact, such as his landlady
and her lodgers.

He had never been attentive to small economies ;
but now he showed so new an interest in the cost of
commodities, and was so very frugal, that his servant
came to the conclusion that he had lost heavily, and
that want of money was the key to all his peculiari-

ties. It did look as if this were the case, for his business correspondence had certainly increased, and his letters took up much of his time.

But when Ruth's letter, telling of her happiness, came to him, it was like a dash of cold water. He seemed to suddenly wake up to the fact that his whims had swayed him too long, and that his ward's claim upon him had been neglected. To his serving-man's surprise, he gave orders to have every thing in readiness for an early steamer. He was going to the United States.

After this he was his usual self again, — went to the Travellers' Club and everywhere else that he had the *entrée;* and on his list of people to visit or leave cards for was Miss Alden.

Thus it was that late in the chilly afternoon of the day that Grace had been so startled by her home news, Mr. Barclay made his appearance. She showed her surprise quite artlessly ; but he arose in his quiet way, and greeted her as if they had met the day before.

Miss Alden was nonplussed ; but, as she had never understood the cause of their separation, she made no attempt to fathom it now. She had been talking of every thing and everybody as of old, heartily glad to see her friend again, and hoping much from his coming, when he had told her of his intention of going home. This had dispirited her, and so checked the flow of her ideas, that it was a relief to have Grace enter.

But Grace did not instantly recover from her surprise. She was constrained and perhaps a little awkward. She took off her gloves and stood before the fire, as if too chilled to speak.

"Mr. Barclay has brought a budget of news, Grace," said her aunt, "quite a godsend to us in our dulness. And the most charming news too — about Ruth " —

"Yes, I know about Ruth," was all Grace replied, looking far into the fire.

"How long have you known? Why didn't you tell me?" cried her aunt; then turning to Mr. Barclay, she said, —

"Ah, Frank, young people are so selfish. They think we have no romance left in us, that we are contented to plod on the latter half of our lives in stupid senility, *sans* eyes, *sans* teeth, *sans* every thing."

Mr. Barclay smiles faintly, and looks at Grace, as if he agreed with Miss Alden; but Grace does not respond. She is thinking how really ill Mr. Barclay is looking, how changed he is.

"But charming as the news of Ruth may be, in the light of a love-story," Miss Alden resumes, " I hope there is to be a substantial pecuniary foundation to her happiness."

"I hope so," Mr. Barclay says.

"Mr. Marsh is really one of the Romano family, is he not?"

"Without doubt."

"Then he has but to assert his rights, and get his money."

"If he will."

"Oh, pshaw! of course he will. He is no fool. You must insist, if he is squeamish, on Ruth's account."

" Ah, they must decide for themselves ! "

" But Ruth is, as it were, your own daughter : you must look out for her interests."

Why would Miss Alden persist in putting Mr. Barclay into the position of a *pater familias ?* thought Grace. She quite resented it, and strove to turn the talk into another channel. But Miss Alden returned again and again to the subject, and went even farther into reminiscences and recollections, and reminded Mr. Barclay of a dozen things he had forgotten. And then she came back to the present again, and told Grace that their friend had come to say good-by, that he was going to New York.

They had all drawn about the fire, in the dusk, and no one saw Grace shiver and turn white as her aunt gave her this item of intelligence. She murmured something indistinctly, and Miss Alden went on with her monologue.

It was about their unhappy lot, their reverses, her sadness at having to part with her old friend, her general dissatisfaction with every thing and everybody; and it ended in tears, which obliged Miss Alden to leave the room suddenly for the want of a handkerchief.

" Does your aunt not know, has she not heard, that your father's business-affairs have been arranged, and that the worst is over?" asks Mr. Barclay, now addressing Grace for the first time.

" I have not told her," responds Grace. " I have but just heard it myself, and I have been afraid of raising false hopes. Can you tell me any thing? Is it quite true, Mr. Barclay ?"

"So far as I know, yes."

"And who has been so kind to him?"

"Ah, there you ask too much!"

"But I never heard of any friend of his that could have or would have done such a thing. It is altogether unusual, — something chivalric."

Grace clasps her hands in front of her, and gazes more steadily than ever into the fire. Mr. Barclay sees that her eyes are moist, and notices that her low voice trembles ; but he answers calmly and coolly, —

"No, it is nothing remarkable, — just one friend assisting another. It is done every day."

"Oh, I beg your pardon! I am sure it is not, and I know but one person in all the world capable of doing such a thing."

"You overrate it. But I trust it may be the means of making you happier; though work is, I believe, your panacea."

Mr. Barclay says this a little satirically, and Grace hesitates to speak again ; but she remembers that he is going away, and she may never have another opportunity.

"Mr. Barclay," she begins, but her voice falters.

"Well."

His tone is not re-assuring, it is curt and cold.

"May I thank you?" she says, with great timidity.

"For what?"

"For every thing."

"No, Grace."

"But, Mr. Barclay"— She stops. It seems impossible to go on, and he does not help her. He just glances at her, and that is all. He has no desire to repeat his foolish absurdity; and she looks so prettily girlish in the firelight, so winning and lovable, that he dares not trust himself to be very kind. Of course she is grateful; that is taken for granted: and it is going to be very hard for him to say good-by to her. But what is the use of all these words? An old man like him should have known better than to have thought it possible for her to love him.

"Don't feel obliged to say any thing, Grace," he at last takes pity on her to reply.

"But I must," she persists: "I have been so proud, so mistaken, so ungrateful."

"In what?" he asks, as coolly as ever, but with inwardly rising excitement.

"In every way. I thought you pitied me only, and that, perhaps, if your sympathy had not been taxed, you might have chosen Ruth. I did not want to stand in her way. I did not want to be pitied; and — and — O Mr. Barclay, *do* forgive me!"

Mr. Barclay rises now, and takes the sobbing girl in his arms, as he whispers, —

"Am I not, then, quite the mistaken one? Is it possible that you do love me, Grace?"

He hardly believes her when she says, "Yes;" but he is contented to let her remain sobbing on his shoulder, where, to her intense astonishment, Miss Alden finds her.

"My dear Grace!" she exclaims, as she stops with a tragic gesture in the middle of the room. "What *is* the matter?"

Grace hurriedly rushes from the room, and Mr. Barclay leads Miss Alden to a chair, saying, —

"She will be better soon; her nerves are over-
taxed. When she is composed, may I have a little
quiet talk with her, and with you?"

"Certainly, certainly. I have wanted to tell you
how exasperated Grace's conduct made me, but I
have had no chance. I knew how unwise she was,
but I thought she had sense enough to appreciate
the honor of being your wife, Frank."

"I have something else to speak of," replied Mr.
Barclay; and then he told her of her brother's better
fortune. Miss Alden received it with more equa-
nimity than might have been expected. She was
glad, of course, but she should never go to California
or Colorado under any circumstances. For the rest
of her life she should devote herself to literary pursuits, but Grace might join her father as soon as she
pleased.

"I will attend to that," replied Mr. Barclay, which
somewhat confuses Miss Alden, who cannot make
out just how matters stand. But the tea-tray now
comes in, and the housemaid lights the lamp; and,
after a while, Grace returns, with re-arranged toilet,
and flushed cheeks, and a little tremor that makes
her seem sweeter than ever to Mr. Barclay.

Miss Alden has letters to write, and goes to her
bedroom, leaving Grace and Mr. Barclay to themselves; and then comes a long explanation which
satisfies both of them, though Grace cannot forgive
herself for inflicting so much pain, and she is more
than ever convinced that no one in the world can
equal Mr. Barclay's tender, generous kindness. He
does not tell her what he has done. He does not

acknowledge any thing. But she knows that he has been guarding her for weeks; that she has never gone out alone in the crowded thoroughfares, that he has not been near; and that he has almost impoverished himself to help her father. She finds it out in the subtle way that is attributed to a woman's instinct; and she no longer hesitates to tell Mr. Barclay that he is a prince among men, and that she has never loved, and never can love, any one else half so much.

It is compensation for all he has undergone. He is happier than he had supposed it possible for him ever to be, with a fulness and a depth that is quite different from the ecstatic joy of youth; and he is quite untroubled as to whether Grace's gratitude is the spring of her affection. He knows better. He sees her beaming eyes, her vivacity, hears her soft, ringing laugh, and is sure that her pure gladness is caused by his return to her, so quick has been the revulsion from doubt to trustfulness. When Miss Alden has finished her letters, she joins the happy pair again, and Grace whispers to her aunt the glad tidings.

Miss Alden is more stirred by this than by what has gone before. She pressed Mr. Barclay's hand, and kissed Grace with a degree of fervor that had been absent from her caresses a long while.

When Mr. Barclay has at last left them at a late hour, Grace feels obliged to inform her aunt that he is no longer a rich man. This is rather a sobering fact, but Miss Alden bears up wonderfully.

"No matter, child; you and I have gained some

strength by our vicissitudes. So long as he is not absolutely indigent, we must not let this be a barrier to your happiness."

Grace smiles, as she thinks how differently her aunt now regards these matters, and immediately enters into her aunt's plans for visiting the duchess, —plans which gild Miss Alden's dreams by day and night.

Mr. Barclay lingered in London, but no longer a sad and weary man in quest of something to fill his vacant hours. All his days were full with an interest which only a wholly new and fresh hold upon life could have given. Grace would not consent to leaving her work unfinished, or her engagements broken; and Miss Alden was deeply immersed in the construction of a series of essays which she proposed to publish under the title of " English Country Homes."

It may be surmised that her experience was not as wide as many would have thought necessary, and that her observations were rather limited, since her visit to the duchess at Longwood was the basis of her book. But Miss Alden had already discovered that the literary faculty is one that will not allow itself to be circumscribed, and that a large class may be judged from a single species. She therefore gave free rein to her imagination, and made much use of facts conveyed to her by others; but her visit to Longwood remained the solid structure of her book. And the visit was truly a delightful one. Grace made wondrous efforts to have her aunt's toilet all that she desired: so Miss Alden's mind was at ease to enjoy the distinguished society which paid her so much attentive consideration ; and the duchess, being a really good woman, was as simply gracious and hospitable as Miss Alden could desire.

She staid ten days, and made diligent use of her opportunity, coming back to her plebeian lodgings with as much literary enthusiasm as if she were a Goldsmith, and wondering how she could ever have been contented in not having a hand at forming people's opinions, or stimulating their ideas. So entirely absorbed was she in her new career, that she forgot to make inquiry of Grace as to just how Mr. Barclay's fortune had so dwindled.

Letters from the Potters came with every mail, describing their curious Western experiences ; the chaotic state of affairs in which mining life had thrown them being always a subject of congratulation with Miss Alden, in that she was not weakly drawn to follow them.

"Imagine, Grace, seeing women in costumes by Worth, out in that town of Leadville! It reminds me of that verse in Proverbs, — or is it elsewhere? — that speaks of a ring of silver in a swine's nose. The sense of incongruity is the same."

Grace laughs at all her aunt says now-a-days, in that quiet, contented, happy way which makes her so much more companionable than when she was so sadly depressed. But Grace has grown very staid, notwithstanding her happiness, and does not like any allusion made to the difference of age between herself and her lover. She wants to meet Mr. Barclay more than half-way, and is positively glad of all her bitter experience, thinking rightly that it has made her wiser and better. She is wiser and better; but Mr. Barclay finds her none too grave, and is surprised that she so readily adapts herself to him in all his plans for the future, going even beyond him in consideration and prudence.

CHAPTER XXXI.

THE winter sped on, and Mr. Barclay did not return to his native land. Nor did Ruth go to him,
though the choice of doing so was given her.   Under
Sister Camilla's wise and motherly care, she was living a wholly different life from the one of pleasant
wandering she had spent with Mr. Barclay.   Simple
duties, housewifely arts, and thoughtful care of the
ignorant and the needy filled her hours ; saving her
leisure to cheer and stimulate Lillo, whose hard-
working life was a constant denial of the supposition
that an artist's career is one only of dreams and aspirations.

A letter of hers to her guardian, however, must
now be given, to show how she was developing.

" You know all about my leaving Mrs. Vedder, and the fearful occurrence which so soon followed that affair. But you can
hardly know how much I dreaded ever seeing her again. I flattered myself that there would never be any necessity for my
doing so ; and that she was as glad to be left alone, as I was
willing to leave her. But Sister Camilla could or would not
look at the matter as I did. She implored me to see my aunt,
and do what I might to soothe her sorrow. It was an ordeal
which I wished to evade. But Sister Camilla never lets a duty
rest ; and at last I yielded, and wrote to my aunt, asking if I
could see her. To my surprise she assented, and appointed a
time for me to visit her. Lillo would not let me go alone,

though I insisted that he should not appear as my escort. We therefore started one cold morning, on an early train, and reached Berryville in less than three hours. No one but a hired man met us at the station, which was wrapped in snow, and had few signs of life about it, standing, as it did, on the edge of a little village which seemed another Sleepy Hollow. We drove about two miles out of the town, over a hilly road, which in summer must be very picturesque, and came to rather an ornate villa-sort-of-a-place, with a pretentious gateway, and an abundance of deciduous trees. Here I made them let me walk, leaving Lillo with the man who had driven us; for, much as I feared to meet aunt Abby, much more was I unwilling to have Mr. Marsh possibly insulted by her, when she knew (as I meant to tell her) that he was to be my husband.

"Well, I reached the house, and was shown to a gaudy parlor, full of useless and hideous *bric-à-brac.* Vulgarity was in every line of its satin and velvet furniture, in its glaring color and absence of taste; and I shuddered to think what would have been my fate, if a kind Providence had not rescued me from the hands that had fashioned this. Not a book was to be seen, unless you call those gilt-hasped albums which contain the caricatured features of fat and lean humanity, simpering on their pages, books. (O *dear Mr. Barclay*, how I thank you for not leaving me to my rich relations!) If all had only been plain and poor and clean, how much sweeter my thoughts would have been! I was all in a ferment by the time I was allowed to go up-stairs. Aunt Abby had been making her toilet, and I could hardly see her for the folds of crape which swept around her and in yards on the floor behind her; but the flashing light of her diamonds helped me on a little. And I looked in her face to see that she had sent for me, not to soothe, not to sympathize, not to let me see that sorrow was refining her; but to rebuke, to reproach, to sting me! I looked in vain for the suffering I really expected and hoped to see. It was not there. She answered my look with positive defiance, as she said, —

"'So you've come at last, have you?'

"'Yes,' I replied, 'Aunt Abby; and I would have come before, if I had thought I could do you any good.'

"She laughed contemptuously as she said, 'Do *me* good! I think you need to do that to yourself.'

"'There's no doubt of that,' I answered; 'but I meant something rather different, — I know yours was a sudden and terrible sorrow.'

"'Oh, there, there!' she cried out, 'for pity's sake, stop! You might have prevented it all: it was your hatefulness to Charley that made him more than ever careless and wild, — you, with your stuck-up, proud notions of being above us all. Cauldwell was right, for once, when he gave you that lecture. Mr. Barclay spoiled you out and out. Charley was a fool for his pains, and so was I. I wish I had never seen you, I wish you had staid in Europe, with all your high-falutin ideas. And then to have you come and tell me you want to do me good, when you know you hate us all; and think'— But here her sobs made her inarticulate.

"I was so horrified that I could not move. I longed to rush from the room. I felt as guilty as if every word she uttered were entirely true, and I suppose I looked as I felt; for after a while she ceased crying, and said in a voice less sharp, but still angry, 'I suppose you'll marry that Italian count, now; but I don't see what you find in *him.*'

"The quick revulsion of feeling that this caused enabled me to speak; and, summoning all my dignity, I said as gently as I could, for all my indignation, anger, and a sense of the absurdity of the situation, now that she had turned with so evident curiosity to my affairs, —

"'Aunt Abby, you and I have both made serious mistakes; pardon me for supposing, even for a moment, that I could be of any use to you now or at any other time. I thought that I might offer sympathy without offence, but I see my error. I have but added to your troubles in coming here. I will go now. Good-by.'

"At this she relented a little, and looked ashamed; but still she said, 'You might have saved Charley; you might have given him a chance. I don't see why you couldn't have been kinder, and I don't know what you find in that footy painter. It's all because Mr. Barclay hadn't the sense to bring you up as he ought to have done. He's got all those stuck-up Boston notions, and he's spoiled you; and, after all, I don't know whether you are going to be his wife, or the other one's. Whichever it is, poor Charley might have been given a chance.'

"All this tirade gave *me* a chance to collect myself, and be cool: so I repeated something of the same sort that I had said before, and tried to get away; but now she softened still more, and wept and wailed and deplored her miseries.

"Will you, can you, believe me when I tell you that in another hour I had begged Lillo to go to the city without me, and that I staid in that wretched house a whole week?

"When the crape and diamonds came off, aunt Abby was another woman. She begged my pardon; she implored me to forget every thing she had said; she unearthed all her treasures in the way of photographs of her children, and souvenirs of their infancy: and she so drained my sympathies that I was as limp and lifeless as a rag. For a whole week I staid, and listened to ber monologues. I received Mr. Boggs every time he came to see aunt Abby; heard all his boastful harangues with all the patience at my command. I hope he did not detect my weariness, for I really tried to be interested in what he talked about. Sister Camilla says we must forget the outer rind of the individual, and remember only his spiritual essence. But I find it so hard to do this. We are not all as able to do it as she is. Every one interests her, because she is always thinking of souls more than of bodies.

"But, my dear Mr. Barclay, I now fully realize what a kindness yours has been. What if I had been living all these years under these influences!"

Again she wrote, —

"I have been to see my grandfather. It is a curious sort of thing to look at one's blood relations from such an outside point of view. Sister Camilla went with me. He lives in one of the old houses on V. Square, alone, with only strange old colored servants, as queer as himself. The house is very spacious, but very bare of every thing but books. He is a man of fine presence, but reminds me of one of his own volumes, uncut. He may have plenty of wisdom within, but no one is the better for it; and the reserved cover is stiff with want of usage. Imagine what I would have been, left to his untender mercies! I should have grown into some sickly specimen of sun-deprived plant, without force enough of my own to find sun and air and moisture; and so again I thank you, dear Mr. Barclay. Sister Camilla and I strove to interest him in St. Armand's, whose bell has rung in his ears year in, year out, without producing so much as an echoing tinkle in his heart. He listened to us politely, expressed some cut-and-dried platitudes about religion, and turned at once to show his fine stock of Bibles in all languages and bindings. The print, the covers, the edition, were all in all to him; but no farther did he go. I never saw so near an approach to a look of despair on Sister Camilla's fine features. I think, if she had been alone, she would have made some attempt to probe into his poor old heart, and stir it to some purpose; but having me with her restrained her zeal, for she hopes that in time I may gain some good influence, but I see no chance of it. He is as fixed and firm as an old fossil."

Thus ran the letters. Mr. Barclay read them aloud to Miss Alden and Grace.

"My dear Mr. Barclay," commented Miss Alden, "you made a mistake in letting Ruth go home with that horrid woman. But how sweetly grateful the child is! and how fortunate that she should have met Miss Deforest!"

"Yes, it is more than fortunate, for I never could have given her half so much help in all her difficulties. But I do not regard her going as a mistake. In no other way could she have gained quite such an experience. A human life is a serious trust. I never realized the fact so entirely as now."

He looked at Grace contemplatively, and she responding, said, —

"Few men would have accepted the trust so generously."

It is a soft, early summer morning, the sky flecked with white clouds, and the air full of promise and balmy freshness, — a morning when Nature rejoices that the winter with its dreariness and darkness is over, and the time of singing of birds has come. The neighborhood of St. Armand's, having a square with plenty of velvet turf and shady trees, is very pleasant in the early summer; though St. Armand's itself is no brighter, tucked away as it is among the poor, dismal little houses that have seen better days a very long while ago. It does its best, however, to be cheerful this morning; and its old cracked bell has rung as usual for prayers, and its few old women have been devout worshippers. They stop and talk, and look wonderstruck, to see several carriages driving up; and all the poor children from far and near throng about its entrance as Sister Camilla appears with large baskets of flowers, and gives them right and left to the forlorn little waifs. The flowers seem to instantly invest them all with an appearance of festive preparation, which atones for ragged clothes and unwashed faces, and the shrill little voices rise as joyfully in the air as those of the twittering sparrows. The old organ raises its voice too, and peals forth the "Wedding March;" and, though the guests are not very many, the fact that there are two brides quite overawes the spectators.

The group about the altar is a picturesque one, in spite of the prim snugness of the men's morning-coats: for the brides are all filmy lace and shining silk; and Sister Camilla, in her nun's dress, stands beside Ruth; and Miss Alden, in turquoise-blue velvet, hovers over Grace. The chancel is filled with graceful plants, and the votive offerings beneath the picture of "The Empty Cross" are of fairest and purest blossoms.

After the ceremony they leave St. Armand's to its silent pews and much better filled than usual alms-box, and all drive over to the north side of the square, where an accommodating architect has fitted up one of the old houses with the brick and marble fronts into an artistic haunt for a colony of people who want something green for their eyes to rest on when they look out of their windows, and where Mr. Barclay, as well as Mr. Marsh, have suites of apartments. Strange to say, it is just beside the house where Ruth's queer and crusty old grandfather lives, whose acquaintance has been made so recently, and who, though he does not come to the wedding-feast, sends a gift of old folios which Mr. Barclay pronounces very unique. Some one suggests that checks to Ruth's order would have been of more immediate and practical value, which Lillo indignantly repudiates. Well he may, now that orders for pictures are coming in so fast he can hardly fill them; this he attributes not to his genius, not to any of his own ability, but to the lift his romantic story has given him. Americans, he says, care more for romance than for art, though why they separate the two is not so palpable. Another giver of gifts is Mrs. Vedder, who was in the church swathed in crape blacker than midnight. She was not to be outdone by the duchess, who gave Grace some beautiful lace and antique *bric-à-brac:* so she sends diamonds, — big blazing brilliants, for Ruth to wear when (as she insists) she is the Countess Romano.

The house on the square has been re-arranged and re-built under Lillo's eye. All its wide space has been compressed into suites of apartments, full of quaint conceits and pretty devices for making small homes convenient. There are all the cosey corners for lounging-chairs or tea-tables; the *portières*, the brasses, the stained glass, the tiles, rest and refresh the eye upon the interior as do the old trees and clipped grass and waving shadows upon the exterior. But in addition to all these the Romano cousin has sent over old chairs and tapestries from the Italian palace. He is only too glad to be left in undisturbed possession of the estate, and willingly cedes all else that Lillo asks, — which is only enough for artistic "properties." America is more to him than Italy, and Ruth more than America, and she has decided that their lives shall be spent here, between this city home and the old house on the sands, which holds still for them its charm of silence and rest and simplicity; a place where their love may brood and grow strong of wing; where the spirit of faith and peace and hope shall prepare them for the conflicts of the outer world, and contemplation shall enrich and ripen their souls.

Children's Stories.

BY MRS. WILLIAM J. (HELEN) HAYS.

I.

A DOMESTIC HEROINE. A Story for Girls. 12mo, cloth. $1.00.

"This story is in the order of Mrs. A. D. T. Whitney's works, and is intended especially for girls in their teens. . . . The story is a very pleasing one, told in an attractive style." — *The Denver Tribune.*

II.

A LOVING SISTER. A Story for Big Girls. 12mo, cloth. $1.00.

"Those who read Mrs. Hays's pleasing story of 'A Domestic Heroine' will be glad to greet this its sequel." — *The Living Church.*

III.

CASTLE COMFORT. A Story for Children. 12mo, cloth. Illustrated. $1.00.

"This is one of those pleasant stories of child-life which always delight the little people of a family." — *The Independent.*

IV.

CITY COUSINS. A Story for Children. 12mo, cloth. Illustrated. $1.00.

"In 'City Cousins' we have a daintily told story by Mrs. W. J. Hays, who has the 'open sesame' to the childish heart. Mrs. Hays writes well, and her stories always have a purpose." — *The Sunday-school Times.*

New York: THOMAS WHITTAKER, 2 and 3 Bible House.

Historical Tales.

BY LUCY ELLEN GUERNSEY.

I.

LOVEDAY'S HISTORY. A Story of Many Changes. 12mo, cloth. $1.50.

"A very clever romance of the middle of the sixteenth century." — *New York Times.*

"It is delightfully written, and has the genuine sixteenth-century flavor." — *The Congregationalist.*

II.

THE FOSTER-SISTERS; or, Lucy Corbet's Chronicle. 12mo, cloth. $1.50.

III.

THE CHEVALIER'S DAUGHTER. Being one of the Stanton-Corbet Chronicles. 12mo, cloth. $1.50.

IV.

LADY BETTY'S GOVERNESS; or, The Corbet Chronicles. 12mo, cloth. $1.25.

V.

LADY ROSAMOND'S BOOK. Being a second part of the Stanton-Corbet Chronicles. 12mo, cloth. $1.25.

VI.

WINIFRED; or, After Many Days. 12mo, cloth. $1.25.

New York: THOMAS WHITTAKER, 2 and 3 Bible House.

Stories

TO BE HAD AT ALL THE LIBRARIES.

I.

HER GENTLE DEEDS. By SARAH TYTLER, author of "Citoyenne Jacqueline," etc. *Just out.* 12mo, cloth. Illustrated. $1.50.

II.

THE STRENGTH OF HER YOUTH. By SARAH DOUDNEY. 12mo, cloth. Illustrated. $1.25.

III.

OLDHAM; or, Beside all Waters. By LUCY ELLEN GUERNSEY. 12mo, cloth. Illustrated. $1.50.

"Her story is pleasant, her description of characters and places excellent, and her lessons pure and good." — *The Christian at Work.*

IV.

THE HOME OF FIESOLE. A Story of the Times of Savonarola. 12mo, cloth. Illustrated. $1.25.

"It is an intensely interesting story of Savanarola and his times, which it would profit any one to read." — *Sunday Gazette* (Akron, O.).

"Skilfully wrought, and full of beauty and historic interest." — *The New York Observer.*

V.

HEROES OF ANCIENT GREECE. A Story of the Days of Socrates the Athenian. By ELLEN PALMER. 12mo, cloth. Illustrated. $1.25.

"A pleasant love story of the Peloponnesian War. The social and political manners of Athens and Sparta are well depicted. There is a little of Herodotus, something of Thucydides and Xenophon, a touch of Greek religion, philosophy, and Socrates." — *The Literary World.*

New York: THOMAS WHITTAKER, 2 and 3 Bible House.

www.ingramcontent.com/pod-product-compliance
Lightning Source LLC
Chambersburg PA
CBHW020934030726
47496CB00005B/1180